A
DOG
IN
GEORGIA

A
DOG
IN
GEORGIA

A NOVEL

Lauren Grodstein

ALGONQUIN BOOKS OF CHAPEL HILL
LITTLE, BROWN AND COMPANY

Algonquin Books of Chapel Hill / Little, Brown and Company
Hachette Book Group
1290 Avenue of the Americas, New York, NY 10104
algonquinbooks.com

First Edition: August 2025

Algonquin Books of Chapel Hill is an imprint of Little, Brown and Company, a division of Hachette Book Group, Inc. The Algonquin Books name and logo are trademarks of Hachette Book Group, Inc.

The publisher is not responsible for websites (or their content) that are not owned by the publisher.

The Hachette Speakers Bureau provides a wide range of authors for speaking events. To find out more, go to hachettespeakersbureau.com or email hachettespeakers@hbgusa.com.

Little, Brown and Company books may be purchased in bulk for business, educational, or promotional use. For information, please contact your local bookseller or the Hachette Book Group Special Markets Department at special.markets@hbgusa.com.

Design by Steve Godwin

ISBN 9781643752358 (hardcover) / 9781643757360 (ebook)
LCCN 2025933705

Printing 1, 2025
LSC-C
Printed in the United States of America

◆ For Julie ◆

ONE

NEW YORK

ONE

THE WOMAN—LONG GRAY COAT, enormous scarf—scuttled toward Amy just as she and Roxy were leaving the dog run in Tompkins Square Park. It was another blue morning in an unseasonably blue February.

"Hey!" the woman called. She had a vaguely familiar face, and for a second Amy thought she was a student—but no, she generally remembered her students. Or maybe someone from the neighborhood?

Or did she work at the restaurant? She had a tired, reedy voice.

"Excuse me! Hey!" the woman called again.

It was so early, though—not even seven-thirty, and restaurant people generally didn't wake up this early. Amy and Roxy had just finished their morning kibbitz with the regulars: Rufus the Lab, Jazz the mutt, Morty the half-blind pit bull.

"I'm sorry," the woman said, when she was close enough to Amy to be heard over the whine of rush hour and dogs barking inside their oval run. "I have to tell you something."

"Me?"

"Something terrible." The woman had an enormous tote bag on her shoulder spilling over with scarves, leaflets, bits of fabric. "I'm really sorry."

Amy was too tired for this; she hadn't slept the night before. "I'm not interested," she said. "Whatever you're selling."

"No," the woman said. "It's your dog. She's yours, right?"

WHO ELSE'S COULD SHE BE? Roxy, kind-hearted rescue, smallish German shepherd, the worst defense imaginable against thieves or crazy people. She stepped toward the woman for a pat on the head.

"She's sweet," the woman said, obliging.

"Can I help you?" Amy tugged on Roxy's leash. *Heel, girl.* But Roxy was blissed out from the woman's attention, leaning up against her skinny legs.

"I'm just—I hate to tell you this. I'm sorry—I always hate telling people. But your dog is about to—you see, I'm kind of a pet psychic." The woman said this gently, rubbing the sweet spot in the middle of Roxy's bony head. "And I think you need to know that your dog is miserable."

"Excuse me?" Amy straightened, offended.

"No, I'm sorry—not miserable, exactly. Just, like, kind of lost. Kind of directionless."

"She's a dog," Amy said. "That's not a way a dog can feel."

"Actually, it is," the woman said. "It might sound crazy, but I've always had a true connection with animals. I know what they're thinking. Like their deepest emotions."

"Okay, but in fact," Amy said, tugging harder on Roxy's leash, "that's impossible."

"It's been my curse since I was a child," the woman said. She smiled ruefully, and Amy could see a swipe of maroon lipstick on her teeth. "Sometimes people think I'm crazy."

I think you're crazy, but Amy kept it to herself.

"Anyway, something truly metamorphic is coming for her, but it's going to be very difficult. Very heavy. I think she knows it, too," the woman said. She switched her massive tote bag to her other arm. "You can tell by the way she walks, her gait. Something needs to be fixed. Please don't ignore it."

"Nothing needs to be fixed," Amy said. "She walks fine. When did you even see her walk? We've been at the dog park since six-thirty—"

"I've been watching you all morning," the woman said, and this was when Amy blinked. *Run, girl!* She must have said it out loud, because Roxy took off like a jet, pulling Amy with her, the leash taut, and even as they ran she checked Roxy's hips and her gait was *fine*, thank you, and when they were fifty yards away, the edge of Tompkins Square Park, Amy turned around.

The woman had disappeared.

A bad dream. Insanity. Roxy was panting.

"Roxy," Amy said. "Roxy girl. What the hell was that?"

She sat down on a bench, and Roxy sat at her feet. (Gently, not in pain). She looked around again: students and commuters and dogs and their owners and joggers. Two cops. She knew it made her a bad liberal but Amy felt better once she saw the cops.

The woman had not reemerged, and Amy thought that this was what a sleepless night could do to a person in middle age. Waking nightmares! Hallucinations!

"You want to go home, Rox?"

Roxy looked at Amy with a cocked eyebrow. She was a dog. Where they went wasn't up to her.

"Do you?"

Roxy shrugged her body downward, rested her heavy head on her paws.

"Do you feel miserable? Lost? Directionless?"

The dog yawned.

Sometimes after the park Amy and Roxy would walk to Union

Square, especially if the Greenmarket was on, or sometimes they would stop for breakfast at Veselka, or sometimes they would go home and Amy would work on whatever small projects she had created for herself for the day. There was less and less to do, really. She wasn't teaching anything this semester. She didn't have any new writing assignments. No invitations, no appointments, no openings.

Ferry was at school. She could barely even look at Judd. The cats would be sloshing around in the kitchen sunshine like drunks.

"I kind of want a drink," Amy said to Roxy. "But I guess it's too early."

Still, when they got back to the apartment she checked to see if there was any open Scotch, and there was, and she poured that into the coffee that was in the coffee maker from the day before and she microwaved the two together and glugged in some hazelnut Coffeemate and sat down at the kitchen table and took a sip that was disgusting.

Light streamed in, oppressively, through the wavy casement windows. Their building had been a factory one hundred years ago—or okay, a sweatshop, immigrant girls producing umbrella frames sixteen hours a day. But eventually the girls got married and manufacturing moved to the boroughs, and the building survived intact through mid-century abandonment and 1970s squalor before finally succumbing to a bourgeois rehab in the early nineties: brick walls, hardwood floors, original windows and radiators, high ceilings. In 1994, twelve years before they'd met, Judd had had the foresight to purchase one with his parents' money.

He'd also had the foresight to purchase a former crack den on Tenth and A, also with his parents' money, and turn it into Le Coin (pronounced "Le Kwahnh," in the French way), where crowds still gathered most weeknights and all day weekends to eat oysters and drink champagne. Amy and Judd had first laid eyes on each other in Le Coin's sweltering kitchen one Wednesday in November 2006. She'd come in to apply for a job on the line, and in the way of these things a line cook had no-showed that very morning.

"You can cook?"

The first thing he'd said to her.

"I can," she said. He handed her an apron and a hairnet and she got to work.

When they got married at City Hall two years later, Ferry and Jorge, the dishwasher, were their only witnesses. They honeymooned at Le Coin, which was where they liked to be anyway.

And over the years his apartment had become their apartment, his child their child, his life her life, his indiscretions her heartbreak.

Her mother had asked her, was she sure? He has so many—tattoos. And Bernstein? Is he—

Yes, Mom, Jewish.

Well, her mother sighed. I do hear they treat their wives nicely.

Amy poured more Scotch into her coffee, wiped some crumbs off the table onto the floor for Roxy to lick up. Like many restaurant professionals, Judd rarely cooked at home, but still he'd fixed up their kitchen little by little whenever they'd had extra cash: upgrading the stove to a Viking 6 (almost too wide to fit in the freight elevator), installing John Boos butcher block counters and a secondhand La Marzocco espresso maker. She used to love to cook there.

But now, eyeing it through her weariness, Amy saw a half-cocked kitchen that remembered it had once been a sweatshop. Piles of recycling gathered around the espresso maker, and daisies wilted in a tomato can on the windowsill. Pet food was scattered about the floors; they were all sloppy eaters in this house. The kitchen table was scratched from endless breakfasts and craft projects and Ferry's grade school homework.

The scent of high-octane kitty litter wafted through one door; Judd's snores wafted through another.

The loud snoring was new. She had read that it could be a sign of heart trouble, or was it that snoring could cause heart trouble? Judd hadn't been to the doctor in—years. Close to a decade. He hadn't gone even when he promised he'd get that mole checked out, the colonoscopy you were supposed to have at forty-five. He was bad at promises. Also, he didn't think he would ever die.

The last time this had happened, four years ago, he had promised her that he would change, that he would never do this again, but— well, bad at promises. And now, listening to him snore: she wanted to wake him and scream at him, but she had already done that. What was there to say that she hadn't said before? That he could respond to intelligently? What did she want from him anyway? It was a question he used to ask her all the time.

Her mother used to say that if you couldn't take things day by day, you should try to take them hour by hour, and if that proved too much you could just take them minute by minute. Get through this minute, and then the next, and soon you'll have made it through an hour, then a morning, then a day. Her mother wasn't much for good advice, but this nugget had proved useful over the years.

It was 8:12 in the morning. She could make it till 8:13, and then 8:30, and then reassess her life. Her mother would also have told her not to be an asshole, to grow up and move out, but her mother had died nine years ago on the couch in the tiny Minneapolis house where she'd lived for forty-one years. (Her brother had found her, peaceful, under a blanket, as if napping. A Stephen King book on the coffee table, coffee gone cold. The cat nowhere to be found. Her mother had been seventy-six and deserved the rest.)

Amy missed her more than she would have expected.

She clicked on her phone's photo app and reversed the lens so she could look at herself from a weird angle, one of her favorite punishments. Faded circles under her eyes, a curly blond ponytail going gray. Broken blood vessels on and around her nose. Once upon a time, in this generally unflappable city, strangers had stopped her on the street to tell her how beautiful she was. She had her mother's wide mouth and robin's egg eyes. But now she was halfway done being forty-six, and nobody had stopped her in years.

"Judd?" she whispered. "Judd?" She said it a little more loudly, an invocation. Without Judd, what would have happened to her? She'd grown up a too-tall, too-poor nineties kid, beset not only with a bitter single mother but also a twin brother who was gay at a time when being gay was not a social asset. Minnesota winters with the heat turned up to fifty-eight, just enough to keep the pipes from freezing; endless meals of plain pasta with shake cheese. Free breakfast at school, free lunch at school. The other kids so unceasingly mean.

Even then, her truest companions had been animals. A small branch of the Hennepin County shelter was around the corner from her house—a couple of cat rooms and pens for the dogs—and she hadn't walked in with a plan to volunteer as much as she had just escaped there one day, fourteen years old, her mom railing about a doctor's bill and the electric shut off again. Looking for rescue herself. The old ladies at the shelter were not kindly, exactly, but they were matter-of-fact: "if you're going to hang out here, you're going to make yourself useful." And therefore Amy learned to trim claws and wash blankets, to mix up feed.

Every day after school, and some days when she didn't go at all, she was at the shelter, bottle-feeding the kittens whose mothers had rejected them and trying to comfort the pitties nobody wanted. Reuniting her neighbors with their lost pets. The look of gratitude on the owners' faces, their pets' licks and sloppy kisses.

And then, seventeen years old, she was finally saved herself at the Mall of America one chilly October morning. The shelter was closed to volunteers—another ringworm outbreak—but she couldn't face going to school, so she decided to spend the day trying on sweaters from the sale rack at the Limited. She assumed the guy who approached her was a truancy officer. She was willing to take her punishment, call her mother from the PD in the basement of the mall.

"Can I take your picture?"

Oh, not a truancy officer; a perv. "Sure," she said.

He was tall, shaggy haired, could have been anywhere from twenty-five to forty. He took a few shots with a Polaroid he happened to have in his backpack, pictures of her just standing in the dressing room with the curtain open. Nobody at the Limited seemed to care.

He shook out the Polaroids and they looked at them together as they came into focus. Amy was so tall and so skinny that it was impossible to find an oversize sweater that would hang the way she liked.

"Sorry," she said. Whatever the man wanted in her he wasn't going to find.

"Listen, how old are you, nineteen?"

"Seventeen."

"Seventeen? That's great—but why aren't you in school? Okay, who cares, listen, I'm a photographer, I think you have something here."

"What kind of thing?"

"Modeling—what did you think? Surely you've been approached before."

Amy shook her head, dumbstruck. Modeling. She had a face like a pie plate, huge eyes. The only models she knew were Claudia Schiffer and Cindy Crawford—women who were, above all else, *pretty*. Whereas in an unofficial vote in the sixth grade Amy had been selected Ugliest Girl at Mondale Middle.

She picked up one of the Polaroids from the bench in the dressing room. What did she see? Unruly blond curls, flat chest, scared expression.

"You can't see it?"

She shrugged.

"You ever been to New York?"

She barked a laugh.

His name was Scott, and he was really just an aspiring photographer, but he took her to TGI Friday's and by the time lunch was over, she had an entirely new idea of her future. Fuck Minnesota, fuck her miserable mother, fuck even—well, it was sad, but she'd have to leave her animals. She had no other choice if she wanted to be saved.

She left a note for her mother on her eighteenth birthday: *I'm taking the bus to New York City, since I'm an adult now.* She wondered if her mom would be mad or relieved. She did not call to find out, and then they didn't speak for three years.

And while the modeling thing didn't, in the end, exactly take off (a few jobs here or there, a catalog, a stocking ad, and then, for months, nothing at all), in New York she still found herself as happy as she'd ever been. It turned out that everything that was wrong in Minnesota was right in New York: the music on the streets, the endless variety of people, the ability to be seen or not be seen, depending on her mood. And there was a shelter right there on Avenue D that needed her to do laundry, to walk dogs, to reunite lost cats with their owners in whatever time she had to spare.

It was one of the ladies at the Avenue D shelter who asked her if she knew how to waitress—her brother's diner was short-staffed and Amy seemed quick on her feet. She had never done it before but how hard could it be? Turned out hard, but not impossible. And then, after three months, one of the cooks OD'd during a dinner shift and everyone was desperate. Could you try? the owner asked. Turned out she could work fast, didn't mind sweating, learned knife skills by osmosis—and before she knew it, she was a line cook. She was skinny but she'd always liked to eat. She knew how things should taste. She stopped going to pointless casting calls, spent mornings, instead, on her mise en place.

The diner changed hands, so she moved to a Mexican joint; the Mexican joint went out of business. Then her roommate ditched their lease and her mom *still* wouldn't take her calls and her brother sent her twenty dollars after she confessed she was broke. The twenty left her feeling even more broke. Nobody at the shelter knew of any openings anywhere. So, with the courage that came from being out of options, she walked into Le Coin's glamorous dining room to find a job.

At a table in the back of the room sat Judd, casually riffling through papers. When he looked up at her she fell speechless: those eyes!

What did he see when he saw her? Tall, blond, attractive in an off-beat way, said she could cook.

"Have I seen you before?" he asked.

Amy took a moment before finding her words. "Maybe," she said. Then: "I doubt it."

"You're a cook?"

"Yes."

"Show me."

One minute became the next minute, one year became the next. She had never stopped loving him, she was sure.

Roxy drank steadily from her bowl. Judd's snores receded. After a moment of quiet, he called out from the bedroom.

"Babe? Are you there?"

"I'm here," she said.

"What? I can't hear you."

"I said I'm here."

"Are you all right?"

"I'm fine."

He was quiet then, and she knew he was deciding whether or not to believe her. It would be easier to believe her, but: they had been married for years, and had been through this twice before. Still, Judd liked to do what was easy, or what was readily available. She heard him pee with the door open.

"Could you close the door?"

Instead he flushed.

One of the cats leapt onto the kitchen table, Sir Licks-A-Lot, named by Ferry when he was in the fifth grade and now a source of much mirth at the cat's veterinary appointments.

"Hey Licky," Amy said as the cat sniffed her coffee.

It wasn't that she didn't understand. It wasn't that she expected better. She had spent her whole life protecting her low expectations. Childhood Christmas presents of socks and underwear; the friendless school years; ushered out of modeling before she'd ever really gotten started. She had never asked for much.

But still, she had asked for better than this, and he consistently refused to deliver. Moreover, just because they'd been through this twice before didn't make it easier to know what to say to him now. I'm leaving? She wasn't leaving. We need to go to counseling? They'd already tried that. More counseling? What else was there to talk about?

She rejected the obvious choice—to leave, of course—because she was weak (this is what her mother would say). Or because she loved him, although her mother didn't believe in love. And/or because the pain of living through this again was preferable to the pain of losing him forever (again, she was weak).

And she knew that Judd didn't want a divorce, because down deep in his faithless heart he loved her, too, despite the fact that he was an unrepentant poonhound.

"Hey," he said softly, standing in the doorway, uneasy. At least he had the good sense to be uneasy. He was wearing flannel pajama pants, an unbuttoned shirt, wide hairy belly, wild brown hair standing up in all directions. He was massive, six-five; he almost filled the doorway, and she had always felt safe in his enormity. He was the rare man who could make her feel small. Her initials were tattooed on his forearm amid a wreath of flowers.

"Hey," she said.

"Want some breakfast?"

She didn't answer.

"You aren't hungry?"

"A woman came up to me in the park and told me Roxy was miserable."

"What?"

"A woman," she said. "Came up to me in the park. And told me—"

"That's insane."

"It was upsetting," she acknowledged. Sir Licks jumped off the table.

Judd sat down opposite her, reached for her hands.

"I don't know," she said, letting her hands go limp in his.

"Know what?"

"I don't know what to do."

"You don't have to do anything," he said.

"Well I should probably do something," she said. "This keeps happening."

"Nothing happened."

"Judd."

"Nothing—"

"Please, stop it. I saw what I saw. Stop telling me I didn't. I'm not a child."

"I'll fire her."

She took a yoga breath. "You could be sued."

"She's a shitty employee. And nothing happened between us that could be construed as—"

"I told you to stop saying that."

He rubbed her fingers with his own meaty fingers. She did not pull away.

Stubble, thick eyebrows, ice wolf eyes. That's what she told her friends after she first met him at the restaurant, *he has ice wolf eyes.* Nobody knew what an ice wolf was but they could imagine those eyes, how crystal their blue. He had a nose that had been punched a few times, a chef's bonanza of scars and burns up and down his arms and even on his neck. A deep crease between his eyebrows.

"I wanted to call my mother today," she said, which was a lie, but Judd was attached to mothers, his own, even Ferry's—so she knew he'd feel bad when she said that. "I forgot for a second that she's dead."

"Ame," he said.

"She's been dead for almost a decade."

"I know," he said.

"Which is good because if she knew about this it would kill her."

Heavy sigh. Impossible rogue.

"Amy—"

"You have to fire her."

"Of course, I know."

"Someone with that kind of judgment cannot be your employee."

"I thought you were worried she'd sue."

"You'll countersue."

He was still rubbing her fingers. "Can I make you some breakfast?"

"You forgot how to cook," she said, which was an old joke between them. She didn't know why she was relenting; she always relented.

He smiled. "That's not true."

Two nights ago she swore she'd never look at him again. Now they were holding hands.

"Ame," he said, letting his voice go husky, "I know—I know what you saw. I know what it looks like. I know it will be impossible for me to convince you—"

"I don't know what to do, Judd," she said. She had wanted breakfast; now she realized she was about to cry. She looked at the table to keep from crying, but still her eyes were starting to sting. "Can you tell me what to do?"

"Just believe me," he said.

"What would you do?" she asked. "If you were me?"

"I would believe me."

She had already let him back in. She had already let him sleep in their bed. Was it really so much to ask, to break the promise she had made to herself two nights ago?

On the other hand, she kept breaking promises to herself and this was where she ended up.

Was it such a bad place to end up?

Roxy, asleep in the corner of the kitchen, her usual spot. The cats lolling. The refrigerator humming in its corner. The scuffed floors. This beautiful man who still loved her. Ferry, the child they had raised together, a sophomore at Cornell. Books, record collections, a million nights in a steamy kitchen, an apartment they had lived in together for seventeen years.

A frightening woman had told her that her faithful dog was miserable.

Perhaps the woman had mistaken Roxy for Amy's heart.

TWO

TWO NIGHTS AGO.

A text at one-thirty in the morning. Then another and another.

Judd was snoring beside her and the phone just kept pinging and pinging. She knew better than to look at his phone, what awful secrets could be hidden there, but she also believed he wouldn't dare fuck around anymore. The last time had been so terrible—how could he do that again? Who would choose to go through that again? Also she really wanted to sleep. Which were all reasons not to pick up the phone.

But: Roxy was breathing deeply at the foot of the bed. The pings were going to wake her up, or the cats.

"Judd," she shook him. "Judd, your phone."

Ping ping ping.

"Judd—" But nothing. Like the dead, this one. So finally—what if it was Ferry?—she picked up the phone and her reading glasses.

She didn't scream or bite her lip bloody like she had the last time. Instead, she rubbed her eye and brought the blue light of the phone closer to her face. Meret, the new hostess, naked as the day God made her and doing something extreme with her fingers and her labia.

Ping ping ping more photos.

She had amazing, enormous breasts, and now a finger in her mouth.

This, or something like it, had happened before *(twice)*—but that didn't make it any easier.

First the hideous chill creeping from her hands to her heart. Then the fight-or-flight panic deep in her gut. She threw the phone so hard across the room that it cracked on the brick wall, cracked loudly, which of course didn't wake Judd, but did wake Roxy, who let out a sharp bark.

Then she finally allowed herself a scream—a long high one, like she was being stabbed in the chest—and then she flipped on the lights, started grabbing clothes, his clothes, why should *she* go anywhere at one-thirty in the morning, and threw them into a Whole Foods tote bag that happened to be on their closet floor. Underwear, socks, a stinky T-shirt, another stinky T-shirt, fuck him and his dirty laundry.

"Amy?"

A pair of running shoes. He would never step foot in this house again.

"Amy?"

Now Roxy was up and yelping madly. She jumped up onto the bed for Judd to comfort her because when Amy was in distress Roxy was in distress. "Amy, what's happening?" Judd with a sixty-pound German shepherd in his arms.

"I saw your texts."

"What texts?"

He sounded confused instead of worried.

"Your texts—"

"What texts?"

Was she wrong? Had she not seen what she had obviously seen? She picked up the phone from the other side of the room; the screen was spider-webbed with cracks but still functional. Meret's naked body frozen in fractals.

"What the fuck?"

"Look at it," she said.

"Jesus," he whispered, scrolling.

"I didn't look at the history to see what you'd sent her first."

"Nothing," he said. "You can look. I've never sent her anything."

"I don't believe you."

"Amy, I—"

"I need you to leave, Judd."

"Please. I mean it. I never sent her—I've never sent her a thing. I swear to God. Amy, you have to believe me, I don't know what the fuck she thinks—maybe she thinks this is funny? Or it's for someone else? I don't know why she's sending this to me, I really don't—"

Amy sat down on the floor. She was still holding the bag of his clothes. Maybe she should leave? If he was going to make this hard?

"I'm begging you not to make this hard in the middle of the night. I'm really tired, Judd. Please."

"I swear, listen—" He got down off the bed so he could look her in the eye, but she refused to return his gaze. "Ame, I know you don't believe me, you don't have to believe me, but I swear to you there's nothing—"

She forced herself then to look at him. "I am exhausted. I am truly and totally exhausted. The least you can do for me is just take your stuff and go. Go to her house. Please."

"I don't—Amy, I—"

"Please. If you can't do anything else for me."

He didn't move or say anything. She didn't either, kept her eyes trained to the floor.

A silent standoff. On the street a group of drunks sang Billy Joel. *Anthony works in the grocery store.*

"Please go."

There was nothing more embarrassing than watching a huge man in his underwear try to find some clothing on the floor. She went to the bathroom, washed her face for full minutes. When she looked at herself, she was relieved to find that her eyes weren't red, she hadn't broken out in hives. She would survive this one, too.

"Amy," he said, behind her, his beautiful face in the mirror. Those cheekbones. "I have no idea how to make you believe me, but nothing ever—I mean *nothing*—I would never do that again to you. To us."

"Leave," she said.

"Please—"

Roxy was whining. She hated disruptions, bad energy. "You're upsetting the dog," she said, and he closed his eyes for a moment, but just a moment, and then he picked up the Whole Foods bag and left the bedroom. A few moments later she heard the front door open and shut.

He had taken his cracked phone with him.

Amy sat back on her bed, her face stinging from the retinol scrub she had just vigorously applied, and also from tears, because now that he was gone she would let herself cry. Because she had to figure out how to get through the night. And also, how to unsee Meret, her perfect tits, her shaved vulva, the whole of her human anatomy posing in what looked like a shitty bathroom, probably somewhere in the bowels of Brooklyn or maybe Queens. Kids couldn't afford the East Village anymore. Roxy put her head on Amy's lap and looked up at her miserably, like she was the one who had just had her heart ripped out. Fine, it was fine, she'd be fine. Wasn't she always? Roxy too. Amy stroked the dog's side and tried to match her breathing, but it was impossible. Her heart was still racing. Fight or flight, although she'd never really allowed herself to do either.

But after a while, her heart calmed, and Roxy settled in her spot at the foot of the bed and soon the room filled with her gentle snores. Amy knew it was hopeless to wish the same for herself, even with the help of Xanax. She picked up the laptop from her bedside table and turned off her phone so if he called she wouldn't be tempted to answer, and she turned to her animals.

In her twenties it had been drugs and in her thirties the occasional cigarette and a whole lot of wine and now, in her forties, Xanax and animals.

She scrolled through the Dodo, trying to focus on videos of puppy rescues and unexpected wildlife encounters. A baby goat befriended by a lonely donkey. Rescued bears frolicking in a North Dakota sanctuary. A stray kitten nursing on the teat of a terrier whose puppies had been stillborn—a little disturbing, frankly, but sweet in its way, and the terrier clearly loved nursing the kitten, and watching that strange nurturing, the kitten rubbing its paws into the terrier's black fur, the terrier's little maw crinkling and relaxing, the kitten falling asleep in the curve of the terrier's belly—Amy almost felt the acid in her gut give way.

An hour of this, and then another: an elephant pulled out of the mud, a Bernese mountain dog who wouldn't cross the street without an adorable struggle, an Australian cockatoo who sang alongside his owner, a litter of kittens found under a trailer, an elderly man finally realizing his dream of adopting a puppy. An injured bald eagle rehabbed and released. An injured wild horse rehabbed and released. Ukrainian zoo animals evacuated to Poland. Outside, the sun rising. No news from Judd. She hoped, despite herself, despite everything, he'd found somewhere decent to sleep.

A woman raising a baby squirrel. After she returned the squirrel to the wild, the woman sat in a beautiful chair in her beautiful house and sobbed.

Judd could have gone to Meret's apartment, but she doubted he would: Meret probably had roommates and he wouldn't want to look desperate, showing up with a Whole Foods bag of smelly laundry. Judd had always maintained a very specific image at work, very in charge, friendly but distant, demanding, a perfectionist. Spot checks in the kitchen. Spot checks behind the bar. A curated playlist, for which he paid a consultant $23,000.

On her first day at Le Coin he'd barely talked to her, just asked if she could come back tomorrow, if she needed regular work. Sure, she said. Bring your paperwork so I can pay you, he said, and again she said sure, then stood there, waiting for the attention she was sure would come her way (he was straight, wasn't he?). She didn't know then that he wouldn't give her that kind of power in his restaurant, he wouldn't let anyone know—much less a line cook off the street—that she was worth more than the five minutes of time he had for her. That this was part of his whole power thing, how he made the women who worked at Le Coin want and fear him.

She stared at him, at his ice wolf eyes, and waited for the pick-up she thought was coming.

When it didn't come she felt almost giddy. A game! She came back the next morning with makeup on, and still that day, nothing. Instead he ordered her around the kitchen, not screaming like some hack chef on TV but sometimes looking at one of her plates, shaking his head, silently handing it back to her like she should know what she did wrong. "Taste it," he'd say. "Taste." While she went weak in the knees.

He negotiated with suppliers, he hired and fired waiters, he drank wine at the bar and sometimes he would talk to her and sometimes he would spend the entire day not even seeing her, while she watched him and lusted. And then, finally, in a burst and a rush so intense she could still feel it in her stomach, he took her to his apartment and fucked her standing up in the kitchen and again in the bedroom and once more in the bedroom and she would have taken more, *she wanted more*, which was like nothing she'd ever felt in her life.

Her first orgasms administered by someone else.

It was a disaster to think of those early days with Judd. She'd never sleep again. So she turned to the Justice for Angel website— Angel, her beloved Georgian mutt—but there was no news. She sent another five-dollar donation to the rescue group, via Paypal, along with a short note (*with love from your friend Amy in New York!*). Five dollars equalled about fourteen Georgian lari. Judd would have had questions, maybe, if he ever looked at their credit card statements. "Samartlianoba Angelozi-istvis," she said out loud: justice for Angel. Sending the five dollars, an almost daily ritual, calmed her heart a bit. A little thing of her own, something Judd didn't know about, and of course the help for poor Angel, lost somewhere in Tbilisi.

If she were in Tbilisi, she would know how to find Angel. It had become her sub-specialty, the locating and securing of lost pets. Ever since her time at the shelter around the corner, she'd been doing it: using an owner's old T-shirt to lure a blind Doberman out of hiding, tracking a parakeet through the holly bushes that lined her childhood sidewalks. And then, volunteering at the Avenue D shelter, she'd learned to night-vision video. She'd reunited more tearful, grateful people with their lost animals than she could count.

But she was here, and the people in Georgia were there, so all Amy could really offer was money and goodwill and her own heartache.

AT SIX-THIRTY IN the morning Roxy stood up abruptly, which the cats took as their cue, meowing and trotting toward the kitchen, and Roxy stood there patiently while the four cats got their kibble and tuna and then started inching toward the door, she had to pee, *please please I gotta go.*

"Okay, okay," Amy said, in her slippers and her pajama pants. They trudged down the stairs, Roxy too polite to pull on her leash but doing that waddle she did when she really had to pish, and then outside to her favorite sidewalk linden, the one that had its own tiny gate and a sign that said "please be respectful" over a silhouette of a squatting dog with a red line through it.

And when she was done peeing, Roxy barked, barked, turned to the left.

"Judd?"

"Ame," he said. He was holding the Whole Foods bag, his khaki barn jacket, his ratty pajama pants, his running shoes, red eyes. "I've been walking for five hours."

"You don't have to be a martyr, Judd," she said, which was something her mother liked to say to her when she was a child and trying to make her mother understand that life was hard.

"I didn't know where to go."

"There are a lot of hotels in this city."

He looked at her bleakly. Roxy tilted her body toward the apartment building's door: she had watered the linden, time to go back inside. Amy and Judd stood there, looking at each other, both sleepless, both exhausted in every possible way. They were too old to keep going on like this, weren't they?

Roxy, still too polite to really pull, started to nudge.

"Come on," she said.

The three of them trudged up the stairs silently, Roxy in the lead. Amy thought: Why hadn't he gone to a hotel? Or to the restaurant? He had the key to the restaurant—well, maybe he had. Gone to Le Coin. Maybe he was lying, trying to make her feel bad for him—

It was strange, she thought—she thought this often—how out in the world he was so gregarious and in command, but at home he was so often needy, almost childish, and, like a child, prone to breaking things and then thinking he could be forgiven by looking at her pitifully and saying he was sorry. The ridiculousness of the charming man.

In the apartment, in the kitchen, they set about their regular routines: Judd fed Roxy, Amy swept the cat food off the counter into the sink. "Coffee?" she asked, out of habit.

"Did you sleep last night?" he asked.

She shook her head.

He was quiet for a second. "Come," he said.

She stood frozen by the sink.

"Please," he said.

He was, to this day, the only man she'd ever loved. She was too tired to think.

She followed him to the bedroom. She took off her slippers. He lay down under the comforter in the big oak bed that was one of the only things she'd brought to the marriage, the big oak bed that her mother had kept in storage and shipped out to them as a wedding present. It had been her grandmother's.

She looked at his huge body under the comforter and waited for her stomach to roil, but instead all she could think of was the white kitten curled up in the embrace of the grieving black terrier. She got in the bed, curled up next to him.

"Amy—" he said.

"Not now," she said.

And within minutes they both were asleep.

THREE

TWO MORNINGS LATER, Judd made her a sandwich and she ate it in Ferry's room. She sat at his old desk, gazed out his window without seeing. The sandwich was perfect: Roasted peppers and egg scrambled with Vermont cheddar on a toasted slice of baguette. Well. Anyone could build a delicious sandwich out of ingredients like these, and she tried not to moan in delight in front of Judd when she took a bite. He smiled anyway, knowing her too well. She wrapped a paper towel around the sandwich and while her back was to him he reached out and stroked her side the way he did when he wanted sex and she shrieked *"no"* and left the room and he said, "Okay, okay. Amy, I'm sorry."

They were living in a cautious détente, unsure—or at least Amy was unsure—what to do next or how to do it. She had options: go to the restaurant, find Meret, demand *what the fuck*; go to the restaurant, find Meret, slap her in the face; go to the restaurant, find Meret, ask her in the conspiratorial way of women to tell her the truth about what had happened between her and her husband.

Go to Meret and say: "Hahaha, you foolish girl, you know

nothing." Which is what Jackie Kennedy evidently said to any number of her husband's lovers, unsettling them with her smile.

The hostesses at the restaurant, Meret and the dozens before her, were always gorgeous and always cavalier in the way that gorgeous women were, the way Amy herself had once been once she realized that, no matter how she saw herself, other people responded to her presence in a very particular way. Soon after arriving in New York, she began to stand tall, almost imperiously, and to move gracefully. She could have slept—she often did sleep—with many of the straight men she'd encountered in her twenties, sometimes a bartender, sometimes a finance guy. Not for the sex (she generally didn't care much about sex one way or the other, and maybe that's what Judd knew about her, what he was always looking for elsewhere? But *no*, they'd worked that all out in therapy) but for the pleasure of the attention, and for the even more ecstatic pleasure of waking up in a beautiful apartment, floor-to-ceiling windows or a big marble bathroom, and she could just *stay*, sometimes for days, because these men loved having her around like a beautiful ornament and she loved the full refrigerators, the sushi, the fancy bedsheets.

She probably could have married one of them. Many of her acquaintances from that time did, and went on to have kids and live in Westchester and send her Christmas cards, and in those first years Amy felt nothing but good feelings toward them knowing that because she had married Judd, she had won.

Anyway, the hostesses were never as striking as she had once been, and she still knew how to hold her body imperiously, still knew how to make a shorter woman flinch, even if she rarely used those skills anymore. But—but she still had them. They were somewhere. She could put on some makeup and the black Yohji Yamamoto coat she'd been given twenty years ago and storm in there like a fucking stallion and demand Meret quit, leave town, kill herself.

Maybe she would do that later today.

Outside, pigeons cooing. Sir Licks jumped on Ferry's desk to inspect her sandwich, because she had no boundaries; all the animals in the house felt entitled to her food. She ripped off a tiny piece of egg for Licky and then another, slightly bigger, as she did not want to seem parsimonious. The cat purred and pushed his wet nose on her arm, which was a certain kind of love. Amy felt tears start to percolate again and refused to indulge herself. She took her phone from the pocket of her hoodie and dialed Ferry. It was nine a.m., which was probably too early, but on the other hand she and his father were picking up the whole of his $300,000 college tab so he knew enough to either pick up the phone or call her back.

"Ferris," she said to his chirpy voicemail. "Nothing urgent."

Thirty seconds later, her phone rang. Thank God. "Dos," he said, which was what he often called her, a nickname stemming from the fact that his biological mother, Judd's first wife, was also (hahaha life is funny) named Amy. Her nickname was Uno.

"Ferry," she said. She could almost smell him through the phone, soap and musk-scented body spray. It was a mystery how he was the way he was: his father was a cad and his biological mother a belligerent addict, yet somehow he had grown up to be six feet two inches of grace, possessed with a wisdom beyond his years and Confucian patience and American good sense. Everybody loved Ferry but she loved him the most; it knifed her how much she missed him.

"You okay, Dos?"

"I woke you up," she said.

"You didn't," he said. "I'm at the library, actually."

"At nine a.m.?" she asked. "On a Thursday?"

"Along with half my chem class."

Amy had gotten her BA four years ago from Baruch College, having finally completed her GED; what she knew of traditional undergrad life came from movies and her friends' nostalgia. When they'd dropped Ferry off at Cornell, hundreds of acres in the middle of God's own country, Amy felt something snap hard inside her, a surprising longing for everything she hadn't done the right way. Beautiful kids in sweatshirts, their businesslike parents spreading sheets and folding towels. Amy stood among all the move-in chaos like she'd just landed on Mars. Judd, who had a BA in film studies from Dartmouth, took charge of the sheets and towels.

"What's it like there?" she asked. "The weather?"

"It's been nice," he said. "Not too cold yet. I'm still in shorts."

"You're always in shorts."

"I guess that's true."

She was quiet for a minute. She wouldn't rat out Judd. She *wouldn't*—Ferry had also been through all this before, terrified she and his dad would get divorced, terrified that somehow this meant he'd end up living with his biological mother. She'd stayed with Judd the first time mostly for him.

"Everything okay, Dos?" She *would not rat out Judd*. She would *not*.

"There's a dog," she said, "in Georgia." It was the first thing she thought of. "And she vanished."

"Okay," Ferry said. "Is this a story?"

"I guess it is."

"Let me go out into the hallway," he said. "I shouldn't really talk in the reading room."

She hadn't told anyone about the dog in Georgia but if she were going to tell anyone it would be Ferry, and if there was a time to tell anyone it would be now, while she was not talking about Judd.

"Okay, I'm here," he said. "Shoot."

"There's a dog in Georgia named Angel, which is *Angelozi* in Georgian."

"What do you mean in Georgian?"

"In the language—I'm talking about Tbilisi, Georgia, in the Caucasus—I'm talking about the country."

"Okay," Ferry said. "I'm recalibrating. Continue."

"Right, so this dog was famous for walking kids across the street to school. Angel would be there every morning and the parents would leave their kids with her, and she'd wait for traffic to stop and then cross with the kids. All the cars would slow down. It was a thing. People posted a lot of videos. I watched them all the time."

"She was a stray dog?"

"I guess so, yes. She lived on the corner. The grateful parents built her a dog house."

"This is weird."

"There are forty-six thousand stray dogs in Tbilisi," Amy said.

"Okay," Ferry said.

"So this has been going on for years, Angel walks the kids back and forth across the street, and then one day she's not there, and nobody knows what happened to her, but there's some blood on the inside of her dog house and people say they saw teenagers throwing rocks at her, but it might not have been teenagers, it might have been Russians."

"Russians?"

"There are a lot of Russians in Georgia right now, because of the war with Ukraine."

Ferry let the line go quiet for a minute. "You sure everything's okay, Dos? Is my dad okay?"

"He's fine," she said. "I've been watching Angel's videos and I just—I am just so heartsick over this dog. There are missions right now in Tbilisi, like search and rescue missions, all these parents and kids roaming all over the city looking for this one dog in forty-six thousand. But who knows if they're even searching the right way? Like if they even have drones?"

"Drones?"

"You need drones to cover wide open areas," Amy said.

"I see."

"And if the Russians did it, so help them—the Georgians hate the

Russians already because they've been staging this low-key invasion since 2008, not like what they're doing in Ukraine but still bad—"

"I know about the Russian invasion of Georgia," Ferry said.

"Anyway," Amy said, "I wanted to tell you about it."

"Thanks?"

"It's just been on my mind," she said. "I guess I should find more to do."

"You teaching?"

"Not this semester. I don't even have to get dressed if I don't want to." Every so often, Amy taught Food Writing at the Cooper Union Extension, her credentials being her years at Le Coin and the occasional food article she'd published in the local press. But this year the enrollment hadn't been there.

"But everything else is—"

"Everything is fine, sweetie. I shouldn't have bothered you. I just keep thinking about—"

"Angel."

"*Angelozi*," she said, which was the way she'd heard it pronounced on YouTube.

"So then you should do something about it. Join one of the search and rescue missions."

"Haha right."

"No, really," Ferry said. "It would be a good project."

"What are you talking about? I'm not going to Tbilisi."

"Why not?"

"I am *not* going to fly all the way to the Caucasus."

"Well you're certainly not walking."

"Correct," she said. "Anyway, I should let you get back to your— could you come with me? If I went?"

"I have midterms."

"After midterms?"

"The dog might be dead by then."

"Oh God," she said. "Oh Ferry." Jesus. Was she crying again? *Again?*

"Dos," he said. "Mom, I was just kidding. Mom. Come on." Sometimes he also called her Mom.

"A strange woman told me something was wrong with Roxy today. At the park."

"Is that what this is about?"

"Maybe," she said. "I don't know."

"Is Roxy okay?"

"She's fine."

"But you're not okay."

"I guess I'm not," she said, and she hated herself for relying, once again, on his good sense and his intuitive nature and his calm. It wasn't fair—she was his stepmother! A parental figure!

"You should go find the dog," he said. "You know how to find lost dogs."

"I do."

"Seriously. You're probably the only person in the world who could help them."

"Lots of people know how to find dogs, Ferry."

"Yeah, but you have like—have a sixth sense."

"I'm not going to Georgia, Ferry."

"You're not teaching this semester," he said. "You should think about it."

"I'll think about it."

"Good," he said. "I gotta get back to studying. Love you."

"I love you too, sweetheart," she said, and then she hung up the phone and gave Licky the last bite of her sandwich.

She flicked back to the Justice for Angelozi page, a rudimentary website that listed the various efforts to find the dog alongside increasingly incendiary theories about who might have done such a thing to the children of Tbilisi's noble furry friend (hoodlums, vandals,

Russians, Russians). A new update: rumors that Angelozi was kidnapped and was going to be held for ransom by a group of Russian defectors who desperately needed money to afford Tbilisi's exorbitant rents, the cause of which was, of course, the Russian defectors. A preposterous theory except—except!—that rents really had tripled in Tbilisi.

A photo of Angelozi: Lab-shaped, expressive brows, off-white fur, fluffy and soft.

She couldn't stand it. She couldn't! The pain that humans inflicted on one another was bad enough, but the pain they inflicted on animals—the habitat loss, the factory farming, the heartless neglect—She was feeling too much today, she needed a Xanax—

And then the chat feature came to life on the laptop. "Hello good evening is this Amy Webb of New York City?"

Scammers had figured out how to access her email chat?

"I am Irine Benia from Justice for Angel."

Amy felt her big eyes get bigger behind the screen. She blinked hard. "Angel?" she typed. "Did you find her? I've been watching the search from New York—"

A pause. She should probably try using Google Translate, it wasn't fair to ask this person to write in English.

"I want to thank you for your generous donations, Miss Webb," Irine said. "You have given so much to our cause and helped our volunteers purchase torches and make flyers. And purchase food to keep them from hungry while they search. Thank you."

"No, thank you!" Amy typed back, amazed that there seemed to be someone real on the other side, embarrassed to be thanked for doing virtually nothing. "Thank you for what you're doing for poor Angel."

"You have donated over three hundred US dollars," Irine Benia typed.

She had? It was so easy to lose track.

"Well, I just want to help however I can," Amy wrote. "It's really nothing," and then felt profligate and ashamed. To tell this woman in Georgia that $300 US was nothing.

"I am writing to see if it would be all right with you if we used some of the money to help provide support to the other dogs in our care," Irine wrote. "This is a lot of money for us and our organization is rather small."

"It is?" Amy wrote. "I thought lots of people were looking for Angel."

"Yes"—Irine, after a pause. "Many people have Angel in their hearts, but it is hard to give up everything and look for a dog. People are quite busy after all."

"Yes, but what about the parents?"

Another pause. "Parents are busiest of all."

Well.

"It is mostly me and my daughter. When she has time."

"Yes, of course." For some reason Amy had convinced herself that Justice for Angel was a real movement, that there were leagues of Georgians searching the streets and the shelters for their poor injured friend, that the dog was a national animal hero along the lines of Smokey the Bear. But where had she gotten that idea? The videos she watched on repeat really told the same story in slightly different ways.

"Have you tried a drone?"

"What is this?"

"It's like a camera that flies—or maybe you could use a stop-motion camera? By an outdoor food bowl?"

"I do not understand," Irine typed, after a moment. "Perhaps we do not have these things in Georgia."

No drone, no camera. These were serious handicaps.

"Maybe you could set up a station by her old house? Use some of the clothing of the kids who went to school with her?"

"I should use kid's clothing?"

This was going nowhere. "I will come," Amy typed, surprising herself. "To help with the search."

"From New York City?"

"Yes," Amy typed. "I will come this week to find Angel."

"But—" Irine wrote. "You live in New York City."

"Yes. I will take a flight."

"To Tbilisi?"

"Yes."

"You have a place to stay?"

"I will find a place to stay."

"You stay with us," Irine wrote.

"I couldn't put you out," wrote Amy, automatically, while thinking: *Jesus what am I doing?*

"You stay with us," Irine wrote. "I have room. Tell me your flight information when you receive it. I am very happy you are coming. You are the patron saint of animals."

"Thanks, but I'm not," Amy wrote, although there were indeed several rescued cats gathered around her. "Is this the best way to find you?"

Irine sent her email address and her phone number and "god bless you Miss Webb," and Amy wrote, "really, you can just call me Amy if you want" and Irine wrote "Okay Miss Webb," but then a smiley face to show she was kidding. And Amy thought how remarkable it was that this person across the world could make jokes in English, and had also offered her, a complete stranger, a place to stay, and that she probably wasn't a murderer. Also, she had already spent $300 on Angel and thought: well then she might as well spend more.

Her passport, refreshed three years ago for a wine-tasting trip to Italy. Her suitcase: a bit dusty but the zippers still zipped. What was the weather like in Tbilisi in February? Astonishingly, according to the internet, exactly like the weather in New York. When should she leave? Tomorrow? Could she leave tomorrow? No—that was too soon. Wednesday then.

Was she a fool, leaving Judd alone in New York City with Meret?

Encouraged by her suitcase, her passport, her newfound purpose: she would take care of Meret before she left. Were there ATMs in Tbilisi's airport? The internet confirmed that there were. Was Georgia a safe country? The state department website confirmed that it was, one of the safest in the world. Surprising. Could she really book a ticket?

Flights through Istanbul, but they left from Newark, and she hated going to Jersey. A flight from Kennedy through Paris was $1100. A flight on the same day through Warsaw was $200 cheaper. Oh, but she loved Paris, it had been the only city she had ever truly *loved*, when she first went with Judd she'd felt like she'd not only died and gone to heaven but risen from the ashes—and even though it cost $200 more, she could smell the croissants rising in the airport kiosks. And as she was thinking about it, Google was filling her stored address and credit card number into Kayak and then the flight was booked. The flight was booked!

Was Irine Benia even a real person?

She clicked over to the *Brittanica* Country Guide. Georgia's climate was warm and pleasant, "Mediterranean-like," on the Black Sea coast. The main economic drivers were agriculture, mining, and the production of alcoholic and nonalcoholic beverages.

Their government was an unstable coalition between pro-European centers in the cities and Soviet nostalgists in the countryside. Since 2008, Russia had occupied parts of Abkhazia and South Ossetia. But otherwise, the country was peaceful, holding regular elections and boasting a "vibrant civil society." And although the birth rate was lower than the world average and the death rate was higher, Georgians were known for their "hospitality, love of life, lively intelligence, and sense of humour."

Well, that sounded nice.

Over on YouTube, she played a few introductory lessons to the Georgian language, which sounded, to her ears, like a very Slavic German: lots of multisyllabic words, looping vowels, and heavy throat-clearing sounds. *Hello* was "gamarjoba" and *good-bye* was "nakhvamdis," which was hard to say but not impossible. *Thank you* was "madloba." *Bodishi* meant "I'm sorry."

She texted Ferry: "I'm going. To Tbilisi. To find the dog."

He didn't text back, which was okay—which was good! He was in class or he was studying. "Judd!"

He came into Ferry's room; he was showered, he had shaved. He bent down and kissed her on top of her head. "You okay?"

"I'm going to Georgia."

"Georgia? Really? What's there?"

"The country."

"The country?"

"I'm visiting a friend."

"You have a friend in Georgia?"

"You're not the only one with a secret life, pal."

"Amy," he said. "What are you talking about?"

"I'm going to Tbilisi, Georgia, on Thursday to visit a friend that you don't know."

"I see," Judd said. He sat down on Ferry's bed, which sagged under his weight.

"I just bought a ticket. I fly through Paris."

"Do you want me to come with you?"

"I do not."

"I love Paris."

"I'm not really going to Paris," she said. "I'm going to Georgia."

He rubbed his eye with the heel of his hand. Ordinarily, in conversations where he didn't know what to say, Judd got up and walked away or poured himself a drink. When Uno needed a liver transplant, when they thought she might die, he sat down to tell Ferry but then got up and drank an ounce of bourbon instead and then realized that might look bad to Ferry, who was old enough to realize his mother's own drinking had put her in the position of almost dying. So he left the room entirely, and Amy explained the transplant to Ferry, gently, and held him in her arms while he tried to figure out whether or not to cry. He didn't like his mother very much, but—he did start to cry. He knew what death was. He was eight years old.

The cats crept toward them on little cat feet. Three cats, then four.

"Amy, I understand that you're mad at me, I understand that you don't want to deal with me right now, which is fine. I don't want to deal with me either. But I don't think you have to go to some Russia-adjacent terrorist state because we're having an argument—"

"It's not a terrorist state at all," she said. "Tbilisi is a very safe city, one of the safest in the world—"

"How do you know that?"

"The State Department website."

"I'm not sure we're going to believe the internet on this one."

Last week Judd's disapproval would have made her reconsider her plans. Today she felt both tired and free. "My friend Irine is letting me stay with her."

"I had no idea you had a friend in Georgia."

She shrugged to imply there's a lot about me you don't know.

"When are you coming back?"

"If I do everything I set out to do, I'll come back in two weeks."

"Set out to do?"

"Yes."

"Do you have a return ticket?"

"I do."

"So?"

"So I'll be back in two weeks."

He sighed, performatively. "And what, exactly, are you setting out to do?"

"I really don't feel like getting into it, Judd," she said.

"Is it for an animal?"

"It's for me," she said.

"Okay," he said. "But this seems . . . extreme."

"I suppose it does."

"You sure it's not for an animal?" He had always supported her love of animals, had let her turn their apartment into an animal shelter (Ferry had calculated that, over the years, they'd fostered sixteen dogs, thirty-nine cats, five rabbits, four guinea pigs, and, for a few weeks in the early teens, twin pot-bellied pigs) but also always treated her love of animals like it was a sort of cute, sort of unserious hobby (yet what could be more serious than saving a life? She did not know). He didn't condescend, exactly, but he sometimes called her the Family Zookeeper in public.

Judd, meanwhile: ate animals, cooked animals, occasionally hunted animals; had taken a course in whole-animal butchery up in the Catskills; had deep-sea-fished off the coast of Baja California, slaughtering majestic bluefins right there on the boat. Crabbed in Maryland, clammed in Maine; killed lobsters by plunging knives into their heads. Amy tried not to think about the complexity there (he loved Roxy, tolerated the cats), but she herself hadn't eaten meat in years. She just couldn't. These were animals that *nursed their babies*.

"Okay, listen, I know you don't want to tell me everything right now—" he said. "I mean I know there's a lot that we have to work out—"

She looked at Judd then and wasn't sure if the person she saw was the actual person in front of her or an amalgam of every role he'd ever played in her life. Was he as beautiful as she thought he was? Was it his physical beauty that tied her to him like a cord?

No, it wasn't that. It was everything else in her life. Her food, her shelter, her child.

"You can ask me whatever you want," she said, magnanimous.

"I would just feel—I would just feel a little safer if I knew more about this trip."

"I understand that," she said.

"But you're not going to tell me."

"I will give you Irine's address and phone number so you can reach me if you need me. Or if Ferry needs me."

He leaned back on the bed. One of the cats, Magnus, came over and sniffed him. "Are you sure you don't want to go to the Caribbean?"

"I don't."

"St. Barts?"

She was silent. Magnus settled himself on Judd's broad chest, his tail up against his chin, a feline beard.

"Kripalu?" he said. "You could take Lynne." Lynne was Amy's closest girlfriend, but they weren't enormously close. "You could take your brother."

"Why on earth would I take my brother to Kripalu?"

"You could take me," he said, sounding forlorn enough that she actually felt sorry for him for a split second, so she lay down next to him and Magnus on Ferry's bed and took his hand. Ferry's ceiling was still spackled with the glow-in-the-dark stars they'd plastered up there when he was a child.

"I'm sorry I can't tell you more," she said. "I won't be in danger. It will be perfectly safe. But I have to do this. And I'm an adult. So I'll be fine."

"Are you going because you're angry at me?"

"Judd, you're an adult too," she said. "Act like one."

He squeezed her hand.

"When I get back we can go to Kripalu if you still want to."

"I don't think the food's that great there," he said.

"That wouldn't be the point," she said, and he turned to her and smiled, his way of admitting he was kind of an idiot, and they kissed for a while even though Magnus refused to move, and then they went to their own bedroom so as not to desecrate Ferry's. And afterward, as he showered and got ready to go to the restaurant, she lay in their bed and felt scared: scared at how easily she had forgotten Meret but also scared that she had extracted something from his transgression. The only thing she had ever extracted before was a promise from him to be better. To do better. Now she had gotten something else—a secret of her own—and she thought of the women she had met or heard of whose husbands cheated with impunity but rewarded their forbearance with diamonds, cars, personal pilates instructors.

She had never exacted revenge before. Not that the trip to Georgia was revenge, but it was kind of a mindfuck, and that had never been her thing.

Or was she scared because in the decade since she'd stopped cooking at the restaurant, she'd stopped thinking of herself as intrepid and started thinking of herself as a wife and a stepmother and a teacher and a rescuer of stray dogs and feral cats, none of which seemed particularly brave no matter how much Glennon Doyle she read, and now here she was, going to a place she had not really even heard of before last month. Because of a dog.

It had been a year and a half since Ferry had left for college, a year and a half since her days had been structured around keeping a teenager fed and schooled and healthy. Why hadn't she worked harder to raise enrollment for her class? Why hadn't she gone back to the kitchen at Le Coin? She could have done anything—why had she done nothing? But now—now she had something she could do.

Judd came out of the steamy bathroom wrapped in a towel, his hair matted to his forehead. "Georgian food is great," he said. "They have these breads, they're called khachapuri, they're filled with cheese and egg. And dumplings. Huge ones, like Turkish manti but much bigger. And Georgian wine is incredible, some of the oldest vineyards in the world."

"Sounds good," she said.

"You should take notes on the food," he said. "You can use it in your next food writing class."

"I don't think I will," she said.

"Well, if you think of it," he said.

She nodded. She was still wearing the T-shirt she'd slept in, her underwear kicked down somewhere toward the bottom of the bed. "Should I hire someone to feed the animals or will you come home to do it?"

"You should probably find someone," he said. "And a dog walker too."

Of course he wouldn't leave Le Coin for all of twenty minutes at night to come home and feed everyone. But there was a limit to how many battles she needed to win in one day.

After he left, she showered and threw a load of T-shirts and jeans into the washing machine, then dusted off her suitcase and pondered exactly what she should take, what she would need. Comfortable shoes, a flashlight, a slip leash, dried pig ears, bully sticks. Her drone, a charger, a fresh notebook, and some pens.

She thought about it for a second and then removed her ATM card and credit cards from the accounts she shared with Judd from her wallet. She stuck them in the desk and replaced them with the under-used ATM card that connected to the little account of her own, the one she'd always kept secret, the place where she squirreled away her occasional paycheck or stipend. This was the other piece of advice her mother had given her that she had chosen, for some reason, to follow: make sure you always have a little something of your own.

This trip could not be on Judd's dime.

Her phone pinged: "Proud of you, Dos," Ferry texted. "You're going to find that dog."

"Proud of you too, Ferry," she texted back. "You're going to ace that chem test."

"We're both heroes," he wrote.

"I think you're right," she wrote, then followed up with eight million hearts and stars.

FOUR

THAT NIGHT, EMBOLDENED, she put on lipstick, leather leggings, finger-combed her hair, called Lynne and asked if she wanted to hit Le Coin to inspect the new hostess who had been flirting with Judd. Lynne, bitterly divorced and always looking for a reason to get out of the house, said "damn straight I do" and showed up at the apartment in black jeans and a black beanie like she was prepared to commit violence.

"We're not shooting anyone," Amy said. "We're just there for some surveillance."

"These are my surveillance clothes," Lynne said. "I'm fifty-two years old and invisible."

They arrived at Le Coin a little after seven, the bar crowd already spilling into the narrow space around the front banquettes. Meret stood at the hostess stand, black dress, leather boots.

"That's her," Amy said.

"Obviously," Lynne said.

Had this woman been fucking her husband? She seemed so extraordinarily—young. That unlined face, the cheap shine of her dress;

Judd didn't pay his staff enough, really. She was attractive, obviously—almost cruelly attractive—but also somehow unformed-looking. Her face had no lines whatsoever, no depth. Of course that didn't mean Judd *hadn't* been fucking her, only that Amy probably wouldn't have, in his place.

"You okay?" Lynne asked.

"I'm okay," Amy said, and took a deep breath. She probably was okay. She nodded at Meret quickly, walking past her like she owned the place—which in a way she did—and Meret had the good sense to blush and step aside.

"And you're sure nothing's happened between her and him? I mean nothing physical?"

"I'm sure," Amy lied. Well, she wanted to be sure. Amy and Lynne took a two-top by the windows that was usually held empty for impromptu VIPs. Judd was nowhere to be found: probably in the kitchen, then, or the office upstairs, paying bills. Or was he somewhere else? A secret place of his own? Amy gestured to Fred, the bartender, for a martini; he sent two over promptly.

The restaurant had gone through a few understated renovations since it had opened: the key was to keep it timeless without also making it look like a period piece. The zinc bar with Fred in his white shirt and black apron behind it, mixing cocktails with a silver shaker, the broad framed mirror behind him like the one in the Manet painting. The brass shelves of top-tier alcohol, including bottles from brands nobody had ever heard of or, if they had, couldn't find in their average liquor stores. The round tables, a little too close together, to give the room some energy. The noise bouncing off every surface.

"So what'd that busty cunt do?" Lynne asked, sliding olives off her martini's stirrer. She had a trace of an Irish accent from a childhood in Belfast.

"Sent a naughty pic," Amy said.

"Can I see?"

"On Judd's phone," Amy said.

"You didn't forward yourself a copy? You should always forward yourself a copy."

"I was too traumatized."

Lynne shook her head. "She probably looks amazing naked."

"She does."

"But you probably do too, you skinny twat."

"Thanks," Amy said, sipping her martini, so icy it crunched. "But I'm not twenty-three anymore, you know?"

And then the waiter came around—Neil, a few years ahead of Ferry at St. Ann's, an aspiring modern dancer—and Amy ordered the risotto for Lynne and the agnolotti with chanterelles for herself plus a bottle of Bruno Duchêne Pét-nat ($180 on the menu; Judd's supplier charged $22). Carbs, alcohol, butter, foods of strength.

"Can we get the oysters? I love the oysters here." The kitchen did a fiery oysters Rockefeller: garlic, spinach, Calabrian chiles. Amy either did or did not eat shellfish depending on the company she was with and her mood; today she did not feel like she could face them, but ordered six for Lynne.

"I can pay for this, you know."

"You won't pay."

"I know," Lynne said. "But I feel like less of an asshole if I make it clear that I *would* pay."

Amy was watching Meret across the room. Meret leaned over a lot, more than you'd think a hostess would need to. She gave great cleavage.

"So what are we going to do about her?" Lynne asked.

"I haven't decided yet." Fuck the wine, Amy wanted another martini, but she didn't want to alarm Fred. Anyway she was already buzzed enough to be as curious about Meret as she was disgusted by her. She watched as the girl gracefully managed the crowd at the hostess stand, the pushy men, the women who were already a little drunk. And then

Meret's ass in that tight black dress, swishing past as she led a trio of finance bros to their table.

"I miss that feeling," Lynne said as the oysters arrived on their artfully tarnished platter.

"Of revenge?"

"No," she said. "No, you know. Of being wanted."

"Wanted like—"

"Like wanted," Lynne said. "Like—being flirted with, being needed. Having a man make a fool of himself over me. Back when I was young, it was so intoxicating—I would sleep with the silliest men just because they wanted to sleep with me, because they went too far to have the chance to sleep with me."

Amy kept her eyes on Meret's ass.

"That probably happened to you all the time," Lynne said.

"I guess it did," she said, turning her eyes to her friend. "But it's been years."

"I used to think—" Lynne said. She was still wearing her black beanie, but loose curls had escaped from underneath, girlishly. Lynne's eyes were sparkling with loss. "I used to think I really lusted for these puny little men. Even when Peter and I were married, when we were married for ten years, fifteen, and the sex was just—whatever it was, something we did with our shirts on—every so often, there'd be a guy at a bar or a man I'd meet a conference and he would be just *ridiculous* over me, and I'd convince myself that I wanted him. But I just wanted to see myself reflected in him. Do you know what I mean?"

Amy did.

"I wanted to see myself as someone worth acting ridiculously for."

"It doesn't happen much anymore, does it?" Amy said.

"It doesn't happen at all," Lynne said. "Men who were in no way as handsome as Peter, as—as sophisticated as Peter. Men without money, without anything. But they wanted to fuck me—they were, in fact, desperate to fuck me, texting me at weird hours, and I just—I melted for them. It didn't even matter who they were. They made me look so good. To myself."

"Did you sleep with them?"

"Never," Lynne said. "Never. When it came to that I ran away. I couldn't risk everything I had built on a stupid ego trip."

"It's not such a little thing though," Amy said. "Feeling wanted."

"Feeling want-able."

Amy nodded.

"It was my last gasp. Forty-seven. Forty-eight."

"You think that's a last gasp?"

"For some women. For me, that's how it felt."

Amy understood. Her mother's last gasp had been when she was thirty-five, the year before she had her kids; she often told them that.

"You never cheated," Amy said.

"I never did—I mean not technically. Peter did."

"The nanny."

"Oh, he slept with lots of women before her. She was just the one he wanted to blow up our lives for. And listen—" Lynne slurped an oyster—"I get it. I get it! I even got it *then*. She was gorgeous, and she wanted him so much, and reflected back in her eyes he must have felt like a god. He didn't care about her, not really—he cared about what she saw in *him*. You know? That she thought he was perfect. Which I didn't anymore. I knew him too well."

"Of course. You were married for twenty years."

"Twenty-four," Lynne said. "According to my kids, they fight all the time now. He doesn't want to go to her family events, doesn't want to go to her best friend's wedding."

"That's not what it was about," Amy said. "He didn't really want to be her partner."

They were quiet for a while, drinking and staring into the past.

"I remember that feeling too," Amy finally said.

"Wasn't it the best?"

And now—what to say about who she was now, how she felt now? The crazy mood swings, the faltering marriage, the trip to Georgia, which was insane. And she was almost certainly perimenopausal, which was something she would never talk about or even think about. Her body was a secret she liked to keep from herself.

"Did you ever cheat on Judd?"

"Never," Amy said.

"I didn't think so," Lynne said. "Would you ever?"

"I doubt it," Amy said. "It's hard to imagine a man who would make me want to. Even after all these years." She finished the dregs of her martini. "Isn't that crazy?"

"The problem is, Amy, if I may—" Lynne said.

"You may not."

"The problem is that you still think Judd is some kind of star. You're still a starfucker."

"Lynne, cut it out."

"You still feel like you owe him something for marrying you when frankly it's the other way around. He owes you! You've stood by him all these years, despite all his—missteps—"

Amy lifted her finger for another martini. "That's not exactly how it's been."

"You don't owe him anything. I'm telling you. Men who are married live an average of eight years longer than unmarried men. They owe their wives everything. They owe us their *lives*."

"I'm not a starfucker."

"Do you make his doctor's appointments? His dentist appointments? Did you raise his son? Still raising him? I mean I know you love that kid, but you took on an awful lot of work for someone else's baby."

"Come on," Amy said, feeling her neck prickle. "Don't say that." Lynne was a mean drunk, which Amy often forgot until it was too late.

But she took it down a notch. "All I'm saying is you should make that bitch pay."

Amy sighed. "Judd says nothing happened."

"Doesn't matter," Lynne said. "If we roofied her we could tie her up in the basement and give her a really good scare."

"I'm not here to go to jail."

"Then what did you mean when you said you wanted vengeance?"

"I'm not sure I said that at all? I think you said that?" Amy sighed. "Anyway I'm leaving."

"Now? After you've just been defending him for the past twenty minutes? You're really going to leave?"

"No, I'm not leaving Judd. I'm just going away for a few weeks. To Georgia. Not—" she said—"not Atlanta, Georgia. I'm going to Tbilisi, Georgia. In the Caucasus."

"Why? What on earth is there?"

Amy sighed. "A dog rescue. I think."

"A dog rescue?"

"I think," she said. "I'm not entirely sure. I just—after all this, I just need to get away for a little while," she said. "And I want to be useful."

"So you're going to Tbilisi," she said.

"There's a dog," Amy said. "Please don't ask me anything else about it. It's too ridiculous to explain."

"Aren't there dogs in, like, the Catskills you could rescue? In New Jersey?"

"The people in Tbilisi don't have any of the tools they need to find her. And it just feels—I can't explain it, but it feels like something I've been called upon to do."

"A mission," Lynne said.

"That makes it sound religious."

"It's not?"

Amy sighed. "This is for an animal," she said. "Not for Jesus."

"A mission's a mission," said Lynne, a lapsed Catholic who still saw God everywhere. "Does Judd know you're going?"

"Yes."

"And does he care?"

"He likes that I have something to accomplish," Amy said. "I think, anyway. Or I guess *I* like having something to accomplish."

"That's so American of you," Lynne said.

"What can I say?" she said. "I'm American."

Then Neil returned with the wine and a minute later with the food and a fresh basket of warm sourdough and cultured ricotta. Amy tore into a piece of bread, Lynne guzzled the wine, Meret passed by again, this time with a group of jubilant-looking tourists, maybe Brits, maybe Midwesterners, and Lynne stuck out a toe but pulled it back before Meret took a spill, and then Judd appeared out of nowhere by their table and pulled up a chair.

"I didn't know you were coming in," he said. "I would have come down sooner. Neil took care of you? Lynne, you like the Pét-nat?"

"It's gorgeous," she said, dialing up her latent brogue. She talked a good game but was as susceptible to Judd's charms as any other female. She smiled impishly, took her cap off.

"Did Amy tell you where she's off to?"

"Tbilisi, Georgia, she just told me," Lynne said. "That's incredible. So brave."

"Well, we all know Amy's a brave girl," Judd said, patting her knee. How had she let this happen? How had she let them diminish her in this way? Calling her a brave girl like she was a child about to go on her first bike ride, like she wasn't a fully actualized human being who had left home at eighteen, built a life, raised a child, raised a *husband*, saved a million dogs, cooked a million meals, held up her world again and again and again? Something inside her clenched and unclenched, a fist punching from the inside.

"I've got to go," she said, standing.

"Already?" Lynne said.

"Babe, you okay?"

"Yes," she said. "It's time for me to go." She thought, briefly, that she should apologize, but she didn't. She had nothing to apologize for: she'd had enough and wanted to go home. But then she sputtered out an "I'm sorry, I'm tired," and Judd nodded and Lynne nodded and then Judd said, "I'll be home early," and Amy shrugged as though she didn't care. But she did care. She wanted him where she could see him. Because as she brushed her way out of the restaurant, swishing past crowded tables, she saw Meret leading a group of giggling girlies to the back, and she saw what Judd saw: Meret was so young, she was so beautiful, and so stupid. But Amy also knew that she wouldn't be that way forever.

Amy thought about approaching her, she thought about whispering *you know nothing*, but deep down she knew there was no point. Meret would learn for herself soon enough.

TWO

GEORGIA

FIVE

SHE TOOK THE subway to Kennedy, thinking the minor aggravations of the A train would calm her nerves. Which it did, sort of, giving her time to meditate on the in-car ads for storage units and boner pills and the shifting demographics of the folks who got on and off the train. She wore her passport in a belt hidden under her shirt. Before she left, Judd gave her $1000 in cash, even though she protested that they had ATMs in Georgia. Ignoring her, he lifted her shirt and tucked it into her hidden belt, which made her feel like a child, and the $1000 made her feel vulnerable, as though it were visible through her clothes. Did he know she had left their joint ATM card at home? Was he trying to keep her from taking care of her own damn self?

He and Roxy walked her to the station and she thought about just handing the money back to him but then thought, why make a scene? And she also thought that maybe she could use the extra thousand.

"Are you sure I can't put you in a cab?"

And then she was furious, a fresh wave of fury: it was just a turn of phrase but still the idea that he was going to *put her anywhere*. She hugged Roxy, who licked her face, and tried to let the pressure of the dog's body melt the fury away. It didn't. She kissed Judd quickly and hustled down the stairs, not looking back.

"Amy!" he called after her. "I love you! Be safe!"

"I love you too," she mumbled, then guiltily texted him as soon as she got to the platform. "I love you too." Smiley face, thumbs up, heart.

Then an hour and fifteen minutes of inaudible announcements and the smell of Roxy's breath on her hands and the traces of fur clinging to her parka.

On the AirTrain, which connected the subway to the terminal, new worries: had she packed too much? Not enough? Did she have enough time to make her flight? She had two and a half hours. The sun was setting over Manhattan. What if she never saw home again? Never saw Roxy? Ferry? She did not think of Judd. She was worried that, if she did, she would lose all her resolve. Not just because she was worried about what he would do while she was gone, but because she really was going very far away, and she really had never done something like this by herself.

And in fact she didn't have to do this—she could spend two weeks anywhere. One thousand dollars on her person, clean underwear in her suitcase. An ATM card. She could buy a ticket for St. Barts.

But no: she would accomplish this absurd thing. She said this out loud: "I will. Accomplish. This thing." She was a woman with a passport and a plane ticket and a specific set of expertise. She had found dozens of lost pets since she herself was a child. She was doing this not because it was absurd and not because she was lost; she was doing this because she could. She marched like an automaton through the airport and toward the thing she had set out to do.

Kennedy was mercifully empty.

The woman at the Air France counter checked her bag, checked her passport, asked her no questions. The woman at security ushered her through. There was no delay, nothing stopping her from moving forward.

Earlier in the day she had emailed Irine: "Are you sure it's okay that I'm coming? I'm very happy to stay at a hotel."

And Irine wrote back right away: "It is an honor to host you, Amy. In our country we are very proud of our culture of hospitality. You are doing me and my family a great favor by staying."

So what could she say? At the airport, she bought I Heart New York T-shirts for five people in five different sizes, hoping that would cover whoever was in Irine's family. She had also packed a large bottle of Woodford Reserve, a miniature bronze Statue of Liberty, three New York Yankees caps and a coffee-table book of America's National Parks. And if none of that appealed to Irine, she could give her $1000.

And then the gate: "Flight Eleven to Paris: anyone needing a little extra time?" In a lovely French accent. Amy needed time, she needed time, although she was so often overwhelmed by all the time she had.

She popped her Xanax before she walked onto the plane and was asleep by the time it departed. But her dreams, usually muted by sedatives, were strangely vivid: Judd was in a plane that was following hers, his plane was in fact trying to chase hers, because he wanted to tell her something. He had lied about Meret. They were going to spend the next two weeks in bed together, and he wanted to thank her for leaving. Thank her for giving him what he wanted once again. That was why his plane was chasing hers, so he could thank her in person. And then, as she opened her mouth to say something, Judd's plane went down, and Amy witnessed the plunge from her own plane's small window, saw Judd explode in a lake of fire on the ground.

"Chicken or pasta?"

Amy blinked awake: pasta.

And also a travel-sized bottle of tannic red, then *Marry Me* with Jennifer Lopez and the catastrophically miscast Owen Wilson, and then another nap. And then the strangely endless nowhere Paris of

Charles de Gaulle airport, somewhere outside the city but definitely in *France*, which was made clear by the many tiny patisseries where any US airport would have had an Auntie Anne's or Starbucks. She bought herself two croissants and an espresso in a paper cup and sat down to watch the travelers shift back and forth under the fluorescent lights, trying to delight in the French all around her. How long since she had been immersed in another language? She had taken a few French classes at Baruch, understood enough to order food. And she had watched *Amélie* at the Angelika four separate times.

She'd said to Judd, the first time they went—2008? 2009?—that Paris was the only place she'd ever been that looked exactly like its publicity shots: yellowish white limestone buildings, black shutters, curlicue balconies, outdoor cafes with awnings. And then, turning a corner—the Eiffel Tower! The first time she saw it she couldn't believe it, gasped then tried to cough to not seem like such a rube. But still: the Eiffel Tower, just hanging out in the middle of the city like some kind of ordinary building.

Paris still felt beautiful to her, even from a distance, inside this airless airport: a family in African robes, green and magenta; a family in sweatpants; a confused-looking family pushing four different luggage carts, balancing nineteen suitcases; a couple in chic clothing; a woman with a small dog.

She texted Ferry: "I'm sort of in Paris!" She texted Judd: "halfway there."

Three more hours to kill before the flight to Tbilisi—not enough time to leave the airport, too much time to do nothing. She booted up her laptop to check the latest Angel news and was shocked, on the *Didi Gulabi* home page, to see a photo of her own face from that oh-so-brief period of her life when she modeled. God, from what freakish internet wormhole had they unearthed that? She looked young, beautiful, and surprised, eyes lined with bright blue liner, green shadow, a kind of carnival effect, mouth puckered in a kiss. Blond curls framed her face. The photo, she remembered, had been for an ad for a local video chain. She ran the accompanying text through Google translate: *We are pleased to announce the arrival of Amy Webb, American model and benefactor, to Tbilisi to help in our search for Angelozi. In a time of much sadness, Miss Webb's presence brings optimism and joy.*

Amy couldn't help it; she laughed out loud, and then, when she was done laughing, whispered, "fuck."

BUT AT LEAST it was a different sort of despair that filled her as she boarded the flight to Tbilisi: the despair of knowing how badly she would disappoint Irine. Her tired face, her idiotic gifts, the fact that she had never really been a model and that she could no more guarantee Angel's return than she could guarantee a sunny day.

The preflight announcements were in French, English, and Georgian, the first time she'd ever heard the language spoken live. It was lovely, gentle and lilting. The flight from Paris to Tbilisi was five hours long. It would be six in the morning when she arrived, and Irine said she would meet her at the airport. Five hours before she brought the disappointing truth of herself to this lovely woman in the Caucasus.

Still, as the plane lifted, heading East toward Asia, she felt a brief rumble of excitement in her belly about going somewhere she'd never been before. And the chance to go somewhere and do something helpful! She even indulged in a little fantasy of bringing Angel back to the shelter, muddy and a little scratched up but very much alive, and how excited everyone would be. Which is perhaps why, when the plane finally landed, and Amy again readjusted her watch, she found herself overwhelmed by an entirely new and surprising feeling:

Joy.

Joy!

She was here, had arrived here. Home of Irine and Angel and 46,000 stray dogs and even if she couldn't rescue everyone *she was here to help.* Yes yes I will be of use, she whispered as she waited in the freezing-cold immigration line.

"Address where you are staying?" A stern-faced man at the counter.

"I don't have—let me just find—"

"A private home?"

"Yes. A friend."

"You have a friend in Tbilisi?"

"Yes. She lives—she lives in—" But how to pronounce any of this? She showed the transcribed address to the man behind the counter.

"Okay," the man said, and then he stamped her passport. He smiled at her: one of his teeth was bright gold. "Enjoy your visit."

"Thank you." *Madloba.*

Past immigration, the airport was much like every airport she'd ever been in, glass and steel and plastic, except that the signs were both in English and beautiful flowery Georgian. As she waited for her suitcase, she tried to figure out what time it was in New York (ten p.m. the day before?) and then she went through customs and the sliding glass doors that separated airport world from the real world. And— just as she had dared to hope—there was a beautiful dark-haired woman on the other side of the sliding door, holding a sign: AMY WEBB WELCOME TO GEORGIA! The woman was smiling broadly and was wearing a bright red coat and sunglasses and a smile that could electrify the entire airport.

And Amy felt herself beloved.

SIX

SHE HUGGED IRINE as if they were, indeed, old friends. "You are even more beautiful in person," Irine said, fluently—"and so tall!"

"Oh please, *you're* beautiful! How do you speak English? I'm sorry you had to get up so early."

"I learned it here, everyone does. You are tired, yes? You are hungry? It is not early for me at all, I get up with the dogs—"

"The dogs!" Amy said as they left the airport and walked through a parking lot that was much like any airport parking lot, except the sky was a new sort of pink-purple-gray, a color Amy had never seen in any sky, and in the distance in every direction were snow-capped mountains. The sun was halfway risen, a glimmer in the east.

"Your flight was good?"

"Great! I went through Paris."

"I love Paris," Irine said.

And then a small car, boxy, the seats covered in dog hair and smelling like cigarettes. In the back of the car, a yipping wire-haired mutt.

"This is Zazi. He's one of our rescues, he wanted to say hello."

"Hello, Zazi." The dog was skinny with a badly mangled ear. He was buckled into the back seat like a child, barking frantically at Amy. Irine yelled at him in Georgian until he lay down on the back seat, abashed.

"Very rude," Irine said, "I'm sorry." And then they took off toward the highway, a modern, American-looking highway, but the cars were a wild mix of open-bed trucks and Audis and fragile ancient sedans and buses and 18-wheelers belching up plumes of smoke. The sun was filling the sky now, and the traffic moved in fits and starts, and Amy was startled to see a bright neon Exxon station and billboards for ski resorts slung across the highway. What had she expected? Something less—glamorous. Motorcycles weaving. Birds circled above, what looked like vultures, and then a flock of small dark birds lifting into the sky.

"You are tired?"

"Strangely, I'm not," Amy said.

"You are hungry?"

"Maybe a little?"

"Good, when we get to the house we eat."

"Irine, I want you to know you don't have to feed me or—I mean I am perfectly happy to take care of myself. I don't want you to feel responsible for me."

"I don't know what you mean, 'not responsible,'" Irine said, but she was smiling. "Of course we are responsible. You are our guest!" And as the traffic loosened, she started speeding much like many of the other small cars were doing, skirting past the buses and trucks at what felt like warp speed. She took her hands off the wheel to light a cigarette and pointed the pack at Amy. Amy, who hadn't smoked regularly in twenty-five years, took one. She lit up, inhaled, felt herself suffer a brief pulmonological incident.

They rolled down their windows and held their cigarettes out into the Georgian morning as Zazi barked manically in the back seat.

"He doesn't like me smoking," Irine said. "He worries for my health."

Amy inhaled, suppressed a cough. "That's sweet."

They were entering the city now, more quickly than Amy had expected to. They were descending a hill. On a placard on a stone wall, a bas-relief image of a familiar face. "Does that say this is—Is this George W. Bush Street?"

"It is." Irine gave Amy a sideways glance. "Did you like him? When he was your president?"

"Oh . . ." Amy hedged—was George W. Bush a hero in this part of the world? "Was he popular here?"

They were slip-slapping down a windy street lined with rickety buildings. In the back seat, Zazi's barks became whines.

"Not really. He just showed up in Tbilisi," Irine said. "For an afternoon. We were so grateful we renamed the airport road for him."

Amy nodded like this made sense.

"Many of us are easily impressed. Too easily." And now they were in the heart of the city, or what might have been its heart, grayish apartments with moldering balconies, thirty stories high, spread out in vast blocks. George W. Bush, with his twang and his malapropisms and his Texas ranch and his wars. How impossible to imagine him here.

"What did he do when he visited?"

"He gave a speech and then a man from the crowd threw a grenade at him and his wife. Fortunately the grenade didn't go off, but it was a big mess—you don't remember?"

"Wait, *what* happened?"

"It's true!" Irine said. "A security officer saw the whole thing and disposed of the grenade. Bush never even found out until after he'd given his speech."

"I can't believe I never heard this story."

"Well," Irine said. "The grenade didn't go off. You would have heard about it if it had."

"Yeah, but—"

Outside, traffic roundabouts, a fast food joint, a produce stand, more gray, forbidding apartments. George Bush had survived a grenade attack—here?

"These buildings are ugly, I know," Irine said, gesturing out the window. "I lived in one until I was twelve years old. Three families in one flat." She threw her cigarette butt from the window. "One toilet down the hall for ten apartments."

"That's not a great ratio," Amy said.

"You are right," Irine said. "I still remember the lines in the morning, everyone pounding on the door. And of course the worst was when you had a stomachache. Most of the men would just pee outside."

"Really?"

"Really. They have nothing like this in America. Every apartment has their own bathroom, yes?"

In fact Amy and Judd had three bathrooms in their apartment, including one they reserved for the cats. "When did you move out?"

"After we got our independence from the USSR. 1991. One of the families we lived with purchased the apartment and made us leave. And even though my parents hated that apartment we weren't sure where to go. Nobody knew who owned anything, who the landlords were. There hadn't been private property in so long, you see, so we never even thought about buying a house. It was a disaster. Everybody was happy but everybody was scared. Even the police."

"I've read about that," Amy said. "How hard it was after Communism fell."

"For some people the difficulty continues," Irine said, shifting gears sharply. Amy felt the seatbelts strain against her shoulders. "But for most of us the nineties were the worst. Rolling blackouts, freezing cold. I was in school at the time, we'd be in the middle of a lesson and suddenly no more lights, no heat, nothing. I stopped taking the elevator because you could be trapped for hours if the electricity went out between floors."

"Jesus."

"It's hard to believe it now," Irine said as they paused at a red light, "how bad it could be. One time I was on the Metro with my mother, the Metro stopped suddenly, everything was dark. We waited for an hour, but it was clear the power was not coming back, and we were getting hungry. It was past dinner time. So a few of us managed to pull the car doors open and we walked for two hours through the tunnels to find a way out. The rats—oh my god, they were the size of Zazi."

Amy had been on the F train once when it stalled out for thirty minutes and she thought she was going to have a panic attack. Everyone did. Then a homeless man in the corner of the car told everyone to calm the fuck down and then the train started to move.

"How old were you?"

"Maybe thirteen? The scary thing—even scarier than the rats!— was if the electricity came back on and you were in a tunnel a train would start to come."

"Holy crap!" Amy said. "Did that ever happen?"

Irine laughed. "Not to us." She shook another cigarette out of her pack, handed one to Amy. "And it was rare for the electricity to come back that fast, to tell you the truth. Sometimes it was out for weeks. It made many people long for the days of the Soviet Union. Because even if we had to share an apartment with fifteen people, at least we weren't cooking food in fireplaces. We weren't living in the nineteenth century."

"That's how you cooked?"

"In the fireplace, yes. Sometimes outside on a grill," Irine said. She lit her cigarette with a plastic lighter while keeping one hand on the wheel, squinting against the smoke. She had lovely purple-blue eyes, a deep furrow at her temple.

"Did everyone speak Russian then?"

"Mostly Georgian, some Russian. But not eagerly. And now we learn English."

"Your English is so good," Amy said. "I wish I could speak more than a few words of Georgian."

Irine laughed. "There is no need. The only place in the world where people speak Georgian is right here. Unless you plan on staying here forever, you don't have to learn it."

"I probably can't stay here forever," Amy said. "But I can say a few things. I can say hello! *Gamarjoba*."

"Gah-mar-jobah."

"Gah-mar-jobah."

"Not bad," Irine said, as the car rounded a corner. The Soviet apartment blocks were receding, replaced by smaller stucco apartment buildings and storefronts. There was greenery here, too: trees on sidewalks, rose bushes and other flowering plants.

"Where did you go," Amy asked, "after you left your first flat?"

"Eh, we all moved into my grandmother's house. It was crowded— she had all her sisters there, my cousins, but there was really no other choice. My father didn't like it though. He was always complaining, said it was easier to live in our old flat. There was even more fighting in my grandmother's house over the kitchen and the bathroom than there was in our first flat. But at least I could play with my cousins, which I liked. And we got to have our first dog. Who was also named Zazi."

Zazi let out a bark.

"How long did you stay?"

Irine blew out another stream of smoke. "We're still there."

They were off the main road now, threading through a neighborhood of three- and four-story buildings, many with lovely wooden railings on their balconies. Some of the houses looked well-kept, while others were falling apart, but everything seemed to be inhabited, lively. People on the streets, shopping bags, a café with outdoor tables and diners drinking coffee. Zazi was sitting up and panting: he smelled home. A grocery store, a pharmacy, a roundabout, high-rises disappearing in the distance. And then a small park, and another café, and a string of low-slung apartment buildings. Amy's head was throbbing from the cigarettes and the traffic fumes.

"We're here!"

Thank God. "Oh, it's lovely." Which it was. Irine's house was larger than Amy had expected, although she hadn't realized she'd had any expectations until they pulled up. Pale pink paint peeled off the house's siding, and the window shutters and door were intricately carved wood. There were balconies, also intricately carved, and she could hear the mad barks of what sounded like a dozen dogs coming from inside. Zazi leapt out of the car and up the uneven brick path to the front door; Amy and Irine followed.

"Come in! Come in!" An older woman at the door, gray hair piled on top of her head in a tilting beehive.

"Is that your mother?"

"My aunt," Irine said. "My mother doesn't speak any English."

The woman took Amy by the elbows and smiled at her with silver-capped teeth. She had large brown eyes, a mole on her chin, and the folded, velvety skin that came with old age. "We are so happy to see you!" she said. Amy submitted to a kiss on each cheek and then a hug. The woman smelled like strong detergent. She had a wide, cushiony bosom.

"Amy, this is Deida Bachana. Deida Bachana, es aris Ami, chveni amerik'eli st'umari. Come on, let's go inside."

Inside the house: a huge room, a warm smell of something baking, and coffee, and dogs—the excited yelps of so many dogs, cordoned off behind baby gates, jumping up, while Irine and her aunt yelled at them in Georgian. The room was large and mostly empty except for the gates, dog beds, dog toys, bowls on the floor, and Amy realized: this was the Didi Gulabi rescue itself. How many dogs were there? Enough for her to feel overwhelmed, almost alarmed. Twelve, thirteen? All sizes, no discernible breeds, barking, growling.

"Come on! Come upstairs! You meet them later!"

A wooden door and a rickety wooden staircase up to the next floor: a kitchen tiled in brown and green, a few missing tiles, the dogs' barking filtering up from beneath the floorboards. A small, dented refrigerator. Two older women sitting at the table, smiling broadly at Amy. A round cake on the table, steaming.

"I can't believe you can take care of this many dogs at one time!"

"Oh, they come and go, really. When we can't afford to take care of them anymore we let them go."

"Go where?"

Irine shrugged and gestured at the table. "This is my mother, Natela, and my aunt Marmar. And you've met Bachana." The women smiled at Amy with identical smiles. They were wearing faded house-coats, wire-rimmed glasses; one had reddish hair and one had gray. "Bachana speaks a little bit of English but the others—"

"Welcome," said Marmar.

"Well, I guess they speak a little bit of English, too."

"Your flight?" one of them asked—Marmar? Or what was the other one's name?

"I had a great flight," Amy said, and all at once felt like she was going to fall over. She was exhausted, her brain banged inside her skull, she needed a shower. She had no idea how she was going to socialize with three post-Soviet grandmothers for even a single minute. Irine pulled out a chair for her and she sat down, careful not to collapse. Bachana poured a cup of coffee and set it down in front of her. "Thank you, I—"

Irine cut her a slice of cake.

"You should eat."

"I don't know if I—"

"Bachana baked it. It's orange. I think that's what it is?" A flurry of Georgian as Irine confirmed. "It's actually lemon."

And then the pounding of steps down a staircase somewhere and a shouted conversation and then a long-limbed teenage girl, dyed black hair, maroon lipstick, fishnets, black boots, a pierced nose and lip. She sat down at the table and stretched out her legs. Her fishnets had many artful holes. The elderly women began admonishing her right away. A tattoo of a rose on her neck. "My daughter," said Irine.

"It's nice to meet you."

"Maia. Maia, gagatsani sheni tavi."

The girl sliced a chunk of cake and shoved it in her mouth with her hands. Then, while she was chewing: "You're the American model?"

"Oh god, no. I mean—I was a model for like five minutes, but that was a long time ago."

Maia gave her an appraising eye. "My mother said you were famous."

"Maia," Irine said.

"That's what you said." And then more Georgian. Irine leaned back against a steadily dripping sink, sipped her coffee.

Maia turned to Amy. "You're here to look for dogs?"

"For Angel."

"Because as you can see, we have lots of dogs right here in this house. You don't really have to go look for them."

"Maia!" Irine said.

But Amy sort of liked it, the combative adolescent nature. The older women were murmuring among themselves in Georgian and downstairs a dog was howling and Amy's eyes were watering from sudden-onset jet lag. She felt like she had landed on the world's strangest movie set. "I have a soft spot for Angel."

"Well, she makes a good story," Maia said.

"She does," Amy said. "Your English is great."

"It should be. I've been studying my whole life."

"Maia goes to a very competitive technical high school," Irine said. "She is going to be an engineer."

"My son is going to be a doctor," Amy said.

"You have a son?"

"A stepson," Amy said. "He's nineteen, in college. Want to see?" And she took out her phone and passed around a picture of Ferry, first to the grandmothers, who murmured admiringly even though Amy didn't know if they knew who they were looking at, and then to Irine, and then to Maia. She felt both embarrassed by her own showing off and too tired to stop herself.

"He looks American," Maia said. "Lots of teeth."

Amy took her phone back. "I think he has the normal number of teeth."

"Is he tall?" asked one of the grandmothers.

"He's pretty tall. His dad, my husband, is six-five." She paused. "I don't know what that is in centimeters."

"Why are Americans so tall?" Maia asked.

"They eat a lot," said Irine.

Maia stood, grabbed a backpack threaded with safety pins and headed toward the door. She said something in Georgian; Irine said something back. And then the door slammed, and then the desultory yodels of the downstairs dogs.

"I'm sorry she was rude," Irine said. "She's seventeen, she should behave better."

"She wasn't rude," Amy said. "She was a teenager." The three old ladies were still seated, identical, watching her. The cake on the plate in front of her started to swim. "I'm sorry, Irine—I think—I think the jet lag just hit me. I feel—"

"You are tired now, yes? You will go to your room."

"I'm sorry, the cake—"

"No, please, you will eat it later, we have lots—" and the grandmothers rose and one began clearing the table and the other said something sharp to Irine and the third made a *follow me* motion and led Amy to a passageway off the kitchen, and another flight of stairs, and a hallway papered in green roses that smelled, still, of wet dog. And Amy felt, ungenerously, that she would have given anything right at this moment for a five-star hotel or a four-star or whatever a Hilton was or a Courtyard by Marriott. The house was strange and twisting, passages upon passages, almost certainly built by a lunatic. Amy followed the granny and was followed by Irine, who held her suitcase.

"Your room," Irine said, finally, at the end of a hallway.

How would she ever find her way back? But she opened the door into a small and unexpectedly bright room, a window wide open to the morning air, a wood-framed twin bed with a fluffy red bedspread and a wooden chest of drawers. Towels were folded up on top of the bed, a nice big stack, almost like a real hotel. Amy felt herself exhale. The granny slapped the pillow twice to plump it.

"Will this be all right?" Irine said.

"It's perfect."

"The bathroom is two doors down. Would you like me to show you? The hot water can take a bit of time, and there is a towel heater—"

"I'll find it," Amy said. "I think—I think I might just sleep for a while now. I'll find the bathroom later, I just—" She hadn't slept in a twin bed in years, and she remembered with sudden and surprising ardor the give of her caved-in childhood mattress, her pile of mismatched blankets.

"We will let you sleep," Irine said, and her mother (Amy thought it was her mother?) said "good night," and they closed the door behind themselves and Amy sat down on the bed which squeaked. She took off her shoes. Her shirt was sweaty from travel and her underwear itched. She knew she should change but she was so thoroughly exhausted. But also she had to pee. Quite a bit, now that she thought about it. How long had it been since she had peed? It had probably been hours, and that would keep her from sleeping—but at the same time the thought of going back into that insane hallway, of possibly having to talk to anyone again, and be polite, and smile, and apologize—

She sat on the bed and willed her bladder to stop sending signals to her brain. *Let me sleep first. Let me sleep and then you can have anything you want.*

Sigh. She stood, listened at the door to make sure nobody was walking down the hall, then tiptoed toward where she guessed the bathroom might be. A closet, another closet—a bathroom! Tiled in bright red, looking recently cleaned. The toilet seemed to be pretty much a normal toilet, the flushing mechanism easy to determine. The soap was a small bar, neatly wrapped in paper, sitting on a seashell-shaped dish, just like at her mother's house on the rare occasions when they had guests.

And as she tiptoed back to the bedroom, relieved, *It would be okay, she would sleep and wake up and shower and eat, put one human need in front of the next*, a door she hadn't seen before opened to her left. The door was papered, too, in green roses.

There, in the hallway, stood a man. A man, in this house full of women!

He was shirtless; he wore khaki pants; he held a towel to his chest. He said something in Georgian, and Amy shook her head.

"Oh," he said, "you are the American," and then she looked at his eyes.

Bright blue, startling.

"Yes," she said. "I'm—"

"You're here about the dog."

He had short blondish hair, blurry tattoos across his chest, the kind you'd get in prison or a frat party. Blond stubble, square pug nose. Her exact height. Long lashes. Eyes from a geode, from an ice wolf. Only the second person she'd ever seen with eyes that color.

"Were you going to use the bathroom?" he asked.

"No."

He waited for her to say something else. When she didn't: "Then I go, yes?"

"Yes."

He smiled with one corner of his mouth.

"Okay."

"Sorry," Amy said.

He went into the bathroom and closed the door, and Amy stood there for several seconds, alarmed by the hammering she felt in her chest, until the barking of the dogs snapped her out of it, and she remembered that she was probably just hallucinating, that it was all just an exhausted fever dream, just like the woman in the park, and she went to her room and lay down on the stiff twin bed. She had to start sleeping better.

Where am I and why am I so far from home?

She closed her eyes. Pipes gurgled in the hallway. There was indeed a man in the shower. There was a man with ice wolf eyes naked not ten feet away. Amy peeled off her filthy clothes, the smell of dogs and cigarettes and airplanes and this strange strange place, and slid between the sheets and thought: I will never sleep. How could I ever sleep? But in seconds she was out and dreaming darkly, soundlessly, the dreams of the thoughtless or the dead.

SEVEN

HOURS LATER, AMY woke to the sun blasting her face like a laser and sat up, confused. She remembered where she was (a maze of a house in Tbilisi) and why she was there (to find a dog) but had no idea what time it was or what the weather was like or whether she had eaten recently. She sat like that for a while, blinking at the wood paneling, then considered how much she needed a shower.

If she went to the shower, would she have to make more awkward conversation with the man in the hallway? But on the other hand, the lure of soap and water was too strong to resist. She tiptoed out of the hallway again, clutching a towel—was it this door? This one?—and found herself, uninterrupted, in the red-tiled bathroom and saw that the shower faucet was quite similar in model to the one she'd grown up with, righty tighty lefty loosey. And the bathroom door locked.

A shower, clean underwear, communion with her toothbrush, and then she was tiptoeing back down the hall, following the maze toward the sound of the yelping dogs. Why was she still on tiptoe? How could people live with this many dogs without going crazy?

Of course she herself had always, as an adult, chosen animals. At the Avenue D Shelter, she'd made friends with all the dogs, knew their personalities and their quirks, found herself particularly attached to an older bulldog mix who was too grumpy and growly to get himself adopted. She wished she could bring him home, but didn't think Judd would ever agree to a squat smelly dog in their space.

And then, one day, she found Judd standing with the bulldog mix in front of their building. A ring tied to the dog's collar.

"What is this?"

"What does it look like?"

"A dog?"

He got down on the sidewalk, one knee, the whole bit. "I'm asking you to marry me," Judd said.

"With a dog?" And then of course she said yes, and they stood there kissing on the sidewalk for fifteen minutes, and a tourist took pictures without asking them first.

The bulldog was named Leo and he was grumpy, yes—and also drooly, gassy, and deeply loyal. He slept by her side for the three years he had left in the world, and if she thought about him for too long she'd still cry.

In her bereavement after Leo died, she started spending more and more time at the shelter. She began teaching a variety of classes: how to walk the green dogs, how to walk the red dogs, how to recognize ringworm and feline panleukopenia. She took webinars on rehoming FIV-positive cats and webinars on puppy fostering. She was an expert on marketing pitbulls and, of course, an ace lost-pet locater.

In her decade of animal work she had probably saved one hundred lives. But still, she thought, she had never taken a dozen homeless dogs into her apartment, because if you did that in America you would be crazy.

Still trying to make herself as invisible as possible, she wound her way to Irine's kitchen. She found the loose door that led down the stairs, through the path of baby gates (half the dogs were asleep but the other half were barking madly, madly) and out the front door. She was not getting any cell service in this particular spot, so her map feature was useless. But to the left and down several hundred feet there seemed to be a street with shops and people, so she turned left.

"Amy?"

It was the goth child, Irine's daughter, whose name Amy had completely forgotten.

"Maia," the girl said.

"Right, yes, Maia, hi."

"Feeling more awake? Where are you headed?"

"I'm not—" Amy sighed. On the one hand she would have relished solitude but on the other she had no idea where the hell she was going. "I don't know."

"You want a tour?"

"Not, um—not if you're busy."

"Not busy at all," Maia said, smiling, crooked teeth, and then Amy remembered how charming teenagers could be when they were a distance from their parents. "Is there anything in particular you want to see?"

"Is there a place we can search for Angelozi?"

Maia raised her brows. "That's really why you're here?"

"That's really why I'm here."

"You actually came halfway around the world to find a dog?" Maia's tone was a little amused, a little outraged.

"Listen—"

"How did you even know about Angel? How much YouTube do you actually watch?"

Amy could feel herself blushing. "A lot."

Maia backed down. "I do too," she said. "But still, and I mean no offense, really, but with all the problems we have here you could have probably picked a more important problem to solve than a lost dog."

The way she said *dog.* "All God's creatures are precious."

"Oh shit," Maia said. "You're religious?"

"No," Amy said. "I don't know why I just said that."

Maia started to laugh, and Amy, after a moment, laughed, too. "Maybe let's go to Rustaveli."

They marched down the hill, jagging a little this way and a little that, Maia keeping two steps ahead of Amy, which was a relief because then they didn't have to talk. Amy had never been great at small talk even with other native English speakers on a good night's sleep, and besides, she had no idea what to say to Maia that the girl wouldn't find ridiculous.

A broad avenue came into view, something like the Champs Élysées or another grand European boulevard but with a little Sixth Avenue thrown in there, too. Large marble buildings on either side interspersed with T-shirt and cellphone shops. Amy followed Maia as she threaded her way down the sidewalk, trying to keep up while looking all around her, almost tripping over a dog with a luxurious gray hide just lying there in the middle of the sidewalk, uninterested in anyone's comings or goings. The dog had a tag in his ear, no collar.

"Maia! One second!"

Maia turned around, watched a bit archly as Amy removed a dog treat from her backpack. "Here you go, baby."

The dog seemed unimpressed: in fact, it actually yawned.

"Don't waste your time," said Maia. "He doesn't want it."

"Isn't he hungry?"

"No, people feed him all day. He gets the leftover lunches of every office worker on this street. He's tagged, so they know he doesn't have rabies."

Amy was still kneeling by the dog, fruitlessly trying to get him to show some interest in her treats: they were the expensive kind, dried buffalo, from the fancy pet store on Twelfth Street. The dog rolled over to face the other direction.

"I've been rejected," Amy said.

"We—what is the word?—we spoil our dogs here. People know that about Georgians. We're nicer to animals than we are to people."

"Sometimes it's easier to be nicer to animals."

Maia nodded, scratched at a hole in her fishnets. "I agree with that," she said. "We keep walking?"

The dog had fallen back asleep right where it lay, in the middle of the sidewalk. Amy left the treat by its paws in case it was hungry when it woke up. "We keep walking."

The only way to really get to know a city was to wander it, to let yourself get lost and try to figure out your way back to your starting point by relying on landmarks and signposts. That was how Amy had done it when she and Judd had traveled, and why she had a decent understanding of Miami and Rome, alert to the small changes in neighborhoods, the restaurants and kinds of trees along the sidewalks. Following Maia, however, Amy felt free to look into the faces of the people, under their caps and their scarves, under the bright late-winter sky. Some made eye contact with her, and one or two even smiled, or at least allowed their eyes to crinkle up at the corners.

Different from New Yorkers, she thought. More pale skin, more pale eyes, blue and gray.

"You see that?" Maia asked, coming to a stop in front of a marble plaza fronting a huge columned building. At the foot of the plaza stood a strange cross, its horizontal arms drooping down. The cross was surrounded by a protective fence.

"That's the anti-gay cross of the Orthodox church."

"What's an anti-gay cross?"

Maia took a step back, sighed heavily. "Government homophobes placed it there two years ago. We wanted to have a gay pride parade and instead we got this cross. They put it up the day we were supposed to have the parade. And they warned us if we took it down they would throw us in jail."

"Who warned you?"

"The politicians, the church. People in power." Maia put her hands on her bony hips. The wind blew her black hair back so Amy could see the blond underneath. "Pro-Russian demagogues who want to roll back every small freedom our country has won since 1991."

Amy had read about that in the *Brittanica*: the clash between the EU-centric and the Soviet nostalgists.

"It's the Georgian Orthodox Cross, but they use it for their purposes. As a threat. And the Georgian Orthodox church is one of the most backwards churches in the world. They're Putinists. Colonialists. Power-hungry backwards quasi-dictatorial monsters."

Man, her English was good.

"My grandmother and her sisters still go to church three times a week. Because under Communism they couldn't."

"I see."

"They don't care that they are worshiping at the feet of monsters."

"Well, they're older," Amy said. "Sometimes old people have different ideas."

"My grandmother is only sixty-one. I've tried to get them to understand but they refuse," Maia said. "They're comfortable in their homophobia and their patriarchy. They had self-loathing beaten into them by generations of Soviet oppression and now they don't know how to even say hello without translating from the Russian."

"Well." As they gazed at the cross, Amy tried to figure out what her stance should be. These women were her hosts after all! "That sounds difficult," she said.

Maia gave her a bitter look. "You think so?"

"Look, I don't know as much as I should about the government here, but—"

"I know, I know, you care about the dogs."

Amy sighed.

"Do people in the United States even know who our ruler is?"

What did the *Brittanica* say? "It's a—you have a prime minister, I think—his name is—"

"No, not the prime minister. Our ruler." Maia started walking again, then found a nearby seat on a low retainer wall. Amy took a seat next to her, although she was unsure whether or not she was supposed to. Across the wide boulevard stood an Adidas store, a Nike store. On the sidewalk in front of them, a few more sleeping dogs.

"Our ruler," Maia said, "is an oligarch named Ivanishvili. You have heard of him?"

Amy shook her head.

"Yeah, well, he's very famous here. Our country's richest man, a billionaire. Made his money in Moscow right around the end of the Soviet Union, extracting metals, destroying the environment, then came back here and decided to get into government. He was the prime minister for a year a decade ago, but he still controls everything, bribes all the politicians to do what he wants, or just scares them, or just nods at them. I don't know. The minister of health was his dentist, the interior minister was his bodyguard. The current prime minister used to be on his finance team."

"You know, we have something similar," she said. "Trump made his son-in-law the head of foreign policy."

"That's nothing," Maia snorted. "That's the sort of thing we take for granted. No, here our *own* government undermines the very notion of an independent country. They're supposed to be representing us, but they want us to go back to being part of Russia, you understand? They want us to return to the days of the Georgian SSR."

"But why would they want that? Wasn't life miserable under the Soviets?"

"Because Putin will give them whatever they want as long as they give him Georgia."

Amy had no idea about any of this. "Is there resistance?"

"Some resist," she said. "Many do. But not the ones who are apathetic and uninformed. Or just grateful to get through the day. You know, many people are very poor here. It's a luxury to be able to follow politics."

Amy knew that.

"The problem," said Maia, "is that it's also a necessity."

Amy wasn't used to teenagers who talked like this. Even Ferry, usually so astute—did they ever talk about politics in a way that wasn't ironic or amusing? Did they ever talk about politics in a serious way at all? She looked out again at the Georgians passing her on the busy sidewalk. They did not seem poor or uninformed; they seemed like busy city people, like herself.

"Don't confuse Tbilisi with the rest of Georgia," Maia said as if reading her mind. "You know there's a big part of our country that the Russians actually occupy, and we can't do anything about it. Many people welcome it."

"South Ossetia and Abkhazia."

"You've heard of it," Maia said, and gave Amy her first approving smile. "Good. I'm glad you've heard of something."

Amy considered whether or not to be insulted. She decided against it. Watched the foot traffic pass.

"Ivanishvili's minions put up that cross the day after our canceled gay pride parade, and the next day the government put up the fence to protect it. When we protested, they sprayed us with tear gas. Then batons. Eventually we got tired or injured and we went home. Then a few months later we protested again. And got beaten again. It will happen again soon."

"Does your mother worry about your safety?" Amy asked. "When you protest?"

"Of course." Maia sighed. "She's a Soviet too."

The wind was starting to whip up and Amy zipped her green parka up to her throat. The two stray dogs closest to her lazily got to their feet; feeling oddly helpless, or maybe useless, Amy reached into her bag and tossed a few treats out toward them. She was grateful when one of the dogs stopped, sniffed, deigned to eat it.

How cursory her research had been! Gone to the library? If she hadn't been with Maia, she might have popped into the Nike store, tried to figure out the prices. She would have thought the cross was a symbol of Georgian strength or history or religious devotion. She would never have known that teenagers here got tear-gassed.

"Are you hungry?" Maia asked.

She was starving.

"You've had Georgian food before?"

"Not really."

"I think you'll like it," Maia said. "Most people do. Let's go."

They turned up a small hillside and once again Amy hurried to keep up. The sidewalk was dented and pitted, but the street was full of restaurants, steaming windows, the scent of garlic and onion drifting out into the street. On a wall, English graffiti: PERHAPS LIBERTY IS THE ONLY WEALTH.

"We go here," Maia said, finally pausing in front of a dark blue door. "My friend is the owner. It is the best restaurant on this side of the river I think," she said, and a surprising look of shyness came across her face. "I hope you will like it."

Amy followed Maia into a compact room with a wood-burning fire in the stove in the corner. The walls were stucco, the ceiling was hung with acoustic tile. "It's lovely," she said.

"You have restaurants like this in New York?"

"Of course," Amy said, although in truth the place could not have looked or smelled more different than most New York restaurants— no Fred shaking martinis, no curated clientele. The tables were crowded with people of all ages eating together, coats thrown over backs of chairs, and it was hard to tell who the waiters were since everyone seemed to be wearing the same nondescript clothing. Maia left Amy standing in the corner while she made the rounds, kissing people at various tables hello—how did she know all of them?—and then picking up an empty chair and then another empty chair as if she owned the place, squeezing them in at a table on the far side of the room.

"Amy, you will join us here," she called.

"Sure." She squeezed through the scrum.

Envisioning Maia's friends, Amy had imagined a bunch of punk kids like the ones that patrolled the smoking area outside her high school in the nineties: bad dye jobs, smudged eyeliner, eyebrow rings and ratty leather jackets. But the table was full of average-looking people of all ages—grandmothers and a fat baby alongside two small kids drawing with crayons, and someone who had to be the mom and someone else who had to be the dad, or maybe that other guy was the dad? Twelve of them around the table, and what on earth their connection was to Maia, Amy couldn't guess. But Maia was kissing everyone, and then someone else came to the table and Maia kissed him, too, and Amy again felt like an intruder on the set of a curious foreign film.

"Es dedachemis megobaria, is ak aris niu-iork'idan. Misi sakhelia Emi," Maia said. "Amy, sit, sit."

"New York!" said a younger woman who either was or was not the children's mother. "I have always wanted to go to New York City. Do you know Brooklyn? I want to go to Brooklyn. I've heard it's the coolest."

"I'm actually in Manhattan," Amy said. "The East Village."

"New York, New York!" sang one of the men. "It's a wonderful town!"

"What brings you to our little country?"

She could not bear to explain about Angel again, but fortunately Maia saved her, streaming out throaty sentences in Georgian while

Amy squeezed into a seat between a grandmother and one of the children, who looked at her complacently before turning back to her drawing.

What time was it? Six? Six-thirty? On a Thursday night? And yet she seemed to be crashing a dinner party. Sweating bottles of some kind of alcohol were on the table, alongside salads and dips and baskets of bread, and the grandmother to her left poured her a shot and clinked a glass against hers. "Amis gaumarjos!"

"Yes!" she said. She downed whatever was in the glass and felt a spike behind her eyes. The grandmother refilled her glass. "Welcome to Tiflis!"

"Maia, what is this?" Amy asked when she regained her breath.

"Strong, yes?" she said. "It is chacha. Like our national vodka. Better than Russian."

"It's made from grapes," said one of the men at the table.

"Fermented wine," said another.

"I didn't know wine could be fermented," Amy said. Her tongue felt pickled.

"Sakartvelos gaumarjos!" said the grandmother to her left, and everyone but Amy drank again. The kid to her right crumpled up her drawing and began a new one.

Soon more plates of food began arriving at the table, brought by a waitress who everyone knew, and people were passing them around like they were at someone's home, no particular concern for whose cutlery was whose. Amy would have attempted to at least keep track of her own fork but she was undone by hunger. The grandmother spooned two huge dumplings on her plate, then pureed beets that smelled like a million cloves of roasted garlic, and roasted peppers gleaming with oil, and then there was bread stuffed with—were those kidney beans? And an eggplant salad studded with pomegranate seeds and Amy shoved some food into her mouth, and emitted a tiny but very real moan. She had made eggplant like this before, grilled over an open flame until charred on the outside and molten in, but she had never managed to get it so perfectly smoky.

"Good, yes?"

The grandmother was now nudging her in the arm, pointing to one of the dumplings, miming how to eat it. "Khinkali," she said. She held one by its topknot of dough, took a loud slurping bite, gestured at Amy to follow.

"What's inside?" Amy asked; she couldn't bear to reject the food being offered her but also couldn't bear to eat meat, worried she might barf. How embarrassing, to barf—or to reject food, or to explain herself yet again. How to negotiate?

"Maia, what's inside this?"

"Those are the lamb ones. Oh, you probably don't eat lamb, right? Americans don't eat lamb? Here, take those, they're mushroom—" and another plate came her way, thank god, and Amy followed the grandmother's gestures, held the dumpling by its topknot, took a slurping bite, let the juice dribble down her chin. Cumin, for sure, and maybe some turmeric, and something else, ineffable, slightly musky, and of course the omnipresent garlic. The mushrooms were chewy— probably shitakes, or maybe oysters? She wiped her chin. The child next to her showed her her drawing: it looked like a poodle.

"You," the child said, pointing at Amy.

"Me?"

Another plate came her way: bread filled with molten cheese, a barely set egg on top, *khachapuri*. Oh, how Judd would have loved this! While Amy was herself a mere cook, Judd fancied himself a scholar of international cuisines, could identify the most obscure regional dishes or exotic spices. She had eaten around the world with him, mole in Mexico and dolmades in Greece and that awful time he embarrassed her into eating octopus in Japan. And Judd liked to bring his research home to the restaurant, so that even though Le Coin mostly did your standard French-ish Italian-ish American, the kitchen was unafraid of

Aleppo peppers or Cypriot cheese or tiger's milk ceviche from Peru. The specials board rang with the news of Judd's travels, the junkets paid for by tourist boards and the more obscure places he liked to find on his own. County Cork butter, Traverse City cherries.

But it was funny, she thought, that he had never once thought to visit a place that wasn't on the tourist map or that hadn't been suggested to him by someone he admired. He never would have followed a teenager into a humble-looking restaurant; had he been there, he would have insisted they visit whatever the hippest place in Tbilisi was, the one the travel magazines wrote about. And he would have missed all this.

"Gaumarjos! Victory!" said someone across the table, and they all downed fresh shots of chacha in unison. Amy joined in, and this time it went down a little easier, warm instead of burning.

"So you are a friend of Irine's?" asked a woman two seats down. She was wearing a brightly striped sweater and had the pleasant smile of a preschool teacher, but half her hair was shaved off (the other half fell to her shoulder in a swoop of neon pink waves).

"I actually know her through the dog rescue."

"Ah! You are the one who is helping us find Angel!"

Angel! "You know the story?" Amy said. "I didn't know if everyone—"

"Angel's doghouse was right by our daughter's school," the woman said, motioning to the child to Amy's right, the one who had drawn her as a poodle. "She helped her cross the street every morning."

"You knew Angel?" Amy turned to the girl. "Do you speak English?"

The child was focused on her new drawing but she nodded. "Angelozi," she said. "Our dog."

"Did she walk you to school?"

The girl looked up at her with tired eyes. "Angelozi," she said again, and her mother said something to her in rapid Georgian. The girl nodded, sadly, and turned back to her art.

"It's a terrible story," the mother said. "To think she was hurt. But she could have run away, I suppose. Or maybe someone brought her home to be a pet? It's impossible to say."

"It's not impossible," said the man sitting next to her, refilling their chacha. "She was kidnapped. Everyone knows this. We got that note!"

"It was a joke, Tedo."

"It was not a joke! Who would play a joke like that?"

"Anyone! An obnoxious teenager, someone with a cruel sense of humor. Khalkhi sulelebi arian, tkven es itsit."

"No, no, you're wrong. It wasn't just some dumb kid. It was a deliberate provocation."

"An escalation," said another woman.

"What kind of note?" Amy asked. "What happened?"

The first woman sighed. "One of the teachers was fired. She was very beloved. The parents protested, and there was a bit of a—I don't really know how to explain this in English. I'm sorry." She peeled off several Georgian sentences.

"The note said, 'this is what you get.' Supposedly. Nobody's ever seen it."

"And everything went to hell after that."

"I don't know," the pink-haired woman said. "Things happen to dogs all the time. They probably happen to dogs in New York all the time, too. People take them. Strangers."

"They do," Amy said. Her mind flashed to the woman in the park, and her beloved Roxy. "But aren't people saying she was kidnapped?"

"Yes, well, people like rumors in our country," Maia said. "This is what happens when everyone in power lies. We have to listen to rumor, since there is no truth."

"Maia is right," said one of the women.

"This is always the case," said one of the men.

"Gaumarjos!" said the grandmother, and everyone drank. "Victory!"

"Maia," Amy whispered, "why do people keep saying 'victory'?"

"It is what we say when we drink—you say 'cheers,' I think?"

"Cheers!" cried the entire table in agreement and drank once more.

The first round of food was cleared away, and even though Amy's digestive system was groaning she made room for more: more dumplings, more bread, more kidney beans and cheese. She hadn't eaten like this in years, really, the kind of gut-busting feasting that made a person wish for a dozen more stomachs. How many rounds of chacha had she had? Was the tired-eyed child next to her still drawing? Was food still being passed from plate to plate? The baby—where had the baby gone? Oh, asleep on his father's chest, his head drooping on his father's shoulder. The air in the restaurant was warm, almost humid; the sky outside had turned dark. In the corner of the small room, the wood in the fire glowed and sparked.

"Shemomedjamo," said Tedo.

"I'm sorry?"

Tedo emptied his wine glass, then smiled. "It's our word for when the food is so good, you have to keep eating, even though you're entirely full."

A few seats down from Amy, a younger woman started humming a tune, too loudly to be humming to herself, too quietly to suggest solo artistry. The tune morphed from humming into a song, and the woman tapped her fingertips on the table to accompany herself. Then the grandmother joined in, tapping, humming. Then the man across the table. And then, the strangest thing, but Amy somehow knew the tune, too, or the tune was so familiar it had been in the ether around her since she was a child, but only now was she paying enough attention to listen to it.

Major chord, major chord, minor key. The sound like a butterfly escaping her lips.

Maia started to sing then, words that flew in and around the tune. The whole restaurant seemed to quiet as she sang, and how desperately

Amy wanted to understand, although perhaps, she thought—perhaps she did understand?

No, no, she had been here for twelve hours, she knew nothing.

SHE TRIED TO pay, they would not let her pay, she threw Georgian lari on the table and pretended it came from somewhere else. Someone put her in a car, which was good because when it was time to stand she found she really couldn't. Maia seemed to be in much the same shape.

But if she expected worry or even attention when they got home, there was none to be found. Instead, they toddled in past the dogs in the dark, some whimpering, some sleeping, and tripped up the stairs, and departed each other's company at one of the many mysterious hallways leading out of the kitchen. As stealthily as she could, Amy made it to her room and pushed open the door. Was it her door? It was, wasn't it? Or was it this one? Amy held her breath and pushed.

"Yes?"

The man with the ice wolf eyes was sitting at a desk in his darkened room, an open laptop in front of him.

The face on the screen belonged to a lovely, long-haired little girl.

"Yes?" he said again. "Ty chto-to khochesh?"

"I'm sorry, I'm sorry, bodishi," Georgian for "I'm sorry": she didn't know how she knew it but it came out of her mouth like she had known it all her life.

EIGHT

OUT HER WINDOW, under the moonlight, a garden. One of the grannies and eleven dogs near a tree, foraging, sniffing, sitting near her, gazing up at her, leaning against her heavy legs.

"SO WHAT'S IT like?"

Judd on the phone sometime at three in the morning, when the pounding in her head and the dryness in her mouth woke her up once more. She had missed seven calls while she was asleep.

"It's lovely here," she said. "It's sad."

"Why sad?"

"It's a pretty difficult time."

"What do you mean?"

"I just—I should have done more work before I got here, read up more. There's all this political tension right now, and everyone cares, everyone has a stake. Maybe because it's a small country, but it feels like everyone opts in to politics here. Not like at home."

He paused. Then he said, "I miss you."

She closed her eyes. "Are you even listening?"

He sighed. "Of course I'm listening," he said. "I just wanted you to know I miss you. Roxy misses you. The cats miss you."

"How's Meret?"

He sighed again, more heavily. "Did you go this far away so we can fight?"

"I'm just curious."

"I don't know," he said. "I haven't seen her."

"Is that true?"

For a moment, neither one said anything. Then: "It's true. What time is it there?"

"You don't know?"

"How should I know?"

"The internet would tell you. You could have checked before you woke me up."

"You called me," he said.

"You called me first." Six thousand miles away from one another and this was what they were going to talk about? Well. They had never done very well on the phone.

"Ferry wanted me to let you know he got an A on his chemistry test."

"He could have called me."

"He didn't know what time it was," Judd said. "He didn't want to wake you up."

She was quiet for a moment, then she laughed.

"Tell him I'm proud of him," she said. "We'll be paying for medical school soon."

"Uno can do that," Judd said. "We're spending enough."

"Come on," she said. Judd always acted like they didn't have enough money. She didn't know why. Couldn't he see he had more than enough? This was one of the downsides of growing up rich; you never learned how little a person actually needed.

"He's going to take care of us in our old age," Amy said. "It's a good investment."

"Come home soon," Judd said.

"I will," she said. "As soon as I've done what I came to do."

TWICE SHE HAD saved Ferry's mother's life.

The first time had been simple, almost reflexive: Amy was driving her to rehab somewhere deep in Bucks County when Uno started to choke on one of the Werther's candies she'd been compulsively sucking the entire ride. Although Amy had never performed the Heimlich maneuver, she had studied the posters in every kitchen in which she'd ever worked (NYC Health Department Code 17:172) and therefore moved in balletic form: pulling over, removing Uno from the car, hoisting her up, making a fist between her ribcage and belly button and thrusting one, two, three times on her frail frame until the mostly-intact Werther's flew in a graceful arc toward the trees.

"Whoa," Uno said, when she'd recovered language. She was wispy in the passenger's seat, her once-lovely face lined and worn. "I can't believe that actually worked."

Amy tried not to consider how easy it might have been to let Uno die. Keeping Uno alive had been her project and her promise to Ferry since he'd been old enough to understand promises.

They kept driving west, listening to Steely Dan's *Aja* on CD in the Volvo. Eventually, abashedly, Uno popped another Werther's.

The second time Amy saved her life was more orchestrated, yet also more emotionally chaotic: she'd organized an intervention (this was *after* the liver transplant, *after* Uno's surgeons wouldn't talk to her anymore and her mother wouldn't talk to her anymore and she was by this time so sunken and sallow that she looked like she could be Ferry's grandmother even though she was only forty-one years old).

Ferry: twelve, a sixth grader at St. Ann's, still held her hand when they crossed the street. Ferry, up at night, claiming "headaches," asking if he could go to the restaurant with her and his dad, asking if he could sleep in their room, on the floor, since he knew he couldn't fit in their bed. Not eating or wanting to shower. Even Judd in his bluff obtuseness knew something was wrong.

"He thinks she's going to die this time," Amy whispered. She had cut back her hours at the shelter to be home with Ferry more.

They were at the restaurant, it was ten in the morning, and Ferry had refused, once again, to go to school: the poor exhausted kid was sacked out along a banquette. Judd stared deep into his espresso.

"We can't let her die," he said. "He's too young for his mom to die."

"We'll do an intervention," Amy said.

"Another one?"

"It'll be the last time," she said.

"We can't do it again," he said. "Who'd even come? Who's left?"

"Ferry," she said.

Judd's enormous hands enfolded his tiny cup. "I don't know."

"The alternative is worse."

Judd looked over at his son, asleep on the bench along the wall of the restaurant. His scuffed Nikes dangled off the side. He had his backpack under his head for a pillow. The school's nurse was sympathetic but had also warned that he'd missed fifteen days of school so far and it was only November.

They had never let Ferry participate in an intervention before (this would be Uno's fourth) but now that their choices were so bleak—let him talk to her or let him watch his mother die—

It was just the three of them, Ferry and Amy and the intervention specialist, a no-nonsense middle-aged woman, prim and steely. They were all sitting in Uno's beautifully disheveled townhouse when she came home one afternoon. Uno looked at Amy, looked at Ferry, looked at the interventionist.

"Oh no," she said.

"Uno," Ferry said. "Mom."

Amy and Uno both looked at the boy at the same time.

"Please, Mom."

At earlier interventions Uno had reacted with fury, with iron-fisted rage: she had actually taken a picture off the wall and thrown it at them, had thrown an empty vodka bottle at them, had tried to climb out her bedroom window and down a trellis.

But this time, she just sat on the couch. She was so exquisitely frail, wore such incredible clothes—if it had been another time, Amy thought, Uno herself could have modeled—although her skin was sort of yellowish now and her hair was like straw and her eyes were blood-shot and all in all she looked more tragic than tragically glamorous. She had Ferry's lovely features, though: the full lips, the hazel eyes, the wavy blond-brown hair.

"Okay," Uno said, softly. "Okay, sweetie." She held a cushion from the couch to her chest. "Nobody else is here?"

"There's nobody else," Amy said.

Uno bit her lip, clutched the pillow.

"It has to work this time," Ferry said. "Please, Mom. I'm so afraid you're going to die."

She turned to him with eyes that suddenly seemed huge, then shot a fierce look at Amy, and Amy knew she was rallying herself to yell at her for bringing Ferry to an intervention, for using Ferry this way, as it had long been an unspoken agreement between them that she and Judd would do everything they could to cover for Uno and explain away her missed weekends and recitals and soccer games and that, during the times she was stable, they would release Ferry to her like nothing was amiss, and let her love him and take care of him and pretend it was normal, Amy hovering by the phone, her heart in her mouth until Ferry came home again.

Ferry had learned to love Uno with a sort of wariness, a guardedness that was recognizable to Amy; it was how she had related to her own mother.

But still: when her own mother died she thought she would never breathe again and she wouldn't let Ferry feel that way, not yet. So she met Uno's eyes.

"We're giving this one last try, Amy," she said. "You have to try again."

"I'm so sick of it," Uno whispered.

"I know," Amy said. "He is too."

Uno turned to Ferry again. He was stoic, pale-faced, his hazel eyes the same exact shape as hers. "Oh god, honey," she whispered. "I'm sorry."

"Will you go?" he asked.

She nodded, opened her arms, held him, and Amy looked away like she sometimes did when Ferry wanted his—real, biological, how were you supposed to say it?—

His mother.

And then Uno got up and headed out of the townhouse and got in the car with the interventionist who hadn't said a word but who had already packed up Uno's delicate, beautiful clothing and off they went, back to Bucks County, and this time, like a miracle, it took.

As far as anyone knew, Uno hadn't had a drink in seven years. She hosted Ferry's graduation party with the elan of the high born, top-notch catering and no alcohol, didn't make a big deal about the drinking, just turned the backyard of the town house into a fairy-lit wonderland and served lobster tails and sent everyone home with teddy bears dressed in Cornell T-shirts.

And then she was off to Morocco to supervise a wellness retreat in Agadir and from there to her new beau's house in Singapore; she liked to stay in places where illicit substances were hard to find or vigorously proscribed.

But while she was in rehab, she wrote Amy a letter—the first kind or sincere thing she had ever said to her, and though it was short and poorly spelled, the line that Amy remembered was: "You have saved my life over and over and I don't even know why."

Which was how Amy knew that she herself was Ferry's real mother (was that what you called it?)—because a real mother would know why.

IN THE MORNING she followed the sounds of the dogs to the kitchen, where Irine was getting ready to head out the door. There was coffee on the stove and the remains of the previous day's lemon cake on the counter and a cigarette stub still burning in an ashtray on the kitchen table.

"Good morning!" Irine said. "I hope you were able to sleep. Maia said you went to Nikoloz's restaurant last night." She lit a new cigarette, propping open the kitchen window. "The food there can be a little heavy, no?"

"Maia already left for the day?"

"Her school starts quite early," Irine said.

Amy marveled at the resilience of the young. She poured herself some water from the sink and drank it before thinking about whether or not it was safe to drink water from the sink.

"You had chacha?"

Amy refilled her glass. How dangerous could it be? "Too much."

"You need a paracetamol?"

"I took an aspirin," she said. "I'll just get some coffee."

"Sit, sit. I'll get."

Irine was dressed professionally, in a purple blouse and dark pants, and it occurred to Amy that she hadn't asked her what she did for a living or where she went to work. How could she not have asked these simple things of her host? Or why hadn't Irine mentioned it? In America, a person would come right out with it—you couldn't spend five minutes with Judd without hearing all about the restaurant.

"Ah," Irine said, passing Amy a mug, blowing cigarette smoke in the opposite direction. "I work at Primary School Ninety-eight, just across the river. It's only a very short drive."

"I had no idea," Amy said. "You're a teacher?"

"I was for many years—I taught kindergarten," she said. "And then, because I was good at my job, they gave me a job I did not want, and now I am principal. Which is much harder work, but also of course more money. Anyway, this is how I know Angel—she was the crossing guard at our school."

"That's so funny," Amy said. "I should have asked."

"Why should you ask?" Irine said. "I can just tell you."

"You know, I think I met one of your students last night, a little girl. Her mother is friends with Maia. Or her father?" Amy said. "She seemed to be there with her whole family—I was never entirely sure who everyone was, to be honest. They just kept pouring me chacha."

Irine laughed. "Nikoloz's place is quite popular—many of my students go there with their families. And Maia, of course, she knows everyone. For a while she was good friends with a former teacher at our school. And then—well, they are not friends anymore, which I believe is for the best. Miss Lomidze was a terrible influence. She taught Maia very radical ideas. Now she thinks she can go to a protest or a rave and make the world different."

"That's the way of young people all over the world."

"She should know better, though. Shouting slogans, putting up graffiti. Very stupid."

"It doesn't seem so stupid to protest what you believe in," she said. "Isn't that what kids do?"

"Ha!" Irine said. "The government makes a decision, they protest. The government reverses the decision, they protest. They can never be satisfied. Maia works with a group of students, other young people, I don't know. They make political videos in English. Which is provocative, although she pretends not to know it is provocative."

"It seems kind of impressive to me," Amy said.

Irine gave her a stern look. "Impressive?"

"I mean, just to care so much." She felt herself backtracking. "I don't know that many American teenagers who know enough, who care enough—who dedicate themselves to political activism so—I don't know, so fully."

"Well yes—of course she dedicates herself. She is brilliant. So she thinks she knows everything." Irine took a deep drag of her Crown. "But there is a difference between knowing things in school and knowing them in life, and in life she doesn't know anything. I've had to pick her up at the police station more than once. One time she got into a fight with an officer and ended up with a baton to the cheek. She had a black eye for a month."

Irine leaned back against the sink. In the weak kitchen light, Amy could see dozens of tiny wrinkles around her pursed lips.

"The problem is that she doesn't really understand what the police are capable of," Irine said. "She thinks she does, but she cannot. She has no memory, she wasn't alive before. She isn't nearly afraid enough," Irine said. "And she should be."

Ferry had never gotten involved with the cops. Ferry had never *had* to get involved with the cops.

Outside the kitchen window, Amy could see one of the grannies outside with some of the dogs. The granny had a floral scarf tied around her head, looked like something out of a painting of European peasants. And the dogs just milled around her, content. What a strange place this was.

Irine was pouring herself more coffee, and then she poured more into Amy's cup. Although she was curious, Amy didn't dare ask her about the Russian-aligned oligarch (what was his name?) or the prime minister who had been his money guy or the health minister who had been his dentist. She wasn't sure she wanted to hear what Irine had to say, or know who she sympathized with. Was she really—a Soviet? What did that even mean?

"What I was thinking about, Amy, to be honest," Irine said, stamping out her cigarette, busying herself with a new one. "I was wondering if you thought Maia could go to school in the United States."

"I'm sorry?"

"If she could go back with you to go to school."

"Back with me?" Amy said. "Is that something she wants?"

"Well, I'm not sure," Irine said. "It is something *I* want."

"To move her to the United States?"

"It is the only—" Irine stopped herself. "Regular immigration is very difficult. There is the visa lottery, but the chances there are slim. But for someone like my daughter, the United States would be a much better life. And she can get a student visa, I know she could."

"Well," Amy said. "I think the process is pretty involved. I mean, you're right— there are student visas—but it's quite a process to apply. I don't know how the schools would evaluate Georgian transcripts."

"Transcripts?"

"Her grades."

"Her grades are excellent, I told you."

"I'm sure they are," Amy said. The kitchen was filling up with cigarette smoke.

After a moment, Irine said, "I must be honest with you, Amy, this is what I don't understand. I have looked at the colleges there. On their websites. And what I don't understand is how they could cost so much money. I can't believe it! Every time I look on the website, I think no, this is a joke. How could it be? Is everyone in America that rich?"

"No, of course not—it's expensive for Americans, too. A lot of people save up their whole lives, or pay off loans for years and years."

"But you said your son goes to university, yes?"

"Yes," Amy said.

"And you pay for it?"

"We do."

"And how much does that cost?"

Amy blinked. There was no way on earth she could tell her. There was no way she could say the insane number out loud. "A lot."

"Yes, but how much?"

"Um . . ." She gazed at the scratched formica on the kitchen table. Irine was a woman whose coffee she was drinking, whose electricity she was using. Irine was a woman who had lived in a communal apartment well into her childhood. "Sometimes there are scholarships," she said. "For people who need money."

Behind Irine, the sink drip drip dripped. The floor above them was creaking with the weight of one granny or another.

"Well," Irine said. "It's just a dream, I suppose. I must go to work now. If you want to look for Angel, you might want to head to the area around the British school. It's a place for hiking but many people leave dogs there. I've been going up when I can to look. You can bring Zazi or one of the others if you'd like. They'll help you search."

"The British school. Okay."

Irine gathered her coat, bag, keys, drained her coffee and put her mug in the sink.

"Oh, Irine?" Amy said, wanting to change the subject that lingered in the air, not knowing what would come out of her mouth until she let it. "Is there a—there seems to be a man living in the house?"

"Oh, yes, Andrei," Irine said, briskly. "I meant to tell you. He's our lodger. He works from his room all day, I don't know what he does. Something for the internet. He shouldn't bother you."

"No, of course. I was just wondering."

"Okay," Irine said. Something flickered across her face. "Well, I will be going. Good luck with the search."

The search.

How ludicrous and impossible.

She still had that one thousand dollars in her bag. She could leave it on Irine's kitchen table, get a hotel room, sightsee until her flight home.

But that seemed impossible, too. She was not here to see anything in particular. She was here to do good.

She went upstairs to get her coat and her search supplies—her backpack, her bully sticks, her drone—thinking about the truth of her financial life: Judd's father had been a neurosurgeon in Connecticut and his mother had worked in real estate. Judd and his two brothers had attended boarding schools in New England (Andover, Andover, Exeter) and Ivy League schools, and then Judd's older brothers had gone on to do exactly what their educational and social backgrounds suggested they would do: Mitchell worked in corporate finance in New York and Cal worked in corporate finance in Hong Kong. Judd himself was the black sheep, his restaurant work seen as eccentric, his tattoos and allegiance to the East Village evidence of an idiosyncratic attraction to the down-at-heel. But his parents had nevertheless supported his early ambitions, paid for mechanical and aesthetic upgrades to Le Coin, took him to Italy to source marble for the bar. And there was the place in Southampton where they spent parts of every summer, and the elaborate vacations for Ferry and his cousins.

How to explain this to Irine, or even to herself? During COVID, when they were worried about keeping the restaurant open, Arthur and Donna generously kicked in the funds to build them a beautiful outdoor space on the sidewalk, with greenery and electric heaters.

They lived without fear: perhaps another form of wealth.

She could leave Irine the thousand dollars, which would probably be enough to cover the expenses the stray dogs incurred and Maia's expenses, too, for maybe a month or two. She could even give them more, go to an ATM this minute, empty her small account. But she couldn't pay for Maia's school tuition, or give her false hope about affording an American university. And why would she do that anyway?

Because her mother was worried about her? Because, weeks ago, she herself had been worried about a lost dog?

She headed back downstairs, where a pack of Irine's Crowns still sat on the kitchen counter. Amy took one, lit it and smoked it to distract from the pain in her head, although of course it did the opposite. Then, in the absence of anything better to do, she headed downstairs to select a dog from the dim basement.

Zazi came running to her, so Amy put a leash on him and, noting a look of interest from a dog who seemed to be part retriever, put him on a leash as well. The other dogs, now used to her smell or her presence, drowsed lazily in their various corners. "Don't worry guys," she said. "I'll take you out later."

The dogs did not seem to be particularly worried either way.

THE CAB LET her and the dogs out at a vast green space near, yes, a British school, Union Jacks flapping proudly next to Georgian flags—and also a smallish lake and broad lawns stretching into faraway hills. She seemed to be a world away from the city, although she could see the apartment blocks in the distance.

"Guys, ready to do this?" In her backpack: the drone, the pig's ears, the bully sticks, the treats that at least these two dogs seemed to find mildly interesting when she stuck them in their muzzles. The dogs were polite on their leashes, neither pulling nor stopping suddenly as Amy marched across the grass, sneakers growing damp. It was cool, maybe fifty degrees, but the sun beamed down from a cloudless sky. A nice day for a walk.

Along the rutted path, like everywhere in Tbilisi, dogs lay lazily on their sides, looking basically contented. Her own dogs (Zazi and—who was the other one? A boy: she'd name him Phil) approached a few who stood in greeting, and after a moment of friendly ass-sniffing and circling, the strays would flop down again. They, too, had ear tags on their glossy ears. Amy leaned down to give them treats and felt deep sudden love for them when they accepted and sharp irritation when they did not.

The path merged with a recreation track around the lake: runners, mothers with strollers, and other dog walkers worked their way around the track in opposite directions. Amy was put in mind, pleasantly, of the few times she and Roxy had made their way up to Central Park. She crouched down on the side of the track to set up her drone, a newish Black Falcon, while the dogs waited patiently by her side. This was a good space to get some real imaging going—she could get the drone up to three hundred feet or so here, enough for maybe a two-thousand-foot circular view. And the nice thing about the Black Falcon was that it sent down such clear photos as long as the Wi-Fi was working.

Was there Wi-Fi here? Excellent, a good strong signal.

"Kalbat'ono, es dam't't'itsebuli mots'q'obilobaa?"

"Oh, I'm sorry," Amy said, looking up, shading her eyes from the sun. It was a policeman, having appeared on the track out of nowhere, snappy navy uniform and a serious look on his broad young face. "I don't speak Georgian."

"Tkveni mots'q'obiloba, kalbat'ono."

"I'm sorry, I don't understand."

The policeman held out his hand, expectantly. What did he want? What had she done?

"Tkveni mots'q'obiloba," he said, and now his voice was steely, and Amy felt a bubble of nervousness pop in her gut.

"What do you—"

He grabbed the drone out of her hands.

"Oh no!" Amy said. "You don't understand, it's just a drone, it's not anything—"

The policeman's eyes widened at her intransigence, and he spit out what sounded like a heady stream of Georgian insults, and Amy was both worried and annoyed that he took her drone; how on earth was she going to find Angel without it?

"Es aris uk'anono aghch'urviloba!"

And then a small man walking a large poodle approached them.

"Neba mometsis gadavtargmno," he said. "Inglisurad vlap'arak'ob."

The policeman turned, gestured to Amy, gestured to the drone, railed in increasingly manic Georgian. Once he quieted, the small man turned to Amy. "Evidently private surveillance equipment is illegal in Georgia."

"But it's not surveillance equipment!" Amy said.

"Well," the man said, "it is a drone."

"It's to help me find a lost dog!"

The policeman gave her a disgusted look.

"If I were you I'd apologize."

"Apologize?"

"In English," the small man said. "I'd do that if I were you."

"Then will he give me back—"

"Really," the man said. "I would."

Jesus. "I'm sorry," Amy said. And then, in Georgian, "bodishi."

But her use of novice Georgian won her no favor; the policeman narrowed his eyes at her, said something that sounded both irritated and impenetrable, then marched down the path, her drone tucked under his arm.

"Shit," Amy said.

"You don't know how lucky you are," the man said. He had a neat goatee and a crisp English accent. "That could have gone quite poorly for you."

"Well, thanks for stepping in."

"Of course," the man said, and began strolling along the track; without thinking about it, Amy fell in step beside him, pulling her dogs along with her. "It can be difficult to understand the rules here.

But the general idea is that you should act with extreme deference toward the police. They don't fancy being argued with."

"You live here?"

"I do," the man said. "I teach maths at the British school up the road. Been here for almost a decade, in fact. Fascinating place. One of the most beautiful countries I've ever seen. Although also, of course, the most traumatized."

"What do you mean, traumatized?"

"My guess," the man said, "is Georgia has been invaded more than any other country in the world. Well, except for Poland, perhaps. Maybe Poland. Possibly Afghanistan. But Georgia is certainly up there, invasion-wise."

"More than just the Russians?"

The man chuckled. "My dear, people have been trying to sack Georgia since before Russia was a twinkle in history's eye. Two thousand years ago it was the Romans and Mongols. Then the Visigoths. Then after the Visigoths it was a few hundred years of Ottoman invasion, and then, I believe, the Turks. And *then* the Russians, who are of course still at it. It's the location, you know. Right smack in between Europe and Asia. Which is still why they have so many of these sorts of problems. If they were, say, five hundred kilometers to the south, they'd have different problems entirely."

He paused to let his poodle pish delicatedly by the side of the track. "You know this place was once an SSR, of course," he continued as his dog finished her business.

"One of the first, as I understand it."

"That's right," the man said. "But then the Soviet Union collapsed, and Russia went from being one of the two superpowers on the planet to a banana republic in a matter of weeks. Total catastrophe. A profound humiliation."

"It's funny," Amy said. "I remember that time a little—we watched it on the news at home. But it never occurred to me that it was a bad thing. It was just, like, 'Hey look, the enemy collapsed. I guess we won.'"

"You're from the States, I gather?"

"Minnesota."

"Well, Minnesota won," the man said. "The West, as a whole, it won."

"Believe me, I never felt like a winner," Amy said.

"But that's not how Putin saw it. To him it was a great and tragic loss, a profound humiliation. I believe he called it the greatest catastrophe in human history, or something along those lines. So now, in an act of grandiosity, maybe insanity—now he wants to rebuild what Russia lost. Diplomatically when possible. Violently when not."

"Russia does diplomacy?"

"Well of course it does—it's just a kind of Russian diplomacy. Bribing, harassing, installing their own apparatchiks in the states that used to be theirs and then pushing them to adopt Russian laws."

"I can't believe the Georgians put up with that."

"They have no choice. The Russians are strong, geopolitically speaking, and the Georgians are weak. But it does cause a certain amount of turmoil. Take the foreign agent laws, for instance. Are you familiar?"

She was not.

"They're new laws designed to harass Georgian nationals who have foreign contacts, who get their ideas from outside the country. If you receive any portion of your income from outside the country, you have to register as a foreign agent. Then the government can track you, track your money, who you speak to, everything. The Tbilisi intelligentsia hate it, of course. And the Russians have the same exact law in their own country—the inostranny agent, they call it. They can imprison you for a decade for, say, texting with an American."

"That seems a little extreme."

"Of course it is," he said. "But many things here are a little extreme."

Phil crouched, pooped briskly; Amy stooped to pick up his droppings and spritz herself with hand sanitizer.

"Okay, so here's what I don't get," she said, offering the man the sanitizer. "Russia is such a huge country," she said. "Why on earth would they need more land?"

"They don't just need *land,* my dear," the man said, accepting her spritz. "They need *empire.*"

"But isn't empire just—I mean, at its heart, isn't it just a lot of land?"

"Oh, no, not at all," the man said. "Kazakhstan," he said, "is a lot of land. *Canada* is a lot of land. Russia is, yes, a lot of land, of course that's true. But, more importantly, it's a force bestriding the globe. With its own imposed culture and way of being. That's what makes an empire more than just a lot of land." He looked over at her with small twinkling eyes. "There's a difference."

"But what's the point of it all?" They stopped for a second to let a mother with a stroller pass by. "Why do you need other countries to—I don't know, live under the influence of *your* country? What do you gain from that? It's not like this is the age of exploration anymore. It's not like land equals power or even influence. Germany is influential and it's relatively small! Same with Japan, or France!"

She was unnerved by the man's patient smile.

"What?" she said.

"What?"

"Do I sound ridiculously naïve? I probably do," Amy said.

"No, no, not naive. It's just that—and do forgive me, especially seeing as how we just met, but I must say—this is rather rich coming from an American."

She looked at him as they walked; he was still smiling.

"Surely you know that no other country in the history of the world has dominated every facet of the global order the way that the United States does today. You are a citizen of the most empire-minded civilization since civilization began."

"Oh, stop."

"Did you know that, right now in Rome, the hardest restaurant reservation to get is for a restaurant that sells American barbecue?"

"American barbecue is pretty amazing," Amy said.

"In *Rome?*"

"Okay, fine," Amy said. "But what about England? Did the sun ever set on *your* empire?"

"England, England, yes, of course," he said. "Certainly, we were an empire. But even at our peak, even between the wars, it was nothing like America's world conquest. It couldn't have been. We didn't have the resources you do, the cultural dominance, the military might, the money. We had ships and men with rifles and bush hats. You have Hollywood and Silicon Valley and Wall Street. A very different thing."

"Excuse me, but didn't you guys take over—I don't know, India? And Kenya? And *Hong Kong?*"

"More or less, of course we did, you're right. You're right. And it still stings for us, too—the collapse of empire. I myself felt a little bit teary when we handed back Hong Kong. The lowering of the British flag, the dismissal of the governor. A bit of a punch in the gut, to be quite honest. And what was that, twenty-six years ago? But I feel it still."

"So even *you* lament the loss of British power," she said.

"Maybe I do," the man said. "I suppose I do. But that's because nobody on earth likes to give up power." He tightened his grip on his poodle to keep her from going after a fallen stick. "Even if it's power you had no business having in the first place."

They were three-quarters around the track already, near a little beach on the lake where three kids were building sandcastles in the chilly air. The dogs were jaunty, pulling ahead on their leashes.

From off in the distance, Georgian joggers came toward them, then moved gracefully past: spandex leggings, Nike sneakers. The day still sparkled.

"So what happens now?" Amy asked. "Does Russia win?"

"Probably," the man said, "since Russia wants Georgia more than the West does."

"And then what?"

"Oh, it will be a nightmare for Georgia. No free expression, no rule of law. Violent crackdown against political dissent. Total plunder of state resources," he said. "The usual."

They walked in silence then, letting the dogs lead the way. A murmuration of starlings lifted off into the sky toward the east. Joggers jogged. Mothers pushed their children. A beautiful woman on a bench smoked a cigarette, staring off into space.

"May I ask you a question now?" the man said. "Why on earth did you bring a drone to Tbilisi?"

"Oh, I'm just—I'm searching for a dog," Amy said. "She went missing a few months ago. She belonged to a friend, so I came here to help find her. Drones are useful in animal rescue."

"You must be joking."

"I know how it sounds."

"You came all the way from America to Tbilisi to help find a dog."

"I did."

"That's"—and she was afraid he was going to say *ridiculous*, but instead he said—"very kind."

They came, then, across a group of strays, and the dogs engaged in a bit of friendly butt-sniffing; the strays were brownish and grayish and very much not Angel, and Amy knew, without her drone, that her chances of finding the dog had gone down about 90 percent. "I assume none of these are the one you're looking for?" the man said.

"They are not," Amy said. Then: "Do you think if I'd offered the cop money he would have given me my drone back?"

"Oh dear," the man said. "Oh no. That would have been a terrible idea—"

"But maybe—"

"Truly," he said, "if I can give you one word of advice during your time here, do not ever, *ever* try to bribe a police officer. They're very proud of the integrity of their municipal force. The police were once profoundly corrupt, back in the nineties, and the government did an admirable job rebuilding. One of the best things they've done, to be honest. They would not look kindly on you trying to bribe them."

"Ah," Amy said.

"The consequences could be extraordinarily severe."

"Got it," Amy said.

"Don't try it."

"Gotcha," she said.

"Well, looks like we're back at the end of the road," he said, as the British school emerged in the distance, Union Jacks and Georgian flags fluttering.

"What does your dog do while you teach?"

"Poppy? She sits in the corner." The man patted Poppy on her soft, curly head. "Learns her maths."

"Right," Amy said. She bent to pet Poppy good-bye, and the poodle accepted her pats with equanimity. "Well, it was nice talking with you. Thanks again for your help with the cop."

"No problem," said the man. "Enjoy Tbilisi. Beware the chacha."

"Too late," Amy said.

"Ah well," the man said, then he and Poppy pushed off up the hill.

SHE ASKED THE cab to drop her off in Liberty Square.

The Opel weaved through traffic, endless streets of open-air vendors selling auto parts and construction materials, the dogs asleep on either side of her in the back seat, before they finally crossed over a bridge into the center of the city. Down Rustaveli, past the parliament building with its drooping cross, and then, finally, the square. But despite its grandiose name, the Square was little more than a traffic roundabout, a grassy oval plaza with an obelisk in the middle. "This is it?" she asked the cabby, who didn't speak English and ushered her out with hand gestures.

According to her Google map, this was it. The seminary Stalin had attended as a teenager was just down the street. There was a monument to Pushkin in an adjacent park. On the other side of the oval, a Courtyard by Marriott and a Burberry store.

The square, according to her phone, had been, in its previous lifetimes, known as Erivansky Square, Beria Square, and Lenin Square. It was where George W. Bush gave a speech that afternoon fifteen years ago, where someone threw a grenade at him that didn't go off. (Honestly, how did she miss that?) Georgians liked to throw protests there every few years. During the Soviet period, there had been a large statue of Vladimir Lenin a few feet from where she stood.

Amy tried to feel something, standing in the middle of the grassy oval: gratitude for her own freedom or a sense of being at a crossroads in history or anything, really.

But instead she felt only droneless, homeless—and the fiercely growing cold.

A few feet away, in the tall shadow of the obelisk, lounged a fluffy white dog. Large-ish, Lab-shaped. "Zazi! Zazi!" she whispered. "Zazi, is it her?" Zazi looked up at her, confused. "Angelozi, Zazi, could it be?" The poetic beauty of finding Angel after a day of searching in the wrong place, in this modest historic circle.

Was it possible?

"Angel!" Amy said, then, louder, *"Angelozi!"*

The dog looked at her curiously as she approached. Amy tried to make herself small, praying Zazi and Phil wouldn't scare her away. "Angelozi," she said, removing a pig's ear from her bag—"Angelozi, please come—" and then the dog stood, and it turned out that she wasn't large at all, nor Lab-shaped, and she had reddish-brown spots on her hind quarters, and her ears folded over, which meant of course she wasn't Angel at all. But Amy gave her the pig's ear anyway, and watched, disappointed, as she ate it.

NINE

BY THE TIME she got home she was very cold.

She had purchased a cheese pastry from a vendor on her way back to the house: she had no interest in going to a restaurant or taking more of Irine's food, and remembered, again, why some people found travel so enervating: so much thinking about where the next meal was coming from. The pastry was greasy and sat badly in her stomach, but she thought she'd tell Judd about it anyway. Maybe at home she could recreate it with all-butter puff and maybe halloumi, or something softer. It wasn't a bad idea.

She texted him: "something like a boureka, only puffier, maybe a little saltier." She knew he would know what she was talking about. He didn't text back right away, but that was fine. It didn't necessarily mean he was with Meret.

In her small, quiet room, the wind rattling against the wooden window frames, she changed into sweatpants and an old CUNY sweatshirt. She knew this meant defeat, no more searching for Angel today, but it was dark outside and so cold, and anyway randomly wandering Tbilisi was about as stupid a way of looking for a dog as she could think of.

Tomorrow she would walk around the school's neighborhood and ask some of the students what they knew. Play detective. Discover more about the fired teacher. Maybe there was a lead in there somewhere? It was better than nothing.

She flipped open her laptop to look at an old video of Angel, to refresh her memory about who (or what), specifically, she was looking for.

And there she was, proudly marching across the street with her small charges behind her. The children holding hands, the traffic slowing. Angel waited until everyone was across the street, accepting her pats, her farewells, her thank yous, who's a good girl, such a good girl. She stood erect, her tail wagging, a service animal showing the satisfaction of having fulfilled her service.

Why were dogs this way, so eager and easy to please? Studies had shown that dogs liked to earn their treats rather than just receive them, that the pleasure centers in their brains went off when they solved a puzzle, say, or retrieved a caregiver's shoes. Some quirk in their evolution told them they were best beloved when they were most of use; some quirk in her own evolution, she knew, told her the same.

Amy stretched out on the bed, set her laptop on her hips. Another video of Angel, this time shot in disconcerting, jerky angles, narrated in Georgian, in a child's voice: the work of one of the school's students. She had no idea what the girl was saying until the very end, when she shouted, in English, "I love you Angelozi! I love you I love you!"

The closing shot was a still of Angel happy in her little wooden house on the corner near her school.

Amy was surprised to find tears filling her eyes.

Various legends spoke of where the Pied Piper had led the children when he guided them out of Hamelin. Some said he drowned them all in the river and others said he took them to the end of the earth, playing his flute until they slowly went mad. But the nicer version, the one that Amy liked, was the one where the Pied Piper took them to the top of a magical mountain, the one where they played games and sang songs and learned how to speak different languages and how to tend their farm animals until their parents finally came to fetch them.

A school, in other words. A particular school that was magic.

As she clicked onto a new video of Angel, a text bubble appeared on her screen.

"You there?" Judd.

"I'm here," she said. She assumed he wanted to talk about pastry.

"Uno's in the hospital."

"Oh god," she typed. "Again?"

"Some kind of fungal infection. Asper—aspergers or something."

"Aspergers is autism."

"Something like that."

"Do you need me to come home?" God, it galled her how quickly she typed that. And there was no delete function.

"No, no. Maybe just check in on Ferry."

"Does he know?"

This had always been her job at home, managing Ferry's emotions, making sure he felt safe and loved. She didn't know why Judd was so keen to outsource this work to her, although she had a natural aptitude for it and obviously she did love the kid like he was her own. But he *was* Judd's own. And Judd always shied away from the difficult work of it. He liked his relationship with his son to be easy, football games and restaurant meals.

"Yeah, he knows. I texted him this morning."

"You texted him????"

"He might have been sleeping!" Judd, defensive.

"Well, how bad is it?"

"Unclear."

"Okay," Amy typed, trying to calibrate what to do with this information. "I'll call him."

"Thanks. I love you."

"Me too."

Nine p.m. in Tbilisi meant it was one in Ithaca, a reasonable time to call. Still, Amy paused before picking up her phone. She had done this so many times before. She had said all the things she was supposed to say so many times. It will be all right. It will be okay. She had never known whether she was telling the truth, only that she had to try with all she had to will it to be so. But if she said it when it wasn't true, she would lose all credibility.

She googled "asperger's fungal disease." Up came *aspergillosis*, a fungal infection liver transplant patients were particularly vulnerable to, even years after a successful transplant. Something about the suppressed immune systems. Something about the omnipresence of mold in our ecosystems. It was treatable if caught early enough. It wasn't always caught that early.

The prescription: IV antifungals. Survival rate of almost 60 percent once treatment started. So, okay. She could tell Ferry it would be all right with a certain amount of honesty.

She dialed and it went straight to voicemail. "Ferris, Dad told me your mom was in the hospital. Let me know what I can do."

What on earth could she possibly do? But she had always done something before. She had pulled miracles out of her handbag. Taken Ferry to the magical mountain.

She hung up. In the absence of being able to do anything from Tbilisi, she watched more Angel videos, then followed the trail of YouTube from dog to dog, animal rescue to animal rescue. Usually this sort of thing calmed her heart, but after an hour she still found herself agitated. After all this, a fungal infection! So incredibly stupid. Uno had been born into such privilege and such misery, a childhood of wealth and emotional torment, a sexually abusive stepfather (vile), drug addiction by the time she was fifteen. Her own mother a drunk. Her father never around.

She and Judd had met at Andover, where she'd lasted about a year and a half before getting expelled. Judd liked her, at first, because she could get him coke, and then because she'd have sex with him. And then it became something more, something like obsession with each other for many years. They circled each other around New York for more than a decade, getting back together, breaking up. His parents never approved, threatened to cut him off if he didn't stop seeing her. Which he never did, which they never did.

When she called him and told him she was pregnant, he assumed she'd have an abortion. Instead, she said she wanted the baby, that the baby would help her turn her life around. A lot of pressure, Judd said later, to put on a baby, but neither of them knew that at the time. They managed to stay married for eight months after Ferry was born. Ferry had no recollection of his parents ever sharing the same house. He told her he couldn't imagine the two of them together, how it had ever worked, how they had ever even managed to have a conversation, much less a child. How the only person he could ever imagine his father loving in his entire life was her.

Amy found herself looking at pictures of Ferry as a baby, short videos, which she didn't always indulge in but often tried to savor like chocolate. A video of him in the bath, singing the theme song from *Phineas and Ferb*. "There's a hundred and four days of summer vacation, and school comes along just to end it—"

And Amy, fifteen years ago, her thin voice joining in: "So the annual problem, in our generation—"

And Ferry's little voice: "No, Mom! No! It's *of* our generation! You got the words wrong!" (She loved this video because she could hear his little voice, because he called her Mom.)

She needed water.

IN THE SILENT kitchen (silent except for the drip-drip-drip), Amy was surprised to find the blue-eyed man at the table with his laptop and a beer. She startled. She'd thought for some reason he wasn't allowed out of his room.

"I'm sorry," she said, moving quickly past him.

"Why are you sorry?"

She poured herself a mug of water at the sink. "I interrupted you."

"You did not."

"Aren't you working?"

"If it was important," he murmured, still looking at his screen, "I wouldn't be doing it in public."

She didn't know what to say to that. She drank from her mug, refilled it, turned to head back upstairs, but found that her feet wouldn't move. In the hallway behind her, she heard quiet shuffling. Downstairs, dogs were rolling over, snuffling, sleeping in heaps.

She rinsed out her mug, placed it on the drying rack.

"The water here is terrible," he said. "You shouldn't drink it."

"It tastes like regular water to me," she said.

"It comes through Soviet pipes," he said. "Lead."

"I grew up with lead," she said.

"In America?"

"Minnesota."

The man nodded. She wondered if he had ever heard of Minnesota.

"I am Andrei," he said.

"I'm Amy."

"I know," he said. "You're famous." His voice had a gravelly quality that made it unclear if he was being serious or not.

"I'm only famous in this house."

He nodded, returned to whatever he was doing on his laptop. She wasn't sure if she was dismissed or not, or if she wanted to be. He was wearing a white undershirt, the sleeveless kind, that showed off his strong biceps and his stick-and-poke tattoos. He seemed to be concentrating deeply. A single lightbulb from a ghostly pendant lamp swung gently above the table where he sat. She had felt almost normal today, taking a cab, walking Zazi and Phil around a lake. But now back in this strange house she felt, again, like she was an extra in an art film.

"What are you working on?" He turned to her: those eyes. "I'm sorry, if it's private—"

"I am writing a letter to my daughter."

"Oh," she said. "Where's your daughter?"

"In Moscow," he said. "With her mother."

"Ah," she said. With her mother, she noted. Not his wife. (Why would she think that? Why would that matter?)

While his eyes were still on the screen he said, "I am going to take a break now from writing. Would you like a beer?"

She wouldn't, she had no interest in ever drinking alcohol again. "Sure."

"I'll get you one," he said. "Have a seat."

Although his voice said *boxer* and his tattoos said *inmate*, Andrei moved with the easy grace of someone who'd been trained to use his body professionally—an athlete or a dancer. "Did you dance?" she said.

"My mother was a dancer. She taught me a bit when I was younger." He sat down across from her, slid a beer across the table. "You?"

Under the pendant light, his hair showed streaks of silver. He had a glamorously beaten-up face, like that of a movie star who played action roles or the villain in period dramas. Busted nose, full lips.

"I didn't dance, but I always wanted to."

"You're tall," he said. "It would have been hard for you to find a partner."

"I know." She'd had dreams, as a small child, of wearing a tutu and joining the lineup of sparkly pink girls at the Christmas recital, but even then she'd been much too tall. Which was what her mother said. (Which was a nice way—well, a way—of saying they couldn't afford it.)

"Irine said that you were a model."

"God, I wish she'd stop saying that," she said. "I was a model for about thirty seconds. And it was a very long time ago."

"You still could do it if you wanted." He said it in such a serious, matter-of-fact way that she did not think he was flirting.

Still, a butterfly in her stomach.

"I'm out of the game," she said. "Anyway, I teach now. Food writing at a local college."

He scratched at the back of his neck, languidly. "I don't know what that is, food writing."

"It's writing about restaurants, different recipes, that sort of thing. Where food comes from."

"Where food comes from?" Then he smiled, a real one, revealing chipped teeth. "Americans do not know this?"

"Not, like, the food system. Not farming," Amy said. "My students write about restaurants or about different kinds of cuisine. We'll take tours of, say, Chinatown, and research the different ways that these neighborhoods were built, what the restaurant industry means to different parts of New York City. It's an important part of New York's economy."

"So your students write about the economy."

"Yes," Amy said. She took a sip of watery beer.

"Do you ever make your own food?"

"Sure," she said. "I mean, not as much as I used to, but for many years I cooked in a restaurant." For some reason she did not mention it was her husband's restaurant.

"Did you enjoy that?"

"Oh sure," Amy said.

"But you don't do it anymore."

"My life got busy."

"Too busy to have a job?" he asked.

"Raising my son has been a job," she said. "Rescuing animals is a job."

"Ah," he said.

This was a conversation—she was surely having some sort of conversation—but she had no idea what she was supposed to say next. This used to happen to her all the time when she was younger, but she thought she'd grown out of it. Or, now that she was forty-six, she only spent time with people to whom she had things to say. She should have gotten up and gone back to her room. She didn't have to sit here and wonder whether or not he was teasing her.

If he didn't have those impossible eyes!

And also the fine, stubbly jaw, the full mouth.

She stole a glance up at him and then quickly back to the table.

"Do you miss home?"

"No," she said. "Do you?"

"Of course," he said. "Everyone I love is there." He paused. "You have a husband?"

"I do."

"And he doesn't mind that you are here by yourself?"

"It doesn't matter whether he minds," she said, then looked up at him; he was looking straight at her. "And no, he doesn't."

He smiled, casually, and she felt her heart pulse. How long had it been since she had felt this kind of pull toward a man who wasn't Judd? Alongside this kind of intimidation?

Years. Years. And even though Judd was still beautiful to her, still broad and familiar and safe—how long had it been since she'd wanted to tear his clothes off?

"So then," the man said. He didn't finish.

Amy's husband was turned on by other, younger women (look, even if he didn't sleep with them, he flirted, patted knees, rubbed shoulders, hugged, she'd seen him, he did this in front of her), while she just marched forward with her middle-aged libido and her own understanding of herself as a not very sexual person. The flurry of passion that ignited in her when she first met Judd had lasted a year or maybe more before the genial routines of cohabitation replaced fucking against the bedroom wall—which was how she liked it, coffee in the mornings, clean underwear all day.

But if she wasn't a very sexual person, why did she suddenly feel this way?

"How long are you going to stay in Tbilisi?" he asked, after a few minutes of her being acutely aware of both their breathing.

"I'm supposed to go home at the end of next week," she said.

"And what if you don't find the dog?"

"Oh, I'll find her."

"How do you know?"

"I have a feeling," she said.

"What kind of feeling?"

"Or a connection . . ." she said, "with certain dogs," and she thought of the woman in the park: *I have a psychic connection with animals. I know what's inside them, what they're thinking.*

"I understand," he said, and she was almost certain he wasn't teasing her. "Some people are like that. My grandmother was like that."

An opening to ask questions, but Amy didn't ask.

"There are a lot of dogs in Tbilisi," Andrei said.

"Yes," she said. She slid her beer bottle back and forth across the table. "What's your daughter's name?"

"Faina."

"That's pretty," Amy said. "What does it mean?"

"What does it mean?"

"I don't know," she said. "Sometimes names in foreign languages mean different things."

"It's a Russian name," he said. "It's not a foreign language to her."

"Your daughter's Russian?"

"Yes, of course," he said. "As am I."

"Oh," Amy said—when he'd said they were in Moscow, she'd just thought—"What are you doing here?"

"I live here."

"I know," Amy said, "but if you're Russian, what are you—"

He let the question dangle for a minute. "I came here in September, so that I would not have to go fight in Ukraine."

"Oh. Right."

He shrugged, went to the humming refrigerator, came back with two more beers. "Georgia is one of the only countries you can enter without a visa," he said. "There are a few others, the UAE, Argentina. But it is more expensive to go to those places."

"Of course."

"It is expensive here too," he said. "But not quite as bad."

"How did you find Irine?"

"The same way you did," he said. "The internet."

"She was advertising a room?"

"Help around the house, mostly," he said. "Fixing things that couldn't be put off any longer. I showed up and saw how many rooms there were here and proposed that I rent one. It took some convincing—"

"Why?"

"Not everyone here wants a Russian man in their home."

Amy popped the cap off her beer. The label was red and gold with a block-print design, and under the Georgian writing was the English word BEER. It wasn't very good, but if Judd sold this at the restaurant he could charge ten dollars a bottle for the glamorous label alone.

"I am lucky," Andrei said. "By the time I got here, there was almost nothing left for under a thousand lari a month."

Amy did the math in her head. Four hundred dollars, give or take. "It's kind of an odd house, isn't it?"

He smiled again. What a relief his smiles were. "Eleven dogs," he said.

"How does anyone take care of so many dogs? How do you walk them? How do you *feed* them? And the noise!"

"She gets donations here and there, I believe," he said. "You paid the food bill for several weeks, in fact. Both the humans and the dogs."

"I figured," Amy said, although actually she hadn't really considered how exactly her money had been spent.

"Has she asked you for more money?"

"She doesn't have to," Amy said. "I'm happy to help if she wants me to. Do you think she's in need?"

He shrugged. "Three old ladies, a house that's falling apart, a daughter she is desperate to send to university abroad, and all these dogs," he said. "On one school administrator's salary."

"I should give her some money," Amy said.

"She will be offended if you try," he said.

"I should probably do it anyway."

"As you like," Andrei said.

The faucet dripped.

"How long are you going to stay here?"

"In this house?" he asked. "As long as I can." Beneath them, a dog barked once, sharply. "In Tbilisi? I have no idea. Maybe forever."

She looked at him.

"I can't go home," he said. "I am a deserter. And my wife won't have me back."

"She won't?" Amy said. "Why?"

"Because, as I said, I am a deserter."

"But surely—surely she doesn't see it that way. She didn't want you to, what, go to the front? Wouldn't that be extraordinarily dangerous?"

He laughed, echoing the dog's sharp bark. "My wife is a very strong defender of Russia. She sees the soldiers as heroes."

"Why?"

"They are reclaiming what is rightfully Russian."

"Ukraine is rightfully Russian?"

"Of course," he said.

"But it's not. You know it's not, right?"

He ran a hand through his bristly hair. "For many of us, Ukraine is historical Russia. Many of us do not consider it a separate country. Many of us believe that efforts to create a separate Ukraine are part of a foreign plot, sponsored by NATO."

"But that's insane."

"Is it?" Andrei asked. "It was an accident of history that Ukraine became independent in 1991. They had a referendum, but what does a referendum mean in a country with no infrastructure? With no understanding of what it means to be independent? When half the citizens are drunks?"

"Who says that?"

"Or they are corrupt, or they are Nazis. Or they are Russians themselves, and just don't know it."

"And you believe this?"

He shrugged. "I don't care about Ukraine one way or the other," he said. "I just didn't want to get blown up in a ditch in Zaporizhzhia."

"Right," she said.

Again, the inscrutable shrug.

"So that's why you're in Tbilisi," she finally said.

"That is why."

"Are you able to work?"

"I am," he said. "I can work from anywhere."

"What do you do?"

"Coding for American tech companies. I test their security measures."

"You're kidding."

"Why would I be kidding?"

"I didn't know American tech companies hire Russians."

"We do all the same work for half the price," he said. "It's why I can speak English. Didn't you wonder why that was possible? Or do you just think everyone speaks English because that's what *you* speak?"

"Oh come on," she said. "That's not fair." Although she had, in fact, gotten used to everyone's preternaturally good English.

He shrugged again, picked at his beer bottle's label.

"So that's what you're doing all day, working on American websites?"

"Yes," he said. "At night I usually take a walk, but it was very cold tonight. Tbilisi isn't usually this cold."

"It's not so bad if you have a coat."

"Unfortunately," he said. "I do not." He stopped picking at his beer bottle's label. "And now I assume that you want to ask me why I don't have a coat."

She nodded.

"To get here, I had to drive my car to the Georgian border," he said. "Which is about a twenty-five hour drive, but with all the clogged highways . . . And then the line for cars to cross was three days, and I didn't have enough petrol to last that long. But I couldn't drive to a petrol station because I'd lose my place in line. And then it turned out not to matter, because someone on the line offered to buy my car for ninety thousand rubles, and I accepted."

"Was ninety thousand a fair price? How much is a ruble worth?"

"I needed the money," he said. "It did not matter if the price was fair."

She understood.

"So then I walked," he said. "But, of course, I could not carry very much. And this is why I left my coat."

"Jesus," Amy said. "I'm so sorry."

"You did not cause these problems."

"It's an expression," she said. "I'm not actually apologizing."

He lifted an eyebrow, possibly amused.

"Okay, this is what I don't understand—why did you have to come here? Couldn't you have stayed in Moscow?" she said. "Hidden from the draft? What's the worst that could have happened?"

"The worst is very bad," he said. "And it is hard to hide. If you get called up and don't appear they come to your home. Or my wife would have turned me in anyway."

Honestly his wife sounded like a bitch. "But what about your parents, couldn't you stay with them?"

"My father's dead," he said. "My mother thinks I am a coward."

"Because you don't want to die."

He lifted a finger. "Because I don't want to die for the motherland."

"But what about—" she had forgotten the daughter's name. "What about your daughter?"

"What about her?"

"Wouldn't they want you to stay alive for her?"

He shrugged. "Is it worse to have no father or to have a coward for a father?"

"Trust me," she said, "it's worse not to have a father."

He remained expressionless.

"Does she know where you are?"

"She knows what she needs to know," he said. "We want to protect her. That means that we are—we are careful with what we tell her. And of course my wife doesn't want her to think her father is a deserter."

"I'm sure she'd understand if you explained it to her."

"She lives with her mother and she spends weekends with her grandmother," he said.

"Okay."

"She believes that Ukraine is part of the Russian homeland and that it is currently being overrun by Nazis," he said. "She thinks that Vladimir Putin is wise and just and the protector of her country. She thinks NATO is an enemy collective set on the destruction of everyone she knows and loves."

They were quiet for a minute. His large, scarred hands drew an aimless figure on the kitchen table. Sometimes, they were close to hers.

"I wish I could fix that sink," she said.

"I've fixed it three times," he said. "It never takes."

The dripping sounded mathematical, or like a metronome. Or like it was conveying some sort of secret pattern that they could figure out if they listened hard enough. They listened, hard.

But then downstairs, a dog started to bark through the floorboards. "He probably needs to pee," Amy said.

"Irine puts down—what is the word?" Andrei said. "She puts down pads."

"Ew, gross," Amy said. "I'll let them out to the garden."

"I'll join you."

"Don't you need a coat?" Amy said.

"No," Andrei said. "The beer has warmed me."

She nodded because she wasn't his mother, and they descended the creaky stairs to the ground floor. Before she could even flip on the light, the dogs roused, and started to whine, and then it was a pack of dogs scrambling at the gate.

"This way," he said, opening the gates and then a door to the outside. The dogs stood, some old and slow, others feisty, others barking. They hurried outside, peed against the garden wall or humped each other or circled lazily under the stars. The garden was large enough for a dilapidated swing in the corner, a picnic table in the other corner, and a huge tree in the middle, around which was planted a circle of small white stones.

"You must be freezing."

Andrei lit a cigarette. "You want?"

She took the cigarette and they stood together, in the cold air, smoking erasing the need for conversation, as the dogs milled about, some shiny-coated under the stars, some almost invisible. She could see an impossible number of stars in the sky. The light pollution in Tbilisi wasn't nearly as bad as at home. She knew a few of the constellations, the ones everyone knew, the Big Dipper, Orion. Here they seemed different, in the wrong position in the sky.

"Are you okay?" he asked her. Amy held an arm around her waist in a futile attempt to warm herself. Andrei was crouching down near one of the dogs.

"I could buy you a coat," she said.

He laughed; his chipped teeth glinted. "Is that what you came here for? To fix our problems with your money?"

"No," she said. Then: "I guess so. It's what they expect of Americans, isn't it?"

"People expect less of Americans," he said. But he didn't make it sound cruel.

The cigarette wasn't as strong as the ones Irine smoked, or else she was getting used to them. Still, she felt herself grow lightheaded. She blew a stream of smoke toward Orion. She wondered which way Moscow was. She wondered if his daughter missed him. She wondered if his wife did.

She was so far away from her own home that she felt like she was on another planet entirely. Impossible to imagine Judd, Le Coin, the cooks, the dishwashers, the delivery trucks, Meret, the East Village, the apartment. Impossible to imagine that they could exist at all. Roxy's delicate trot down Fourth Street. The intake desk at the shelter, the dog run at Tompkins Square Park. That the cooks were cooking, that the traffic was honking, the subways were pulsing underneath the streets, none of it seemed real or even possible from this great distance. That the stars were in the right place.

"I think I will take my walk now," Andrei said. "Maybe I'll take one of these guys." And he patted the dog in front of him on the head.

"You can't go out like that, you'll freeze," she said. "You can borrow my coat."

"I'm okay, Amy, truly."

"No, just wait—" and she ground out her cigarette and hustled back inside and upstairs, found her green parka (oversized, it would almost certainly fit), but was unsurprised to find that by the time she returned downstairs, Andrei was gone.

TEN

SHE WAITED UP to hear him come in, but she did not hear him come in.

Midnight, 12:30. One a.m.

And then, still sleepless, and because she assumed nobody would notice, she borrowed another dog.

Most of the Tbilisi strays in the basement—eleven of them, yes, asleep in piles—seemed to be medium-sized, nondescript, but this one was small and soft, a generation or two removed from some pampered Soviet shih tzu. She had liquid brown eyes, a mop of gray and brown fur, and a kind of placid expression that said *I will not be frightened, I will accept my fate.* Amy wondered how this one had ended up here, in Irine's basement (how had any of them ended up here?), as she picked her up under her scruffy belly. The other dogs looked on, curious, but neither barked nor growled. Maybe they understood that this one was the only one who could fit with Amy on a single bed. Maybe they understood that all of their fates were determined by strange middle-aged women who could pluck them up with no warning.

Amy cuddled the placid shih tzu on her way back up to her room, felt the reassuring weight of her like a newborn against her chest. At home, when she could not fall asleep, the steady breathing of a dog sometimes helped, especially when the Xanax didn't, or the animal videos. She plopped the dog (she had a tag but it was filled out in Georgian—fine, she'd call her Georgia) onto the bed and the dog watched her curiously. It was almost two, and the house had settled into its creaky rest. Outside, the moon was just a sliver but the stars glowed like neon through her window. Maybe that was why she couldn't sleep. At home, despite the streetlights and drunks of the East Village, nothing felt particularly exciting or worth staying up for. A good night was a decent meal, maybe something on Netflix, a meditation podcast and asleep by 10:30. A bad night was the same thing but asleep at 3:30 or 4:00, wracked by Judd's snoring or a sense of panic that would overtake her for reasons that, by dawn, had always vanished.

Georgia stretched, lifted her head for a moment, then curled up into a ball on the foot of the bed as if she always did this. What a docile girl! She had a feeling that Angel wouldn't be so docile. Angel was too maternal, too in charge. Angel was a dog with a job, whereas this one had clearly been bred for decor.

At the shelter, Amy was quick to assess the different personalities of her charges: timid or assertive, sometimes unfortunately aggressive, or maternal or yappy or needy. But of course always traumatized; shelter dogs—American shelter dogs, that is to say—were usually stressed out, even in the nicer shelters, because they spent all day separated into small cages with (if they were lucky) tiny individual outside areas where they could get some sunshine or pee in the cold, and (if they were lucky) they were walked once a day, and they were generally only fed once a day (and sometimes not at all on weekends or holidays), and when people came by to visit they were so crazed for attention they would bark their faces off and their eyes would roll back in their heads and they'd jump up and press their bodies against the cages anxiously, aggressively, scaring the nice family that had come in looking for a dog like the ones they'd seen on the Purina bag.

Or they'd be so scared and shut down they'd hide in the corners of their cages and not make eye contact and not even try. "Come on, baby," Amy would say. "You've got to try! Show some initiative!" But the shut-down ones wouldn't even look at her.

The hardest cases, of course, would snap and bite, because they'd been trained to behave that way or because they were just so scared.

But there were always a few dogs that seemed to know what to do, the ones who could perform for people, wag their tails and jump, but just a little, and roll over for belly rubs the second they got outside for meet-and-greets. When Amy took dogs out of their kennels to meet potential owners, she could always tell within three minutes which dogs were going to luck out and which ones were going to return. She thought of the lucky ones as the A students; they were smart enough to have learned how to bark cheerfully (not aggressively), how to lick faces (adorably), how not to scare children or intimidate the moms. They knew they could never seem the least bit intimidating! Even if they weren't really intimidating, only large or bulky or strange-looking; the smart ones would somehow make themselves smaller, make their eyes look especially large. How did they know to do that?

Still, the small dogs always went first, and then fluffy dogs, and then the lighter-colored dogs, since the public saw these sorts of dogs as more feminine and domestic, and of course because of racism (black animals were adopted less than half as frequently as light-colored animals).

Which was why, at the end of the day, it was always the pit bulls who broke Amy's heart, the pit bulls who were rarely pulled from their cages, and when they were pulled they generally got returned. Big, smart pit bulls were the worst, as they were so eager to be with people, so eager to please, that they couldn't help themselves, and would jump and pull on their leashes from the very first hello. And they were strong! And short-haired, and their canine teeth were so prominent, and they weren't cute in that golden retriever way or even in a sort of ugly-sweet bulldog way; they just looked tough and watchful and aggressive. They marketed the pit bulls as "Staffordshire Terriers," but nobody was fooled.

But sometimes—sometimes someone would come in, a single man, tattooed knuckles, boots, and Amy would have a feeling he was looking for a specific kind of dog, a specific *look*. If she was working the kennels that day, or coordinating the other volunteers, she would say, "Pull Babette" or "Pull Samantha" (they always gave the pit bulls girly names), and she'd spend a few minutes with Babette or Samantha before bringing her out, give her some treats, brush her fur and the space between her eyes, maybe even stick a little bow on her collar, anything to say to Tattooed Knuckles, *Look at me, I'm beautiful, I'm your girl.* And when Tattooed Knuckles got to the desk, Amy would be ready, maybe she herself would have unbuttoned the top button of her own shirt. "Do I have a dog for you," she would say.

"Do you?" And he'd look a little lascivious, even though they really were talking about a dog. Nothing else. Even if he were wearing a wedding ring.

And out would come Babette, who had been soothed (she hoped) into a state of relative calm, and because pit bulls were so smart Amy would have already taught her *sit* and *stay* and *paw,* and *watch how gently she takes treats* and *she's been in the shelter for eleven months, and it's just been so unfair, she's such a good girl, but it takes someone really special to notice her.*

It was a thing she was unreservedly good at. Tattooed Knuckles would think about it or say *I really was only looking* or maybe even *You got anything else? Maybe a little smaller?* But then Babette would look up at him with those beautiful gray eyes (most pit bulls did have disarmingly lovely eyes) and Amy could always pinpoint the exact moment it was over. The moment Knuckles sighed. The moment

Babette licked his hand, gently, hopefully. The exact moment that Babette settled into Knuckles's heart.

Pit bulls were still destroyed at three times the rate of other dogs; they were so smart and eager to please and easy to train that they could be trained to do terrible things, and sometimes could not be untaught. But that was rare. Under Amy's watch, the pit bulls of the Avenue D shelter found homes or found fosters or found refuges upstate or in New Jersey or, for a week or two at a time, in her own apartment (the cats hated it, Roxy hated it). Under Amy's watch, the animals who most needed saving were always saved.

Rescue after rescue, she put parts of herself back together. The loneliness of her childhood. The disappointments of her marriage.

"Hey Georgia, what's your story, anyway?"

The dog sniffed Amy's outstretched hand. She seemed relatively well fed, which was good for several reasons—it meant not only that Irine had enough to feed all the dogs but that the smaller ones weren't crowded out during feeding time. She had the tag in her ear that meant she'd had her shots, and protruding nipples that meant that, at least once in her life, she'd given birth.

"When did you have your babies, mama? Were you on the streets?"

Amy let her hand run down the soft fur at the back of Georgia's neck. She felt oily, a little dirty, really, and it would be a nice thing to give this dog a bath, especially if this were her temperament at all times. Would this dog freak out around water? Or would she, like Roxy, love the warmth and the scrubbing and the devoted attention? Grooming Roxy took at least an hour of hands-on work: scrubbing her with special shampoo and conditioner, rinsing her, cleaning her ears, trimming her nails, brushing her teeth with peanut-butter-flavored toothpaste. Blow-drying her as best she could, then wrapping a towel around her warm, moist body and fitting a specially-designed terry-cloth turban on her head. She always posted the results on the shelter Instagram page with the caption "Spa Day."

Hmmm. Georgia did smell a little like pee.

Well, if bathing her made too much noise, she'd simply stop.

She carried Georgia to the bathroom, put her in the tub, started the water running gently. The dog looked confused, but not alarmed, and she thought that she could soap her up with human shampoo (there really wasn't such a difference) and maybe file her nails with her own nail file if she softened them up first and by the time she was done they'd probably both be tired enough to sleep for several hours.

When the water touched Georgia she let out a single yelp and scrabbled at the porcelain sides of the tub.

"Shhh, shhh, it's okay, we're just getting you clean."

Georgia scrabbled. "Shhhh," she said, "please," and then remembered please in Georgian, *gtkhovt*. "Gtkhovt, gtkhovt, come on girl," and the discordant Georgian confused the dog enough that she calmed down a little bit. Amy kept kneading her wet fur, putting well-honed canine massage techniques into practice, and the hidden grit in Georgia's fur came off in grayish streams into the tub. Amy felt nuts, what was she doing? but also gratified because clearly Georgia really did need a bath.

She sang quietly to the dog like she used to sing to Ferry in the bathtub. *There's a hundred and four days of summer vacation.*

She squirted some shampoo into her hand, rubbed it in circles on Georgia's furry head (if she'd had her grooming clippers here she could really go to town) and the dog either enjoyed it or didn't see the point in protesting, just sort of sat there, stopped scrabbling, and Amy wished she knew some Georgian tunes to sing—the beautiful songs they sang at the table the other night, or anything that Georgia might find familiar. But in the absence of anything else: *and school comes along just to end it.*

(Which was where Ferry used to pipe up: "Mama! That's my favorite song too!" When he was three or four. Golden hair, golden skin, golden little boy.)

She rinsed Georgia carefully. One of the nice things about European showers were the detached heads, which were perfect for rinsing dogs or small children or the spaces between your toes, and Amy hoped that she wasn't using all the morning's hot water (god, what if she was?) or that the gurgling of the pipes or her own off-key singing weren't waking anyone up, but she was being quiet, right? Singing quietly? And Georgia was being so good? *Yes, you're being a good girl, look at you all nice and clean.*

"What are you doing?"

She turned around, mortified. "I'm, um—"

"You're giving Nesvi a bath?" Maia was wearing a bathrobe over pajama pants, her hair up in a knot on top of her head, her blond roots showing. She was wearing glasses, looked strangely teacherly.

"I couldn't sleep," Amy said. "Her name is Nesvi?"

"Yes," Maia said. "It means 'melon.' So you decided to give her a bath? Because you couldn't sleep?"

"We woke you up."

"My room is right under yours," Maia said. "I heard all of it. Even the singing." But she didn't look particularly annoyed—in fact, she almost seemed amused. "But you didn't wake me up, in fact. I never sleep."

"You're too young for that."

Maia shrugged, sat down on the closed toilet. "It's been like this for me since I was small. Evidently it used to drive my mother crazy. Even if she put me down for a nap when I was a baby I would just sit in my crib and watch her." She loosened her hair, tied it back up again on top of her head. For a moment, with her hair down, she had looked very beautiful and young.

"Don't you get tired?"

"Not really," she said. "I have too much energy, I guess. Or just too much to do. No time to sleep."

"You're a kid," Amy said. "What do you have to do?"

Maia laughed. "Well, school, of course. And also I have a job."

"You do?"

"I make videos in English."

"Oh, that's right—your mom told me."

"She hates it," Maia said. "But I earn fifty lari for a five-minute video, so I'm going to keep doing it. But of course my employer could get shut down at any minute. For propaganda."

"That could happen?"

She shrugged. "Anything *could* happen. I don't know that it *will* happen." She got down next to the tub with Amy, scratched Nesvi on her damp head.

"Was she dirty?"

"Filthy," Amy said.

"Yeah, we don't ever bathe them," Maia said.

"Do people adopt them?" Amy said. "I'm still trying to figure out how this works."

Maia sank down onto the bathmat, crossed her legs. "I guess people have adopted them in the past. Those friends you met at dinner the other night?" she said. "They brought home one of our dogs. They let her roam around though, so I don't know if you'd say she's really *their* dog. But they feed her and they built her a doghouse in their yard, so. They live out in the country, by the lake."

"I was there today," Amy said. "Or I guess yesterday. I walked around that track there."

"So then you saw all the dogs?"

"I did," Amy said. She didn't want to mention her drone, afraid she'd sound like a fool.

"People dump puppies by the lake, and the puppies become part of these packs," Maia said. "And then people know to leave food and stuff for them. And then the humane society will sometimes capture them for their shots. So they get their vaccines. It's really not so terrible. Like if you have to be a stray dog anywhere, being a stray dog by Visi Lake isn't such a bad life."

"People here are pretty nice to dogs, all things considered."

"I told you. It is easier for us to care for dogs than it is to care for one another," Maia said. She reached out again and scratched Nesvi on the head.

Amy thought about that, about the women she worked with at the shelter; many of them were older, were alone, had struggled with different kinds of addiction or dangerous relationships. They devoted themselves to the cats and dogs more assiduously than many parents devoted themselves to their children. The animals were easy to love, since they were so happy with so little, and it was easy to give them what they needed, food and love.

"So why does your mom take in these guys, then, if they're doing okay out in the wild?"

"I mean they're not always doing okay," Maia said. "They have all sorts of larger animals out there by the lake. That will attack or eat puppies. Or they can get illness or injury. Nature does what nature does. One time when I was little my mom and I went to the lake, there's a beach there, and in the sand was a dog who had clearly recently died, and my mom just lost it. Just freaked out, started sobbing, I didn't understand why. I didn't see what she was seeing. And then she marched me back to the car, and of course I was crying now too because I wanted to go to the beach, and on our way to the car there was this little dog, not much more than a puppy, and she picked it up and put it in the car with us. She said, I'm rescuing this dog. That was our first."

"So that's how it started."

"Yes," Maia said. "And since then, I don't know, whenever she sees a dog who needs help, or who isn't tagged, or who looks too skinny— she just brings them home and adds them to the pack. She spends a lot of time down there with them. I think they make her feel calm, even though to be honest they smell like shit."

"So does she walk them all? How does she take care of them?"

Maia shrugged. "Sometimes, or I'll walk a few when I can. Mostly they just go into the backyard. My grandmother and aunts feed them, or they'll sit down there too, playing with them or just talking to them. I'd do it more but I don't really have time."

"How does she pay for all of their food and everything?"

"I don't know," Maia said. "I mean, I know your money helped a lot. Every time you sent more dollars my mom was like, the American did it again!"

Amy blinked.

"I'm sorry, is that rude? Sometimes I don't know when I'm being rude."

"No, no, it's . . ." If she'd been Irine and some lunatic on the other side of the earth was sending her chunks of money every few days, no questions asked, she'd have been happy, too. "Maybe I should have given more, really."

"That's up to you," Maia said. "I'm not asking for anything."

Amy finished rinsing off Georgia—wait, no, her name was Nesvi— and Maia handed her a towel. Together, they wrapped her up in a big ball and scrubbed her dry. When they let her go, Nesvi shook wildly to get the extra water off, gave them each a sort of disgusted look, and pawed at the door. Enough was enough.

"I guess I should take her back downstairs?"

"I'll do it," Maia said. "I'm headed that way anyway." But they were still both sitting on the bathroom floor, slightly damp. Gently, reflexively, Amy was patting Nesvi dry, and she felt the dog relax a bit. Her tail was wagging, her eyes half-closed.

"I think she is enjoying her massage," Maia said.

"I can't get over how good your English is."

"Your Georgian would be really good too if you grew up watching Georgian movies and Georgian YouTube and Georgian TikTok."

"You get a lot of English media?"

"Of course," Maia said. "We have all of it. Taylor Swift, the Marvel Cinematic Universe. But it's good because it helps me speak better English, and that's what helps me make money."

"What about Russian?"

"What about it? It's the worst. Just—just a hideous language." She made a face. "But my grandmother and aunts still speak it half the time. And so does my mom, which is helpful because she actually wants the Russians to come back in and take over again like it's 1922."

"Maia, come on."

"You have no idea," Maia said. "My mother wants the state in control. She wants to have a strong man making decisions and doesn't want to look too hard at the decisions he makes. And she doesn't want to have to do hard things for herself."

"Maia, she raised you by herself."

The girl grinned. "Yeah, but I made it easy." She stood, picked up Nesvi. "Thanks for giving her a bath. She must have been pretty disgusting."

"She was beautiful," Amy said.

Maia rolled her eyes. "Dog people," she said, but she was smiling, and she left Amy alone in the bathroom, on the floor, wet, a little lonely, still not tired at all.

BUT THEN, LYING in her twin bed, a strange sort of sleep did come. It was not a peaceful rest, but an active one, dreams teetering on the border of the life she was living and a surreal life that could not be. Roxy here with her in Tbilisi, fast asleep among the dogs downstairs, poking her head up in the crowd. Amy, alarmed—how did Roxy become a stray? Had Judd stopped taking care of her in her absence? Did Judd forget to close the door behind him as he headed off to the restaurant? And how did Roxy find her all the way here?

Oh, she must have tracked her smell. She must have known where to look.

Anyway, come on, Roxy girl, it's time to get up now, it's time to come home with me, I don't know what we're doing here anyway, there was never an Angel, there was never another dog, there was never anyone besides you.

And then the woman from the park was sitting in the strange Tbilisi kitchen, saying, *I told you so, I told you so,* and Amy did not disagree.

ELEVEN

DAWN: AMY HADN'T shut the curtain and found herself blinking awake as the first light came through the window. Barking, traffic, the distant smell, perhaps, of dogs. She would not be able to fall back asleep, so she let the feeling of strangeness wash over her. Had she gotten two hours of sleep? Three? At home she would never be able to face a day after so little rest, but here she felt energized, purposeful. She would get up; she would start her day.

Still she tried to glide down the hall to the bathroom as silently as possible, as she could not bear facing Andrei, and only realized that her heart was thumping when she successfully locked the bathroom door behind her. She stood like that, back against the door, relishing her successful escape for several seconds. She should start the shower, she thought. She should pee and brush her teeth. But instead she stayed frozen against the bathroom door, again disoriented. What on earth was she doing? Why hadn't she slept?

She imagined Judd waking up, Roxy waiting patiently to pee. The cats getting fed. The coffee beans being ground, then getting spooned into the coffee maker. The street noises filtering up: kids on their way to school, teenagers playing music while they walked. Street sweepers, double parkers, the usual symphony of honks and barks. Pigeons cooing. Judd in one of his unbuttoned flannel shirts, reading the paper at the kitchen table. An egg sandwich with cheddar cheese.

She tried to imagine herself in that scene. Cleaning up after the animals, folding laundry on a chair. She closed her eyes, could almost smell the coffee brewing, Roxy's hot breath.

And then she heard a riot of barking out the window. Had a dog escaped?

She looked out to the street, and saw Irine walking several dogs up the hill, sprightly, the dogs pulling her forward. There was obviously something delicious in their noses; their leashes were taut. The sun beamed down through the clouds, catching Irine and the animals in its rays.

"Well," she said. That was how it got done, she supposed, the caring for eleven dogs. Her iPhone said it was six in the morning; at home, it was ten p.m., and Roxy was bedding down for the night. As Amy stepped into the shower (how Roxy loved lying on the floor while she showered), she felt an unexpected tug on the thread that connected her to her home.

THE FIRST SCHOOL Amy remembered was the Columbia Street School, which she'd attended from second through fifth grades. It was a small brick building eight blocks from her house whose sign in front offered rotating inspirational messages: "If you can dream it, you can do it!" or "It's a great day to have a great day!" Her stomach used to roil as she approached Columbia Street each morning, trying to keep a few feet behind her brother who was trying to keep a few feet behind her. Slower and slower they walked, knowing they'd get dragged to the principal's if they were more than ten minutes late, knowing their mother would get a phone call, trying to figure out who was more terrifying, their peers or their mother.

Usually they arrived exactly nine minutes and thirty seconds late, melting snow on their cheap boots.

And it was there that Amy learned to distrust school and anything it offered. Education was less learning to read and add and more learning to duck and run from whatever cruelty the day conspired to bring, where she learned that her mother's dire predictions (take care of yourself, nobody'll do it for you) always always came true. Because she was so tall, the teachers had a hard time seeing that she was only nine years old. Because her brother was effeminate, they had a hard time being kind. And while the other kids at Columbia Street weren't exactly wealthy, they all at least used brand-named thermoses, wore Levi's jeans.

And then came middle school, and then high school, about which the less said, the better.

Years later, it took a long time for Amy to gather up the courage to finish her GED, apply to Baruch. She did it mostly to make a good impression on Ferry, so that he wouldn't think she was undereducated—he always did so well in school! She wanted to make him proud. So, with a pit in her stomach, she applied, got accepted (well, almost everyone got accepted), and showed up that September with a new backpack and notebooks, feeling extraordinarily shy. But what startled her, at Baruch, was from the very first day how kind everyone was. The professors seemed curious about what she thought. They guided her through her courses in expository writing and intro psych, didn't laugh at her when she mispronounced a word she'd always thought she was saying the right way. She had worried about being so much older than the other students, but in fact there were many students who were her age or even older than she was, and while none of them became her best friends, there was always someone to have lunch with, grab a coffee. They were interested in her and all she had done. They loved going to Le Coin. She got mostly As and Bs.

And then her History of New York professor told her she was a good writer, and introduced her to a friend of his who published *New York Eats*, and who was always looking for new points of view on the restaurant world, and said it was rare to find someone who could cook *and* write. She screwed up her courage, submitted an article about working in the restaurant industry as a self-taught cook. And *Eats* accepted it and paid her eighty dollars! So she did it again (interviewing women who navigated the sexist world of restaurant kitchens) and again (the impact of low-wage work on kitchen staff), and by the time she graduated she had a nice little portfolio and had earned eleven hundred dollars before taxes from her experience and her writing and her wits. Enough for half her tuition bill that semester. Enough to set her up with a whole new idea of herself and what she could do.

And this was how Amy had learned to love school.

AND THEREFORE, A whistle was on her lips as she headed toward Irine's workplace, threading her way down the hill—she was learning the city, she was learning the food, she was learning bits of the language, the culture, she was *learning.* The Tbilisi sky was bright blue and the wind had stilled, and she felt the warmth of the sun on her scalp. She unzipped her parka to let the fresh air touch her throat. It was seven in the morning on the fifth day of March, 2023.

At the foot of the Dry Bridge over the broad gray Kura River, vendors had set up tables and blankets full of all sorts of wares: folding chess sets and coffee urns and plastic Soviet kitsch: hammer-and-sickle belt buckles, shot glasses emblazoned with Lenin's face. She paused to poke through a display of socks brandishing Georgian dumplings. The saleslady, an old woman with a scarf wrapped around her head, pointed at a sign: THREE SOCK 5 LARI. Less than two dollars. Amy put her three new pairs of socks in her bag and kept walking, crossing the bridge with the morning commuters.

The eastern half of Tbilisi felt more crowded than the west, with narrower, criss-crossing streets, drying laundry pinned to balcony railings, busier sidewalks. Every streetside window seemed to open to a bakery selling stuffed breads: cheese, egg, mushroom, spinach. Dogs were everywhere, too, many of them sleeping on their sides, but some of them briskly crossing streets or marching down sidewalks. These ones seemed to be true strays, skinnier and more forlorn than the ones on Rustaveli Avenue, teats swinging like loose handkerchiefs. Amy bought two spinach pastries, tucked one in her bag for later, tore up the other and offered bits to the next few strays she passed.

But also, as she pressed deeper into the neighborhood: art galleries, vintage stores, record shops. Bars. Signs in English and Russian. A sneaker store with cling-wrapped Nikes in the window. Another store, full of graffiti-print sweatshirts and jeans, and then one selling artfully tattered black dresses. The slow march of the international style: Paris and New York and Los Angeles and even here.

Then, as she got closer to the school, the neighborhood took another turn: off the main road, the apartment buildings turned shabbier, and the sidewalks were jumbled with trashcans and trash bags and beaten-up cars. A huge older woman stood in a threadbare nightgown on the corner, murmuring quietly to herself. Children picked their way through the crowded sidewalks, hunched under their backpacks. Some had parents trailing them, but others, who seemed to be only five or six years old, walked by themselves.

Down the middle of the street a kid whooshed by on a scooter. The woman in the nightgown shouted out what sounded like a curse as the kid peeled away.

Amy followed him.

Many of the shop signs here had faded Cyrillic on them, painted over but still visible on the brick. Amy wondered what the people here thought of the Russians in their midst. Were they aware of them? Did they bother them? Or did they welcome them? If half the population wanted to return to the USSR, maybe these Russian visitors were as welcome as she was. More welcome, even. Or else viewed as invaders.

This was probably why Andrei didn't go out during the daytime.

A few more blocks up a hill and she spied the school, a hulking gray building with a name carved into the lintel in Georgian and Cyrillic. There was nothing to suggest that children learned here, no paper flowers in the windows or children's art, no playground outside. Man. Even the gloomiest New York City schools had at least a few kids' bikes in a bicycle rack up front or a jaunty sign outside. But this place had the look of an old warehouse or a corrupt city hall. The kids streamed in quietly. Parents watched them go.

And on the corner where she was standing, an empty dog house.

It was nothing remarkable: a wooden box with a peaked roof and a rounded opening for its resident to come and go, the size of a mailbox, painted white with red trim. The white paint was scratched; the red paint was faded. She knew from videos that there had once been a nice dog bed inside, but now it was empty. She knelt down to look inside, to see if there was any evidence of Angel—although what? Fur? A ransom note? There had supposedly been a bloodstain once but it had long since washed away. She searched for any crumbs of food, any chewed corners, anything that would give shape to the dog that had once called this little box home. The wooden floor of the doghouse had been sanded down by time and hundreds of nights of sleep; it was almost satiny in the middle, and Amy could imagine white, fluffy Angel curled up in a ball, her tail abutting her nose. What was it like to sleep in this box, under the Georgian sky? Did the traffic die down, or was she never really able to relax, one ear always cocked for a fellow traveler? A lost child?

Amy would have crawled into the doghouse had its opening been a few inches taller or she a few inches shorter, but as it was, she sat crouched on her knees, examining. Dogs, as far as she knew, only tended to run when they were chasing something or they were afraid. But a dog who lived on the street—even enclosed this way—was probably frightened of very little; she was accustomed to the daily clamor of urban living. So then what was it that had sent her running?

"Amy," said a voice behind her.

She turned, surprised, although she shouldn't have been. "Irine! Hi! I thought I'd—" She felt oddly discovered. "I thought I'd search a bit around Angel's former home, see what I could find."

"Angel isn't here, though."

"Well, right, but maybe some clues."

"We've looked all over," Irine said. She ground out a cigarette under her heel. "I don't think you'll find anything. Any trace of the dog has been gone for weeks now."

"I guess I just wanted to see for myself," Amy said.

Irine nodded.

"And also—I mean, I've seen so many videos of her. I wanted to see where she, you know, worked."

Irine blinked. "Did you walk?"

"I did."

"You could have come with me in the car if I'd known you were coming."

"I didn't want to—"

"Well, as long as you're here, come, let me show you inside the school."

They crossed the busy street, just stepping out into it, trusting that the cars would stop the way they had for Angel and her charges; they did. Then they whisked into the school building, past the children filing in. Irine said hello to a few, gamarjoba, gamarjoba. Inside, the school was slightly cheerier than its sullen exterior would suggest: posters lined the walls boasting what Amy could only assume were exhortations to study hard, keep smiling, etc. The floor was dented linoleum, the walls painted an institutional gray-green. "This way," Irine said.

A secretary sat in a cubicle outside Irine's office in what looked like a distinctly 1970s setup, down to the gray filing cabinets and the heavy black phone on her desk. And no computer—or at least Amy didn't think it was a computer? Instead, something like the word processor she'd had in high school to type up her half-assed book reports.

"Eva," Irine said, "am dilit araperi sashineleba khdeba?"

The secretary had hair that was half maroon and half gray, thick glasses perched above her forehead, a Lurex sweater tight across her broad bosom. She spit out some Georgian in a tone that Amy would have assumed was hostile, except that it was impossible to tell what a hostile tone was in Georgian. The two went back and forth for a minute until a loud bell rang. The bell, she was surprised to find, sounded exactly like the bell at the Columbia Street School, a sound she had forgotten until this very minute.

"Here, come into my office," Irine said, motioning Amy past the secretary. Amy squeaked out a gamarjoba as she passed, but the secretary only gave her the side-eye.

"I apologize," Irine said. "Eva does not like Americans."

"How does she know I'm American?"

Irine smiled. "You have clear skin and beautiful teeth," she said. "Also, I told her."

Irine's office was a few years more up-to-date than Eva's—she had a computer, for instance, although it was a bulky desktop with a monitor that looked like it weighed thirty pounds. And beside it, a black bulky phone. On the shelves behind her were framed family photos: her mother, her aunts, Zazi, and a smiling baby, a toddler, a gap-toothed little girl, a squealing ten- or eleven-year-old.

"Maia was so cute," Amy said, trying to warm up whatever was chilly between them.

Irine smiled, then turned her chair to pick up one of the photos.

"She used to let me pick out her clothes. Even when she was eleven or twelve. Now she dresses like a witch."

"She doesn't really," Amy said. "Teenagers all around the world look just like that. The leather jacket, the safety pins, all of it."

"It's terrible," Irine said. "I'm embarrassed to be seen with her."

"She looks great to me," Amy said.

"Is this how your son dresses?"

Ferry, in his vintage sweatshirts and basketball shorts. "All the time."

Irine sighed, put Maia's photo down next to another one, a black-and-white photo of a family: what looked to be a younger Irine, a mother and a father, and a teenage girl who looked somewhat like Irine, but broader, with curlier hair.

"Is that your family? You have a sister?"

"Mmm," Irine said. "I did. She died a long time ago."

"Oh no," Amy said. "I'm so sorry. Was it—"

"It's all right," Irine said. "It's been a very long time." Then she stood, briskly, wiped her hands on her pants. Amy stood too. "All right, you're here, let me tell you about our school."

"Yes," Amy said; they were changing the subject.

"Although this district is not particularly poor, it is not wealthy either, and many of our students come from families with unemployed parents. They sometimes come to school hungry, even though there are services for families to get food if they can't afford it. This can be a problem, because as you know hungry children have a hard time learning."

"The same thing happens in New York."

"I can imagine it happens in big cities everywhere," she said. "I will show you around."

Passing Eva's disapproving gaze, they left the office and turned down a long hallway. Now that the children were in class, there was silence, minus the clack of Irine's heels.

"So what exactly is your job?"

"My job?"

"I mean what exactly do you do?"

"I manage problems," Irine said. "Small problems, two students are beating each other up in the hallway. Big problems, students disappear from school for days or weeks and nobody can find them."

Amy nodded; once upon a time she'd been that kind of problem herself.

"And then we have biggest problems of all. The Ministry of Science and Education wants to get involved in what we teach or what we say. And teachers don't like this, so I have to get in the middle."

"Is there tenure here?"

"What is this?"

"It's a system—in the United States, well in most states, after a few years a teacher can earn tenure, which means he or she can't be fired for what she says. Like she's allowed to express her political beliefs without, you know, being afraid she'll lose her job."

"No," Irine said. "We have nothing like this." She laughed a little. "I have never heard of anything like this."

The building wrapped around a large inner courtyard that was filled with playground equipment, much of it new and bright-looking, a counterpoint to everything inside the building.

"Come," Irine said. She opened the door to the courtyard and led Amy to a large space in the corner that was roped off with sticks and twine. Inside the roped-off area, mounds of dirt were arranged in neat rows, with labels showing off different kinds of carrots and lettuces.

"Every year our students grow all sorts of things and take them home to our families. They have beans here, aubergine. I come in during the summer and harvest the tomatoes for our families. The students love it. For a while we even had chickens but it was hard to keep them alive. Turned out we had foxes."

Amy bent down to look at the miniature garden plot. "When I was little we had a garden like this. We grew lettuce all summer." It was one of her fondest memories of childhood, watching the small green shoots appear from the dirt, heading outside, barefoot, to snip off some leaves for whatever her mom was making (tuna salad sandwiches, bologna and cheese), then waiting a week or two for more leaves to reemerge. They grew other things, too, in the short Minnesota summers: cucumbers and zucchini and tiny golden cherry tomatoes. And there was a crab apple tree in the corner of the yard whose apples her mom sometimes cooked into jelly.

She inspected the small sprouts—these would be the carrots, of course, their tops bright green and feathery; their season must have started earlier in Georgia. Her mother had grown carrots, too, and used their tops in vegetable soup. In fact, Amy had never realized people discarded carrot tops until she watched one of her roommates do it, carelessly, throwing them out along with the halves of the tomatoes she wasn't using, or the heels of her loaves of bread, dazzling in her wastefulness.

"The children call this Angel's garden," Irine said.

The loud bell clanged, and within moments the peace of the garden was overtaken by clamoring children, running outside in their black-and-white uniforms, climbing on the jungle gym, pushing each other on the swings, chasing each other around the perimeter of the yard. They looked to be maybe six or seven years old. They were followed by a pair of harried-looking teachers. One of them, catching sight of Irine, patted the other on the arm and marched quickly over.

"Es sisulelea, Direk'toro, da shen es itsi!"

Irine carefully wiped a speck of dirt off her trousers before responding. The teacher raised her voice, and the conversation quickly grew heated, or seemed to grow heated, before Irine held up her hand. "Sak'marisi," she said.

The other woman started to speak again.

"Enough," Irine said, loudly and in English. "We will go inside now, Amy. You will excuse us."

Amy followed Irine as she click-clacked down the hall a half step in front of her. "Everything okay?"

"Yes," Irine said. "It is a complicated internal matter." She stopped in front of her office. "I'm sorry, but I have to get to work now. You will be able to find your way?"

"Of course."

"If you are going to spend the day looking for Angel, you might want to head north, toward the market," she said. "If she were to be around here, someone would have already spotted her."

"That makes sense," Amy said.

"All right," Irine said. "I will see you at home." Then she turned and headed into her office, a jangling of heavy black telephones and the scowl of her secretary.

Conversations here turned on a dime.

As Amy wandered through the hallways, trying to find her way out (all schools were like this, endless mazes, door after the exact same door), she peeked into some of the classrooms, which looked very much like American classrooms: friendly signs and paintings on the walls, children's artwork. The kids were bent over schoolbooks or standing at broad chalkboards, much like she herself had done once upon a time. Here, though, there were also framed posters at regular intervals on every hallway that had several official-looking symbols on them. And, toward the end of the hallway, framed headshots of several imposing-looking people, like the photos of the governor and lieutenant governor at highway rest stops.

"Edzeb rames?"

"I'm sorry?" It was the teacher from outside, the one who had confronted Irine. She had dark hair cut in a bob, a youthful face, a worried expression.

"You speak English," she said. "I can help you?"

"Oh, I'm just on my way out," Amy said. "I'm a friend of Irine's— of the principal's."

"Yes, I saw you in the courtyard," she said. "I take a break now while the children play. I can lead you outside."

Amy followed her down one hallway and through another—she would never have found it herself—and outside the building. The teacher lit a cigarette on the broad front steps, then tilted her pack at Amy.

God, she was going to come home with such a habit! She took one from the pack—not a Crown, thank God—and they stood together in the way of smokers all over the world, in quiet rapport with each other and the nicotine and their hands. Smoking was so great—why on earth had she ever stopped? And smoking with an informant (she was really playing detective now) was a perfect way to gather some intel.

"I'm Amy, by the way. I'm visiting from New York."

"New York!" the woman said. "Cool."

"Thank you," Amy said.

"I am Marta," she said.

"It's nice to meet you." Then, because what the hell, she said, "You know anything about Angel?"

"Angel?"

"The dog? Angelozi? Who used to walk children across the street?"

"Oh, yes, Angelozi. Well, the children are very sad about it, of course," she said. "It seems terrible to me that someone would do such a thing, but of course there are terrible things happening all over the world right now. Why should our school be spared?"

"I suppose that's true. Still, it's a weird one. To take a dog."

"I do not think it is weird at all." Marta inhaled sharply on her cigarette, gave Amy a look that suggested confidence, even conspiracy. "It could be part of the plan."

"The plan?"

"You haven't heard about the Russians?"

"What about them?"

"Well," Marta said, "It's no secret they have been putting money into our school system to change the curriculum."

"Tell me more," said Amy, a regular Sherlock Holmes.

"You see," Marta said. "They have already done it in the east of the country, changing the history books, making Russian language lessons compulsory. Russian music, Russian art, if you can call their garbage art. But now they want to do that here in Tbilisi, too. And if you make noise about it you are fired. You cannot protest. You must keep your mouth shut. In fact," Marta said, "my colleague was fired six weeks ago for standing up to Director Benia about the Russian program."

"Ah," said Amy. "And what is the program exactly?"

Marta inhaled, looked up the street. "I am not entirely sure what it will be, but," she lowered her voice—"but everyone knows that it is coming. Starting next year, we will be teaching our children Russian language instead of English language. And Russian history instead of Georgian history."

Amy nodded, gestured for Marta to continue.

"My colleague was making a protest about it. And then she was fired. And there is no money to replace her, so now we have two teachers for thirty five-year-olds, some of whom need very special attention. It is quite difficult."

"I can imagine," Amy said, blowing smoke from the corner of her mouth.

"And then Angelozi disappeared just as the parents were going to organize on behalf of Miss Lomidze," she said. "So there was something very new to get upset about. The parents quickly lost interest in Miss Lomidze when it turned out Angelozi disappeared. The distraction was very effective."

"That sounds terrible," Amy said, hoping that she simply seemed curious to Marta—not suspicious or, worse, stupidly naïve. "But you think it was really orchestrated? Couldn't it have been just a coincidence?" How to explain a coincidence? "Like two things randomly happening at the same time."

"Nobody believes in coincidences," Marta said. She pointed her cigarette toward the street, toward the white-and-red doghouse. "The saddest part, of course, is how much the children miss her. Every morning they looked forward to seeing her, brought her treats, made sure she took her—I don't know. Her medicine. To prevent her from getting parasites."

Amy followed the line of the cigarette smoke toward Angel's doghouse. It did look so forlorn, alone on the corner. "So who do you think took her?"

"Probably the Russians," she said. "Or people who want to impart the Russian system on our children. To distract us from what they are doing. They're everywhere around here. The Russians have never left us alone and they never will. They invaded us before they even invaded Ukraine, you know. Nobody seems to remember."

"I remember," Amy said.

Marta crushed her cigarette under her heel. "I must get back to my students," she said. "It was nice to meet you."

"Nice to meet you too." And then Marta disappeared back through the school's front doors.

Amy finished her cigarette on the school steps, watching the street life passing in front of her. If Russians really did take Angel—well, it seemed like such a petty thing. To kidnap a dog! Like the plot of a children's mystery story superimposed onto international relations. At the same time, it was clear that *someone* took Angel. A dog that well-fed, that well-cared for, who never showed a predilection to wander before, who had a job to do—that dog would never just wander away on her own.

But why couldn't it be something simpler than Russians? A family whose child was attached to Angel, say, and brought her home to be a family pet. Or maybe she had, indeed, been hit by a car (but then wouldn't it have been reported? Wouldn't someone have seen?). Or maybe she had gotten pregnant and was off tending to pups?

But no, she'd been spayed, she had had one of those tags—

Maybe she could ask Andrei what he thought might have happened to Angel. As the only official Russian person she knew, perhaps he'd have some ideas? But Andrei was a refugee, an exile, separated from his wife and child. His life had dimensions to it she could not even see. To ask him to weigh in on whether his countrymen would fuck around with a dog felt a little—petty.

She had heard him in the morning, listening to quiet music in his room next door. She wondered if he ever slept. She wondered if he missed his wife. She wondered if he thought about or cared that she was right next door, changing her clothes, breathing, lying in the dark.

The Russia of her imagination, a land of snow-covered steppes and solitary train tracks, onion domes and gulags—what did she know of Russia besides that? At the Columbia Street School, 1986, her fourth grade teacher held up photographs of an American television, an American TV dinner, an American flag, followed by a cardboard box, a large carrot, nothing at all. "This is all Russians have for television. All they have for food. All they have for freedom. So the next time you think you have nothing, think about the children in Moscow with their carrots and their cardboard boxes." And Amy did, and felt guilty deep in her nine-year-old bones, ungrateful for all that she had, only cataloging everything she didn't.

Andrei had grown up in that place, without television or freedom. She knew it was ridiculous, but there was a part of her that wanted to fix it all for him, that wanted to buy him a television. A new childhood.

A grown man walking around in the freezing cold without a jacket.

Inside the school the bell rang, and she could hear the children changing classes, laughing and screaming and pounding through the hallways in the way of children across the world. The front door of the school opened, closed, a clique of teachers joining her on the stoop with their cigarettes. They nodded at her, looking at her like she belonged. But then someone said something to her and she didn't understand and she smiled apologetically and knew it was time to move on.

Down the street, a bit of googling showed that there was an organization in Tbilisi that monitored the health of all the free-roaming dogs, spaying and neutering them, vaccinating them, and monitoring their health. They had a PayPal button on their website. Amy clicked over $50, then thought maybe she could go visit one of their clinics? Or maybe the best thing she could do—the only thing she could really do—was give the people who knew what they were doing some money to do it.

She decided to keep walking. A dog barked across the street. Amy followed the bark to see where it led.

JUDD LOVED A public market. Whenever they found themselves near one, no matter how chintzy or touristy, no matter how overpriced the goods, Judd would usher her through the narrow alleyways separating coffee vendors from lamb cadavers, strings of dried chilies, fresh bread, chocolate. In a particularly gruesome market in Spain they encountered a row of pig's heads lined up toothlessly behind glass. In the one in Seattle, strong young men threw entire salmons theatrically through the air. In Philadelphia, she ate warm pretzels served to her by a dour Amish woman.

The market in Tbilisi was something like all of these, but also more crowded, more chaotic. A sort of flea market spilled out into a plaza, and Amy wove her way past stalls selling counterfeit Levi's, Chanel purses, Air Jordans, Estée Lauder perfume. Headscarved women shouted at men in leather jackets. She passed arrays of toiletries and cheap-looking jewelry, and legions of roaming dogs. Amy lost track of a skinny shepherd, then picked up the trail of another indiscriminate mutt, following them as they scavenged for dropped food on the ground or stopped for pets from the otherwise distracted vendors. She made accidental eye contact with a man who was fishing some dog treats out of a bin; he gestured to her to check out his wares (plastic cooking vessels and coffee makers), but despite her fondness toward fellow dog lovers, Amy did not stop to browse.

Carpets, dried beans, long ropes of something that looked vaguely intestinal, barrels of olives, no Angel. Amy wondered if there was more she could have discovered at the school, if she had done a good enough job searching for clues. Probably not. What had she learned? A teacher had made a stand against Russia. Irine fired her. The students and teachers were upset. Angel disappeared.

"Kalbat'oni? Ginda Stsado?"

An older woman in a floral coat was beckoning to her, holding out a spoon.

"I'm sorry," Amy said. "Me ar vlap'arak'ob kartulad."

"English?" the woman said. "You want to try?"

"What is it?"

"Here, here," she said. "I make myself." She had a modest stall stocked with jars of what looked like different condiments or sauces in shades of red, purple, and green. "You try."

Amy didn't bother to consider whether or not it was a smart idea to try a spoonful of whatever this woman was offering her; she slurped whatever was on the spoon and found it delicious.

"Pepper sauce," the woman said. "With walnuts. You like?"

"It's great."

"Here, try another—" The jars behind her had clearly been repurposed from other uses; they were glass and plastic and labeled with hand-drawn stickers. The woman dug out a spoonful of something from a purplish jar; it was puckeringly sour and a little sweet at the same time. "Good on potatoes," the woman said. "Or meat. You are from Britain?"

"America," Amy said.

"America! My brother lives in New York," she said.

"You're kidding! I live in New York."

"He runs restaurant in Brooklyn. Georgian food. He serves same sauces. Tkemali, my mother's recipe. You should go!" She took out a cell phone. "I text you address."

"Have you been there?"

The woman laughed. "I cannot get visa. It's very difficult. And too much money anyway. But why go to New York? We have everything they have," she said, and she laughed again. "And better weather."

"That's right," Amy said, cheered by her attitude.

"I haven't seen my brother since 1984. But I know everything he does, how he opened restaurant. And how Americans come! Not just Georgians. We can Skype, I see his grandchildren. He is very upset, though, by political situation."

"I know," Amy said. "The Russians in the north, it's terrible."

"Not here!" the woman said. "There! You had Trump, now you have Biden, right? Old men? He says it is very bad. Everyone is depressed all the time. He pours chacha like water to cheer people up."

"People are depressed about a lot of things in the United States," Amy said. "I don't think politics is at the top of the list."

"How lucky for you! You can be depressed about other things!" she said. "So tell me, will you go to restaurant?"

"Your brother's?"

"You go!" the woman said. "You tell me how it is!" She smiled so that Amy could see the gaps in her teeth. "He say he cannot get the right ingredients where he is, so maybe the tkemali doesn't taste as good as mine."

"He's probably right," Amy said, suddenly saddened for this woman and her brother, apart for forty years. "There are a lot of things in New York City I've never been able to find."

Another dog skirted up to them, but it was mud-brown, small-ish, of indeterminate breed. "Hey, have you ever seen a fluffy white dog around here? Sort of medium-sized? She answered to the name Angelozi?"

"Angelozi?" The woman appeared to think about it. "Yes, I know that dog."

"You do? Really?"

"The school dog, yes? The one who disappeared?"

"You know Angelozi?" Could it possibly be?

"Yes, I know the story. That school is nearby. I used to watch her walk the children across the street in the morning. I found it very lovely, you know? To see the way the dog cared."

"But you haven't seen her since?"

The woman shook her head. "She disappeared. It breaks the heart."

The mutt pawed at Amy's jeans. She found a bully stick in her backpack, and gave it to the dog, who seemed startled by the unexpected treasure. He gobbled as much of it as he could in one bite and then raced away to hide the rest. Amy and the woman watched it go.

"Not all dogs can be like Angel, unfortunately," the woman said. "Not everyone is so lucky."

"Can I buy a bottle of your sauce? Actually, two bottles? The ones I tasted?"

"Yes, yes, of course," she said. "One is pepper, one is plum. Oh, and here," she said, pulling out a clear bottle from under the table. "We toast."

"God, I don't know if I can—" But the woman had poured two shots into tiny paper cups and Amy had no choice. She lifted her cup and murmured "Gaumarjos," along with the woman, although victory didn't seem particularly close by.

AS SHE WANDERED out of the market, Amy picked up a bag of beautiful fresh spring peas (so hard to get in New York!) and some feta-like cheese whose name was utterly unpronouceable and, from a stall bearing an Italian flag next to a Georgian one, sheets of fettucine. She hadn't made a real meal in so long but the thought of another pastry for dinner made her feel slightly ill, and the sight of all those beautiful peas—maybe she could make dinner for her hosts when she got home. A way to show her gratitude.

The dogs were eating when she walked into the house, bent over their bowls with a real seriousness of purpose. She liked dogs that ate on schedule. Leo had always refused to, just kind of drifted back and forth in front of his kibble all day, a sort of twenty-four-hour graze, and in this way he put on twenty pounds. ("Get this dog on a diet!" said the vet, but she didn't, and then he died suddenly and Amy never forgave herself.)

Upstairs in the empty kitchen, she set about finding pots and pans. The kitchen was surprisingly well stocked, lots of sturdy saucepans and sheet pans and a large cast-iron skillet.

"Do you need help?"

Amy jumped up; Irine was standing behind her much as she'd been that morning by the doghouse, but now she was wearing sweatpants and a fuzzy sweater, her lovely dark hair in a knot on her head, and she was smiling.

"Irine! Hello! I thought I'd make dinner for everyone."

"You are cooking?" Her eyes lifted when she smiled, and Amy caught a glimpse of Maia's expression in hers. "What are you making? Can I help?"

"I was thinking like a pasta primavera."

"I do not know this," Irine said. "I'm not much of a cook, though. My mother usually makes the food but tonight she has a pain in her wrists, she cannot cook, I don't remember the word—"

"Arthritis?"

"Arthritis," Irine agreed. "So I told her just to go to bed. I was going to have an egg," she said. "But if you are cooking—"

"Just sit!" Amy said. "Relax, I've got this."

Although it had been a while since she'd cooked for someone

else—really, since Ferry had gone to college—for years she'd produced a stream of Spanish tortillas, ratatouille, shakshouka, Caesar salad, pecan-banana bread. She remembered how much she liked doing it, how much pleasure it gave her to feed people. So much of the labor she did at home was reflexive, adopted without consideration, but the cooking had always been a choice, and a delight. Why had she stopped? (Because there was nobody around, she supposed, to appreciate it.)

"So tell me about this primavera," Irine said. "Would you like some wine?"

"I'd love some," Amy said. While Irine got them glasses and a bottle, Amy found salt, oil, a large stockpot. "It's sort of like a vegetable pasta. Some people add cream, some people use just oil and butter."

"Do you need these things?" Irine said. "You can see what we have in the refrigerator. But I should warn you I have no idea. My mother does the shopping."

Irine's fridge was about two-thirds as large as an American refrigerator, and it was filled with ingredients Amy had to guess at—was this butter in this tub or some kind of lard? Was this yogurt or heavy cream? Two plastic containers of sushi, an old orange. Amy dug out bunches of tarragon and parsley, a zucchini, a plastic-wrapped blob of some kind of soft cheese. On the counter there were shallots, garlic. She felt the muscles in her hands start to twitch with anticipation. "You've got great stuff."

Irine waved her glass of wine in the air. "It is all a surprise to me."

Soon the room smelled, if not exactly like a restaurant, at least something like a kitchen, the garlic and shallot exorcising the smell of dogs and old cigarette smoke. Maia wandered in, looking surprised and pleased. "What's going on? It smells so good!"

"Amy is cooking dinner," Irine said. "Come, help me with these peas."

"What do we do with peas?"

"We shell them, like this," Irine said. "I used to do this all the time as a child."

The zucchini went into the sauté pan, then the shelled peas; the fresh fettucine was dropped into the briskly boiling salted water, and Amy stirred the soft cheese into the vegetables so that it melted into a creamy sauce. She sprinkled the herbs and the feta on top of the pasta, while behind her, Maia set the table with lace napkins and pretty flowered dishes. She wished she had a loaf of sourdough or a nice leaf salad to add, but still, the pasta looked appetizing, and both Maia and Irine seemed delighted.

"Bon appetit!" Irine said, refilling their wine glasses. "Gaamot!"

"Wow!" Maia said. "I've never seen anything like this!"

The fettucine had turned out exactly as she'd hoped, slightly al dente; the freshness of the vegetables offset the richness of the cheese and the brightness of the herbs.

"Oh my god this is so good *I am dying*," Maia said, stuffing her face with noodles. "Where did you learn to cook like this?"

"Oh, when I got to New York I thought I was going to be a model, but that was harder than I thought it would be, so I ended up cooking in restaurants. Which was also hard—"

"Wait, you weren't a model?"

"Oh god," Amy said. "Not really. I mean for like five minutes."

"Mom, you said she was an American model!"

"She was!" Irine said. "She's just being modest."

Amy laughed. "Guys, the highlight of my modeling career was a photoshoot for a tire catalog. I was done by the time I was twenty, and then I really needed something else to do, because there was no way I was going back to Minnesota."

"Where's Minnesota?"

"In the middle of the country, yes?" Maia said.

"Way up north," Amy said. "Next to Canada."

"So why didn't you get more work as a model? Why didn't you keep trying?"

"You know, in the end, once I started working in restaurants, I just—I started having more fun. I felt much more at home behind a stove than I did in front of the camera. I liked the people I met, I liked the fact that I could do it. That it turned out I was actually good at creating recipes, or figuring out what people liked to eat."

"Is this what you made?" Irine said. "Pasta primavera?"

"Sometimes," Amy said. "But I cooked all kinds of dishes, a lot of brunch stuff, eggs benedict, French toast. I've always enjoyed it."

"Does your husband cook too?"

"Judd?" Amy put down her fork. "He did, for a little while, but that was never his main interest. He likes the front-of-the-house stuff more, meeting and greeting people, that sort of thing. He works with the chef to design the menu, though. He takes that part very seriously."

"Was it hard for you to cook at the restaurant and raise your son at the same time?" Maia asked.

"Not really," Amy said. "I started working less as he got older. We had a nanny for him when he was young, but by the time he was in kindergarten I wasn't taking any more shifts at the restaurant so I could be there, you know, when he got out of school."

"You could afford to do that?" Irine asked.

Amy dabbed at her lips. "Well—I mean, the restaurant was my husband's. Did I mention that? So it's like, any money I earned there was money we would have had anyway. Because whatever I didn't earn just went back into the restaurant's profits."

"I'm not sure I understand."

Amy decided to just barrel through her half-assed explanation, hoping to stave off more direct questioning. "Well, my husband's parents are heavy investors in the restaurant, so it's really more like a family business. So we worry less about one individual income and more—and Ferry's biological mother has always been, kind of, I don't know, ill. So it's always been important for me to be there for him."

"Deda, it's like how bebia has always been there for me."

"Of course," Irine said. "Although your grandmother worked too, you remember? My mother," she said, turning to Amy, "was an operator at the phone company for many years. During the Soviet era, especially, everyone had a job."

"Everyone in America works too!" Amy said. "We love to work! It's like our thing!" She laughed, but nobody else joined in. "And I've always volunteered at the shelter on top of that. And I teach writing classes when they're available. So that's always kept me busy." She took a long sip of wine.

"Was it easy to work with your husband?" Irine asked. "When you were at the restaurant?"

"Judd?" She thought about what she witnessed during her time at Le Coin: his occasional icy silences or rage at a late supplier, the way he'd turn around on a dime to charm a sexy new waitress or hostess or a well-heeled couple at the bar. It was one of the reasons it had been easy, in the end, to step aside from the stove; working with Judd wasn't a great way to keep their marriage happy. "My husband is, I don't know. Kind of complicated."

"Ah," Irine said. She finally smiled. "I understand."

"I mean, sometimes he's wonderful—"

"But you wouldn't have come all this way if he was wonderful all the time," Irine said.

"Deda, stop that."

"I came here to find a dog," Amy said.

Irine looked at her serenely. Amy took another long-ish sip of her wine.

"Okay, well then, I have a different question," Maia said. "I read that in America, only fifty percent of the population that is allowed to vote actually votes. Is that really true?"

Politics again! "Unfortunately, it is," Amy said. "I think a little bit more in presidential elections, but not, like—not a ton more. Not everyone by any stretch. People take their rights for granted, so they stop using them."

"Some people say that democracy makes you lazy," Irine said. "That nothing ever gets done, and that the people in democracies stop thinking that their votes matter, and everyone runs around in circles but nobody solves any real problems—"

"Deda," Maia said. "Stop."

"I'm not saying that's what *I* think of democracy," Irine said. "Only what some people say."

She had made them dinner. She had been a pleasant houseguest. Why did she feel like she was on the defensive? "Look, democracy isn't perfect, and yes, some things take a very long time, but at least we have a say in our government, right?"

"Which is why you get people like Donald Trump?"

"I guess so—"

"But isn't that not who most people vote for?" Irine said. "Isn't it because of, what do you call it? The thing where the person who gets the most votes in the United States doesn't always win?"

"The electoral college," Amy said. "Yes, it's a confusing system, but I don't think it's a sign that democracies don't—"

"But generally speaking," Irine said, "democracy doesn't even really mean that most of the people get what they want."

"No, no—sometimes it does. Usually it does."

"And it does make some people very rich, correct?" Irine said.

"Sometimes," Amy said, "it does."

Maia forked some more pasta on everyone's plate. "What I think is that any country that could accept so many people from around the world and have them basically get along and also come up with food like this sounds like a great place. Amy, tell me again how you made this pasta?"

She was grateful to Maia for moving the conversation along, and recounted, step by step, mincing the herbs and sautéing the vegetables and folding in the cheese sauce, and then they moved the subject on to other kinds of American food—fried chicken, which they both loved, and meatloaf, which they agreed sounded disgusting—and after a while the pasta bowl was empty and two wine bottles had been tapped. Maia offered to do the dishes, which was good, because Amy was too tipsy to really move. So she and Irine shared postprandial cigarettes in the warm afterglow of a delicious meal, and Amy tried not to think about what Irine really thought of her or where she came from and what she valued and only that she had cooked them something good, that she had done well.

TWELVE

"DO YOU KNOW this story?" Ferry texted.

"In 1184, the king of Georgia died and left the kingdom in the care of his daughter, Tamar. Although she was doubted and undermined by the male nobles of the country, under Tamar, Georgia reached its greatest territorial empire. Her armies reached all the way to Iran and Uzbekistan. Tamar was almost certainly the most lauded of Georgia's medieval rulers and was written about and eulogized by Georgians for centuries. She left a record of liberation and modernization. Some people say she was the last heroic ruler Georgia ever had. She died in 1213, and has since been canonized by the Georgian Orthodox church."

"How do you know all this?" Amy wrote back.

"I went down a Georgian rabbit hole. Also I like the theme of strong women here. Reminds me of you."

Amy laughed out loud in her bed. Strong women. May we raise them, may we be them—was that how the saying went? It was one a.m. and her mouth was dry from wine.

"I'll take that as a compliment."

"You should," he wrote. "It's probably late there. Is it late there?"

"It is."

"Why aren't you asleep?"

IN THE MORNING, Amy sat down on her bed with her water and her ibuprofen. She was going to be more methodical. She sat down with her notebook and her phone, making a list of all the possible places to look (a park, the riverbanks, the hills, a different park). But in the end, none of the routes seemed to be more logical than any other. What was the point of being methodical when she couldn't deduce a method? She pulled on her jeans, splashed water on her face, and decided to do what she had always done when she needed to change up her thinking: get on the train. She had seen signs for the metro on Rustaveli Avenue, so she grabbed her backpack and made her way down the hill, keeping an eye out for Angel, or for any dog who needed a treat. But all she saw was a skinny rat, racing under a car with a wedge of bread in its mouth.

For anyone who had spent her adult life in New York, the Tbilisi metro seemed simple enough: there were only two lines and they intersected only once. But—*but*—the swoosh of getting on the escalator and then the down down down down down! She had never traveled so deep underground before, into the dark gray tunnels of somewhere approaching Middle Earth. She watched, astounded, as her fellow travelers stared at their phones or gazed at their shoes, completely unimpressed by the depths to which they were journeying. Ninety seconds, one hundred twenty seconds, and they were *still on this escalator!*

Then, finally, they were off. She stepped onto a crowded platform decorated with stern Soviet bas-reliefs on the support columns and, on the walls along the tracks, advertisements for Georgian yogurt. Within moments, the train arrived, square and rattling, and Amy embarked with her fellow midday riders. She took the train to Station Square, switched to the other line, had no idea where to get out and ended up returning to Rustaveli. She crossed the tracks and reversed the journey up, up, up, back into the blinking sunshine, having gone nowhere but refusing to beat herself up about it.

She emerged near the parliament building, where more people than she remembered from the day before were milling about in front of the cross. Actually, it seemed like it was a small crowd, people yelling and arguing. Men in suits and ties, a woman in a pantsuit, and kids, too, in all manner of dress and presentation. A television cameraman was recording the proceedings. Amy stood at the perimeter, watching, unsure how to get through. A few people gathered near her, silently watching as well.

"Mat khma unda mietsat," a young man murmured next to her.

Amy had no idea what he was saying.

As more people started gathering by the cross, a police car, siren on, came screeching in from the opposite direction. It was ten in the morning, bright and beautiful, and on the opposite side of the street most people were hustling as if none of this was happening. But a few stopped and stared, and then a few more, and then the crowd started to grow. Someone yelled something. Someone yelled something back.

"Dzalian tsudad gakhdeba," the man next to her said.

"K'ee," Amy said, even though she had no idea what the man had said. *K'ee* meant "yes." She had picked it up somewhere.

The man looked at her and nodded sadly. He had deep brown eyes that were hard to turn away from.

People streamed in from the surrounding streets. Amy realized slowly and then all at once that she was trapped. People were pushing in behind her and there was no way to maneuver herself through or around them. "Uk'atsravad," she said, then, more loudly, "Uk'atsravad!" But nobody would let her pass or even seemed to notice she was there. Her heart started to pound. She had always had a touch of enochlophobia—didn't most women?—and imagined herself getting molested, trampled. Everyone was wearing parkas, dark green, brown, gray, and she couldn't tell if she was being pressed up against by men or women, old people or young. Who was in charge of this crowd? Where were they trying to go?

"Excuse me!" she yelled. "Excuse me!" In English this time. A few turned to look at her.

The crowd seemed to be heaving toward something, moving as a single organism. Amy thought to herself that she could close her eyes and channel better thoughts, let herself be carried, be as free as the breeze, own nothing but her spirit, but of course that was impossible, she was terrified, she wasn't high. The crowd heaved: a huge and wild animal wanting to put something in its maw.

"Please! I'm a tourist! Please! Let me through!"

Tiny steps forward, people pressing against her back, a stranger's hot breath.

"I'm a tourist! *Please!*"

And though there was no reason that being a tourist was enough of a reason to let her pass, she must have startled some of them or at least made them pay attention, because a few people jostled out of her way, and then a few more. She kept yelling *excuse me let me pass excuse me I need to get through I'm a tourist*, and she used her arms a little and her shoulders a little more and she did, somehow, separate herself from the pack. The beast moved in one direction. She inched in another. There were coats in her face, and people hoisting children, and other people yelling what sounded like organized chants toward the drooping cross in front of them.

A panting, thrusting crowd. Amy felt tears spring to her eyes, shame or fear. The person to her right looked at her and hissed. "Ra gaak'eta amerik'elma chventvis, dzu."

She kept inching, inching, shouted again: "Please, I'm a tourist, let me through!"

And then she was at the far end of Parliament Square. The crowd was looser here; there was space to maneuver. She took off her gloves and wiped her eyes. And was stunned, when she turned around, to see that she had made it through a gathering of at least three or even four hundred people, all of whom had assembled in minutes, or even in moments—and the police were there now, too, standing in front of the crowd, protecting the drooping cross, setting up barriers, yelling at people who were yelling back at them, and then one of them shouted something through a bullhorn and the moment seized, the very air seized with what felt to Amy like the throbbing possibility of violence.

But:

But!

It was so beautiful out—didn't the sunshine and the early spring breeze preclude the possibility of attack dogs, tear gas?

Didn't the dignity of the parliament building itself demand civilized behavior?

But!

The crowd was facing off against the police in what seemed like the prelude to a riot. The silence terrifying.

She was at the far edges of the crowd now, inching backward as people rushed in from all sides to join the mass.

Into a bullhorn:

Daarbiet! Brdzaneba gakvs dashla!

The crowd: Tavisupleba! Tavisupleba! Tavisupleba!

And the police again: *Daarbiet!*

The crowd: *Tavisupleba! Tavisupleba! Tavisupleba!*

But more police cars were screeching down Rustaveli, and Amy kept backing up as police seemed to emerge from everywhere at once and stared down the heaving crowd, which was, in the face of the authority, no longer a beast but rather a group of people in parkas and jean jackets and leather jackets and face masks and glasses, no longer moving as one. Just still.

Daarbiet! Daarbiet!

A water cannon on the back of a police truck turned its wide, empty face toward the crowd, ready to spray.

And after a clenched minute, the crowd dispersed.

Amy stood at the corner a hundred yards from the parliament building, drawing deep breaths: counting to four, holding, exhaling for four. The best way she knew to ward off a panic attack. The people of Tbilisi were streaming off now in different directions, but the cops were still there in the angry stance of cops everywhere, and Amy wondered if they would spray the rioters even as they left.

"Freedom."

Maia, standing beside her, out of nowhere. For some reason, Amy wasn't in the least bit surprised. "That's what they were saying?"

"Tavisupleba. Literally it means 'self-rule.'"

Amy nodded. Her breath was regulating. Still, she wanted to hold on to Maia's black-gloved hand.

"We've never really had it," Maia said. "Not for a thousand years."

"How did people know to assemble here?"

"There was a vote in the parliament about the foreign nationals law," she said. "It passed, so now you have to register if you have foreign contacts, or like if your business does, or if you want to study abroad or anything like that. I'm a foreign agent now. It was broadcast on national TV, of course. It's almost like they're taunting us."

"It's amazing they want to antagonize you like that."

"They've been doing it for a hundred years," she said. "Dictators gonna dictate. Imperialists gonna—imperial."

Amy laughed, and after a moment Maia laughed, too.

"I don't understand how people got down here so fast."

"It's what we do," Maia said. "It's all we do."

The plaza was emptying out, and the stray dogs of Tbilisi were returning to their positions on the stairs of the plaza, looking as placid and eternal as the hills of Rome. Amy wondered if the people in the crowd had accomplished anything, sent any kind of message. Their bodies, pressed together, moving toward the police, toward the cross, toward—well, she wondered if they knew what they were moving toward. Or if the point was simply the crowd and the roar and the forward motion.

"We'll be back here tonight," Maia said. "Are you going to come with us?"

"I don't—is it safe?"

Maia gave her such a withering look that Amy felt her insides curdle. "I have no idea," she said.

Amy nodded. And together they watched the remaining protesters of Tbilisi disperse, *daarbiet*, until there was nothing left but the trash-strewn plaza and the sleepy dogs and the snarling cops and, overlooking it all, the tired-looking droopy-armed cross. She wondered why her first response had been to panic, and her second response had been to scream that she was a tourist. Nobody else had seemed to panic. Nobody else seemed to care who she was or whether she belonged. She could be part of the fight or she could remove herself. She had chosen, that afternoon, to remove herself. It had never occurred to her to do otherwise.

AFTER MAIA LEFT—"I better get back to chemistry class"—Amy headed in a new direction, west on Rustaveli as opposed to east. Maybe there was something to be found there? She passed a cinema, a coffeeshop, a store with ugly shoes in the window, and then the broad glass frontage of an extraordinarily chic-looking hotel. She looked up: the Stamba. Very Tribeca-looking, but more spacious than a Tribeca hotel would be, taking up the entire block.

Through the window, she could see a dimly lit bar, and a doorman was helping people in with their oversized luggage, and a Tesla was parked out front, the kind with the doors that opened like wings.

She looked down at her dirt-splattered jeans. Well, the worst thing they could do was kick her out.

But the doorman smiled widely. "Checking in?"

"Just here for a drink," Amy said. After this morning, she thought, she really did deserve a drink.

"Right this way."

The lobby was enormous, had clearly been part of some sort of industrial building, and now was filled from floor to triple-height ceiling with books. She had never seen so many books in her life—there were probably ten thousand of them, hardcovers and paperbacks, shelved to the heavens, ignored by the bustling crowd. How on earth had anyone found that many books?

"It's just decoration," the doorman said as she eyed the massive shelves. "Bar is to your left."

Amy shook out her hair, hoped she looked half human. The bar was all perfect lighting, leather stools, art deco fixtures—like a million bars around the world, but how strange it felt to be in such a place after having just participated in a semi-riot.

"Martini, madame?" asked the bartender.

She looked at her phone; it was only half past noon. "Just a glass of white."

She wondered if she was allowed to borrow one of those books to keep her company at the bar—were any of them in English?—when her phone flashed with news that Lynne was calling. She picked up and then realized she didn't want to pick up. Oh well, too late.

"Jesus, I shouldn't have called, I probably woke you." Well, at least the possibility had occurred to her.

"You didn't," said Amy.

"How is it there? Is it crazy?"

"I'm sitting at a very glam bar drinking a glass of wine," she said. There was no point in trying to explain the rest of it.

"Oh! Well that sounds all right then," Lynne said.

"Everything okay in New York?"

She heard Lynne take a deep breath on the other side of the world.

"I just wanted to let you know—well, I didn't know if I should tell you, but then I thought about what I would want to know if I were you, ten thousand miles away from home—"

"Six thousand."

"Six thousand, ten thousand, I tried to think about what *I* would want, and then I decided—"

The bartender slid the wine in front of her, along with a small dish of spiced walnuts. *"Madloba,"* she whispered.

"I decided, yes, I would want to know—"

"Lynne, what is it?"

The white was absolutely perfect, crisp, dry, cold.

"Well, I don't want to alarm you, but I was walking by the restaurant yesterday and I saw Meret sitting there on that bench in the front of the restaurant. You know that new bench? And then—"

"Actually, I don't want to know."

"No, no, it's not what you think. Or maybe it is? Anyway, she was crying. Like, hysterical. I asked her what was wrong, I couldn't help it. And she just brushed me off."

Amy did an internal check to see how she felt.

She felt nothing.

"I thought maybe someone had died? Or maybe she'd been fired? But I asked her again and she just said *men* and I said, you got your heart broken, huh? And then she didn't say anything else. But, you know, it seems pretty clear she got dumped—"

"Did you ask Judd?"

"Me? Why would I—I mean, I didn't—"

"If you see him you should ask him."

"That's it? You're not worried?"

"I'm ten thousand miles away," she said.

"Six thousand," Lynne said. "But yes, you're right, of course, you don't need to be bothered with this. What's it like there, anyway? How are the men?"

"I have no idea," Amy said. "I'm staying in a house with five other women and eleven dogs."

"Oh Amy, you're mad."

"Listen, thanks for telling me about Meret. I'll speak to Judd."

"I just thought you'd want to know."

"I'm not sure I did," Amy said. "But now that I know, I'll follow up."

"Did I upset you?"

"No, no," Amy said. "It's really fine. It just feels—honestly it just feels really far away."

"It is," Lynne said. "Thousands of miles."

They said good-bye and then Amy clicked her phone's off button.

She almost certainly wasn't going to follow up.

She took another sip of wine, a bigger one.

Under the bar, her knees creaked. Even if she did not feel like feeling anything, her body never stopped wanting, *needing* to feel. Like that was all it was there to do. She had once said to Judd, half seriously, that she would have been perfectly happy to exist as a head in a jar, rolling around on wheels; he'd laughed and said "ridiculous" and hadn't asked her to explain. But what she would have told him, had he wanted to know, was that she didn't understand what all the scaffolding and the wiring, the veins and bones and muck—what all of it was really *for*. It was all going to fall apart eventually anyway. Here it was, the proof! Aching knees and a dull ache behind her shoulder blades that never faded. Gray hair at her temples, gray hair at her part. The deepening well between her eyes. All this while her mind, her spirit, felt as young as ever—as new and inexperienced and demanding as ever.

She had only been alive for forty-six years! With all the experience the world contained, how on earth was forty-six years enough time to really know *anything*?

Her mother had died relatively young, at seventy-six; she hadn't

been ill, or if she had been ill had never mentioned the illness to anyone. In fact, in their last correspondences—they emailed sometimes,
or sometimes still wrote letters—her mother had sounded newly hopeful about life, even optimistic. She was going to take a class on home
repair at MCTC. She was thinking about joining a walking club that
took strolls around the lake.

Forty-six years wasn't enough; seventy-six years wasn't enough,
none of it was enough to learn how to fully live. Her life in human
years was probably more than halfway over but she knew that she had
yet to really get started. It was galling, the parsimony of the human
lifespan.

She wondered if her mother had felt like this. She wished that her
mother had been the kind of person she could have asked. But her
advice had almost always been so glum. "Enjoy it while you're young,"
she used to tell miserable twelve-year-old Amy. "It's not going to get
any better."

Was she supposed to feel sorry for Meret? Or to feel glad that she
was in pain? Was she obliged to feel anything at all? She had spent her
entire life taking care of people, feeling their feelings for them, trying
to assuage or even heal them: her mother's anger and her husband's
ambition and Uno's addictions. But she didn't feel like feeling right
now. She had traveled so far, it had been such a day; at least she could
have that.

She watched the people outside the window for a while as they
went about their lunch breaks, manhandling bags of groceries, dogs,
children.

What was the word again? The freedom to rule oneself?

She chewed mindlessly on some walnuts.

When Trump had been president, the op-ed writers liked to warn
about authoritarianism, or how friendly he was to Putin, or how much
he admired dictators, but the man had seemed like such a clown it was
hard for her to take any of their warnings too seriously. And the thing

that Judd had said to her, which made her feel terrible when he said it, even though it was probably true, was that as aghast as they were that a reality show host with a golden toilet had somehow become president of the United States—and yes, it really *was* appalling—but the thing of it, Judd said, two years into Trump's administration, the thing of it was that actually he hadn't really changed their lives that much. In fact their tax bill had gone down a little, so if you managed to tune out the tweets and the Muslim ban, if you managed not to think about the Supreme Court's rightward turn or the withdrawal from the international climate agreements—if you managed to ignore the worst of it, the Trump presidency had actually been more or less the same as any other.

And even during the heart of the COVID crisis, those terrible months when they worried about the restaurant's survival while they huddled at home, and sirens rang out day and night and New York governor Andrew Cuomo was briefly everyone's crush—even then, Judd hadn't seen it as Trump's fault as much as an act of a vengeful God. Yes, of course Trump managed the whole thing horrifically, Judd said, but people were dying even when their state governments were competent. So could we blame the whole thing on one man?

Then Joe Biden won election in 2020, and Trump was suddenly in the past. They could look toward the future.

But it turned out that Trump was running for reelection in 2024 (he'd announced it over the winter, so very early, which everyone thought was a little sad). And although it seemed crazy to imagine it, he could win again. He had done it once already. And yes of course he was a buffoon, he was a clown—but also he had tried to blackmail Ukraine's president, and he did seem to really love Putin, and he had sent those people to storm the capital, and who was to say—who was to say—

If what these Georgians knew was something that every American should know, too. That the beams of their house were so very fragile.

That there were termites in some of them and dry rot in others. That the whole house was standing on little more than the habit of having stood for so many years.

The word, she remembered, was *tavisupleba*.

Literally it meant "self-rule."

It was the house she had been born in. She had never lived in any other.

She signaled to the bartender to come over, but he was busy with other patrons, so she stood, went to the lobby, and combed through the books like she was in the world's most outrageous library until she found a beat-up English copy of *The Quiet American*, which she'd always meant to read.

"Ah, that's a good one," the bartender said when she returned to her stool.

"I've always wanted to read it."

"It's about a journalist's affair with a Vietnamese woman. And also colonialism and war and American power."

"Isn't that what everything's about?" Amy asked, then smiled like she was making a joke.

The bartender topped up her glass. "Not quite everything," he said. "But many things." Then he went to tend to other customers, and Amy stayed there, thumbing through the novel without really reading, until she decided she'd sat long enough, and it was once again time to search for a dog. The other problems were too big for her to solve alone.

THE HILLS BEHIND Parliament Square were traversed by steep, winding streets, narrow and pitted and draped in shadow. Along them Amy passed gardens, half-abandoned construction projects, secret staircases connecting one cul-de-sac to another. She hiked up the streets, pausing every so often to catch her breath and look out at the city below her. The climb wasn't as easy as she wanted it to be. One of her knees sometimes went tricky for no reason whatsoever. And she could feel the pull in her back. When she was younger she used to be able to climb all day, like a gazelle. Well into her thirties, even. But now she looked around for a place to sit, found a ledge near an ice cream shop. From here she assessed her vantage point toward the Kura River and the castles and fortresses of the valley beneath her. There was a modern-looking steel bridge to the west, near a massive church that seemed, from this angle, to be built into the side of a mountain. In the late afternoon light, the church glowed pinkly.

She hadn't even brought a travel guide with her. On this side of the river, directly below, a dozen small domes emerged from the earth. What were they? People fluttering around them like ants, and to the west a gondola ferrying Georgians up and down the side of the hill.

If she were with Judd, he would tell her the story of the entire landscape. He liked to do lots of research before any trip so he could present himself with expertise whenever they met someone new. He hated the idea that people would think he was a tourist—or, worse, uncool—so he'd drop the names of the latest restaurants or museum exhibits to natives who were usually either impressed or gracious enough to pretend to be. Ferry would often roll his eyes at his dad, but Amy always admired how at home Judd was in the world.

Still, in Georgia, Amy had the sense that no guidebook could lead her to the most crucial parts of the country. And that, if Judd was here, he would notice all the wrong things. Yes, the food was delicious, and yes, the buildings were beautiful, and she was sure the shopping was great, especially if you were in the market for Soviet trinkets or antique rugs. But the real thing that this place could offer, if you were looking for it, was the chance to see a kind of future, and to learn what was necessary to prevent it. To learn how to fight for your home. Judd would not understand that or want to look.

Up a winding street, Amy kept climbing, past kids playing soccer— a lost ball here could fall five hundred feet—a small church, a corner grocery, a series of narrow apartment buildings. She stopped at a bench and sat down once more, pondering the view, this time from an even higher remove.

All those lives below.

Talking to Lynne reminded her of the first time Judd had cheated on her, the first time she'd had incontrovertible proof. Six years ago. She'd thought, after the crying and the wanting-but-not-quite-managing to throw up and the furious confrontation and the histrionic apologies— she'd thought, I will leave now. I can leave.

Six years ago, she was forty, but she knew she wasn't too old to start over.

The question, then as ever, was where to go? Despite her rage and desperation back then, she didn't feel afraid or cut off from the world. In fact, she felt an empowered, embittered ownership of it (or, if not the world, at least half Judd's assets). For an entire afternoon, through tears, she'd imagined her next steps: she'd build a new life in Paris (Paris? Of course Paris!), find a studio in the Eleventh, somewhere near a park and a metro station, with a real washer-dryer and a dishwasher, nonnegotiable. She'd sat at the kitchen table until her ass started going numb, blocking all electronic notifications, phone calls, or texts (she didn't want to hear it, didn't care what Judd was doing or what his excuses were) and planned out what she would need for the rest of her life. They'd been married for eleven years, which was enough for a 50 percent settlement. Would she really take 50 percent of everything he had? No, in fact she wouldn't need that much. She would take only what she needed, and her dignity. Enough money for a studio—fuck that, a one bedroom!—somewhere with a café down the street where she could gather her thoughts in the morning, near a Franprix for groceries and a flower shop for beauty.

Her French was dustier than dust, basically nonexistent. After five seconds consideration she enrolled in an online French course.

A lawyer to help her get citizenship would cost $3000 for an initial retainer. $3000 for a new life! A bargain!

And then, a little past four, Ferry schlumped into the house, dropped his bookbag by the door, went directly to the refrigerator to procure a bottle of Mexican Coke (god, they all were so precious in this house), and then sat down at the kitchen table across from her. He was fourteen then, rangy but with the shaggy hair and doofy smile of a young boy. "'Sup, Dos."

She began clicking down the open pages on her browser. "'Sup, Ferry."

"Why are you sitting here in the dark?"

"Just—researching a trip to Paris." She rubbed her cheeks with the back of her wrist to make any errant tear streaks disappear.

"Paris?" He stood again to rummage through the pantry for snacks. "Sweet. Do we have any Doritos?"

"I don't think we—"

"Oh, never mind, we have Cheetos. When are we going?"

"Going?"

"To Paris? Or is it like a romantic thing? I'm not invited?"

"Of course you're invited," she said. She shut down her laptop. "But I'm really just daydreaming about a trip. I don't have anything concrete."

He had no idea that anything was amiss between her and his father; the discovery of Judd's indiscretion had happened the previous night, while Ferry was fast asleep, and the recriminations had taken place mostly after he'd left for school.

"We should totally go," he said. "I've never been to Paris. I've always wanted to see the Mona Lisa."

"She's small," Amy said.

"So what?" he said, sitting back down across from her. He was eating Cheetos by the fistful from an industrial-sized bag, wearing a vintage Mets sweatshirt and basketball shorts, socks pulled up to his knees as per the mysterious fashion among fourteen-year-old boys that year. He pointed the bag at her with orange-y fingers and she grabbed a handful. She knew she would never leave him.

She had never left him. Had only waited for him to leave her.

Amy stood, thought that she should probably check in to see how Uno was doing, probably make sure Uno was stable, probably see if Ferry was holding up okay.

But over the river flew a solitary hawk, circling, and Amy was transfixed by the way the hawk tilted in the air and then dipped, searching for a mouse, a rat, perhaps an untended litter of newborn puppies.

A city one thousand years old. A warrior queen. A bridge, a church, a mountain, a dome. A white dog somewhere in the distance, or just down the street, waiting to emerge when she was ready to be found.

Amy threaded her way back down the eastern hills of Tbilisi. She would not pick up the phone and check back in with the world. She was invisible, an ant on a hill.

THIRTEEN

IT WAS ALMOST five by the time she returned to the house.

"Shhhh . . ." One of the grannies stood by the door, issuing a warning. She was wearing velour pants and a burgundy coat, and her hair was in its beehive. Amy could not remember for the life of her what her name was. "Fighting."

"Fighting?"

The sky had started to relax into the west, but just barely, tinted at the edges in the same burgundy as the granny's coat.

"Irine," the granny said. "Maia."

"Ah," Amy said.

"You stay outside? With me?"

"With you?"

"Come." The granny beckoned her to follow, and together they walked to the side of the house, to a rusty metal gate half-hidden under grape vines. On the other side of the gate was the house's overgrown backyard. The granny ushered her to the picnic table. "We wait here."

"What are they fighting about?"

"Yes?"

"What are they—do you know what the problem is?"

"Yes?"

Amy wondered if she should pull out her phone, Google translate, but she didn't want to confuse the granny. (God, she should stop thinking of this woman as a granny! She was only fifteen years older than Amy was!) "Do you know why they're arguing?"

The granny smiled, but still looked perplexed. Through the door behind them, the dogs were barking, having sensed their presence or perhaps just needing some relief in the cool March dusk. "I let them out?"

"Sure," Amy said.

The granny opened the door and out came a whoosh of legs and tongues and fur, happy yapping, peeing by the tree, approaching for sniffs and pets and ear tousles and the relative joy of the prison yard.

"You like?"

"Dogs? Oh, I love them," Amy said. "I have a dog at home named Roxy. She's a German shepherd—do you know German shepherds?" She picked up her phone to show the granny a photo, one she loved, Roxy with her big dumb tongue hanging off to the left, wearing one of Ferry's baseball caps. They had wanted to dress her up as a player for Halloween, but she'd resisted wearing the old Dwight Gooden tee.

The granny nodded, pointed at one of the *Didi Gulabi* strays that looked something lke Roxy around the eyes. "Yes," Amy said. "Like her."

They sat quietly for several minutes to watch the dogs accomplish their initial squats and sniffs and assemble themselves in exhausted heaps around the yard, some of them staring up at her with expectant, adoring eyes.

"Ty ikh vyspustil? You let them out?"

Amy turned. Andrei, standing by the back door in a winter coat.

"Hey! You got a coat!"

"I didn't want you to worry about me anymore," he said, but he didn't smile at her and she really had no idea if he was kidding or not.

He said something in Georgian (or Russian?) to the granny and the granny responded fluidly, rapidly. They exchanged several sentences, and Amy tried desperately to pick out a word she knew. She thought she heard Irine's name, she thought she heard Maia's; she knew this conversation wasn't for her.

Eventually, Andrei spoke in English. "Irine and Maia are having a very loud argument upstairs. Irine doesn't want Maia to go to the protest. She's saying she'll stop paying her school fees if she goes."

"Oh, I see," Amy said. "But Maia was already at a protest today."

"I believe that's what the fighting is about inside. According to Marmar it has gotten very bad. Maia is throwing cups against the wall."

"Cups?"

"You know? For coffee?"

"Oh, yes. Cups."

The granny—her name was Marmar, she had a name—said something else to Andrei, who shrugged his shoulders.

"Chto nam delat'?"

"Ona mozhet postradat'."

"Kakaya raznitsa?"

"What's happening?"

"She wants to know if it's World War Three in there or only Afghanistan. A big battle or a long and boring stalemate."

"Which is it?"

"Both," Andrei said.

He and Marmar then began a rapid-fire negotiation, utterly incomprehensible, and Amy turned to the closest dog, a small black-Lab-type creature with beautiful amber eyes and a scar on its muzzle. The dog pushed itself between Amy's knees to better secure a petting position, and Amy rewarded its initiative with a nice long scritch under the chin. Still, although her body was turned away from Andrei, it was extraordinarily aware of him, of his bulk on the picnic bench beside her, the musky smell of him, the soft guttural sounds of whatever language he was speaking. She felt a little bit of a buzz on her right side, the side that was closest to him.

It occurred to her that she had not had a crush on anyone in so long. A thrill! The dog panted gratefully between her legs. Amy rubbed its soft leathery ears between her fingers.

"Yeye doch'—molodoy chelovek. Chego ona ozhidayet?" Marmar was gesturing up to the sky with both hands, the universal gesture for "what do you want me to do?"

Andrei shrugged. "Ono tboya doch'."

She luxuriated in the sound of his voice, closed her eyes and tuned into the prickling of the skin on the right side of her body, the warmth of the Labrador between her knees. "U tebya bol'she sily," he said. "Chem u menya."

It was the sexiest sound she thought she'd ever heard. She drew circles on the felt of the Labrador's ears, the murmur of Andrei's voice behind her, the setting sun, his body on the bench, her eyes were closed, she wanted to—

"Amy!"

"Yes?" God, what was wrong with her?

"Marmar thinks we should separate them if they're going to keep going like this. One time Irine ended up in the hospital."

"What?"

"Nothing Maia did—Irine thought she was having a heart attack. It was before I arrived, so I'm not certain if—"

Marmar interrupted. "You must understand." Amy had not been expecting her to speak English. "What happened for Irine's sister."

"Understand?"—but then she thought back to the picture of Irine's family behind her desk at work, the sister who had died a long time ago. The Lab lay down between her feet.

"Can you tell me?"

Marmar drew a breath. "In April, 1989, yes, you know?"

"When people were killed in the protests," Amy said.

"Yes," Marmar said. "Irine and her sister went to Parliament Square, went to—I don't know in English—" and then she said something to Andrei, who nodded along. It was Russian, of course they'd been speaking in Russian.

"Irine and her sister went to the protest on April nine in Parliament Square," Andrei translated. "They had been protesting for months, their parents didn't want them to, didn't understand what the point was. And it was dangerous. But the girls didn't think so. They were part of a new generation."

"And then the police—"

"Not police. Soviet troops. Gorbachev was rapidly losing control of the situation across the USSR—almost every day a different Soviet republic was declaring independence, scheduling a referendum. Most of the countries managed to secede peacefully, but for some reason in Tbilisi . . ."

"There was violence."

"The Soviet soldiers started attacking protesters with—I don't know what the word is in English, with farming tools, heavy ones. Like steel triangles on sticks. We call them *lopata*. They used them to smash protesters in the head. Twenty people died. Seventeen of them were women."

"And one of them was Irine's sister?"

Andrei said something to Marmar, who responded in Russian, mimed being hit in the skull.

"A soldier hit her in the head many times and then, I don't know exactly what—" Marmar said something else. "She says she was very sick for two years. She could barely walk. She couldn't think clearly anymore. Often couldn't speak, lost her ability to remember words."

"Jesus."

"She lived like this for two years, and then she threw herself out of the window of their apartment in 1991, about a month before the independence referendum. That was when Irine's family moved here. They couldn't stay in that apartment anymore after what happened to her sister."

Irine had told her a different story. Well, that was her right, to prune the truth.

Marmar said something else.

"Da, da," said Andrei. "She was eighteen years old."

"God—what a horrible thing that must have been. I'm so sorry."

"Yes, well," Andrei said. "Everyone has their tragedy from that time. This is Irine's. My family has their own, of course. Even Gorbechev has one, I'm afraid."

"What was her sister's name?"

"Irine's?" He turned to Marmar. "Kak yeye zvali?"

"Maia," Marmar said. "Like Irine's daughter."

Jesus.

"There's often a certain poetry in these things, isn't there?" Andrei said. The sky was darkening faster now, and a few of the dogs were pawing at the door, ready to end their idyll and head in for dinner. "Anyway, you can see why Irine is so upset."

"Maia said that Irine wants the Russians to take over."

"I don't know what you mean by take over."

"I mean—Maia said Irine was supporting the Russian agenda here. And then I talked to someone at Irine's school today and she said that Irine had fired a teacher who stood up against some kind of Russian program at the school." She felt it was important to understand this. To figure out who was right and wrong.

"I don't know anything about that," Andrei said.

"Does Marmar?"

Andrei turned to the old lady, whose eyes seemed wet. She had known the young Maia, of course, and Irine, before and after.

"She says that the teacher who was fired was dangerous. She posed a danger to the whole family."

"To the family?"

Andrei said something else to Marmar, but Marmar said nothing, just made a disgusted face. "I don't really know what she means. Does Irine support the Russians here?"

Andrei gave her a look. "Kak Irina otnositsya k russkim?"

Marmar buttoned her parka up her neck. It was perceptibly colder now. She looked at Amy with pale gray eyes. "We raise our children," she said. "We pray to God. In this way we are happy. Like you."

"Of course," Amy said, not sure if she understood.

She stood, wiped her hands on her velour pants. "I must feed dogs now," she said. "You will help Irine and Maia, Amy."

"Me?"

"You negotiate."

"Americans are the best intermediaries," Andrei said. "They are the only ones other people listen to."

"I don't know—well, I can try."

"Yes," Marmar said. "You can try."

Marmar opened the rear door and the dogs followed her inside to their various bowls, with Amy and Andrei in the rear. Methodically, she began scooping ladlefuls of kibble to each dog, each of whom knew to wait patiently for its turn. As she fed them, she murmured gently, calling each one by a name that Amy could not understand.

"Let's go upstairs," Andrei said.

"Is it going to be World War Three up there?"

Andrei paused. "Just Afghanistan."

But upstairs it was actually Mars—deserted, chilly, dark.

"Irine?" Andrei called out, but the house responded with silence. He flicked on the swinging lamp over the kitchen table to illuminate a mess of papers, an overturned chair, a broken mug on the floor. "Irine? *Irina? Maia?*"

"Oh dear." Amy turned the chair upright, picked up the broken mug and threw it in the garbage.

"They fight like this sometimes," Andrei said. "I've seen it more than once since I've lived here. You know how children are."

"It's not how my child is."

"Yes, well," he said, smiling, "we are more passionate on this side of the ocean."

Under the bare kitchen bulb, Andrei's blue eyes glittered. To distract herself from them, Amy straightened the papers on the table. He watched her for a second, and Amy felt an expectant hum. Something could or would happen between them; she felt it.

She finally spoke. "What should we do now?"

"Hmmm?"

"I mean, should we look for them or—?"

"Look for them?"

"I mean, to make sure they're safe?"

"I'm sure they're safe," Andrei said.

"But maybe we should look?"

"You can do whatever you want," he said. "But I don't think this is really any of my business anymore. I'm going to watch TV."

"TV? Do you want company?" This flew out of her mouth before she could stop it.

"Do you like watching Russian detective shows?"

"Maybe?"

He chuckled as though she had been trying to make a joke. "I'll see you tomorrow, Amy Webb."

She blinked. "See you tomorrow."

But he didn't move.

If she went upstairs after him, maybe she could follow him into his room, ask him to turn on the closed captioning on his cop show and sit on his bed and then—or she could just be a grownup about this, invite him to her bedroom, make what she wanted clear. Wouldn't he respond to that? Didn't men always respond?

"Good night," he said, and then retreated into the darkened hall.

"Good night."

And she sat frozen at the table, staring at the home screen of her phone. Beneath her, she could hear Marmar still humming through the floorboards. She could still go upstairs, she thought. She could knock on his door. She could—

Her phone buzzed and she grabbed it. "Judd?"

"Hey love," he said, and her face flooded with shame.

"What's going on?"

"Just got back from the hospital," he said.

"Oh my god, what—"

"Uno needed to be admitted, and nobody was around for her. She called. I couldn't say no."

"No, no, of course," Amy said. "What now?"

"It's a strange infection," Judd said. "Usually antifungal medications can clear it up, but sometimes it's resistant. The docs don't know yet what they're dealing with, although they sound optimistic. They basically have to throw all the medicine they have at her until something works."

"How long does that take?"

"Days, at least," Judd said. "Maybe months."

"God," Amy said. She had been gone for five days, and this is what happened. Yet it all felt so distant. She couldn't imagine being in their apartment, wiping up the familiar mess on the counter, doing the laundry, walking the dog. But she also knew that as soon as she returned to New York, Georgia would become a dream.

"Have the doctors made any predictions?"

"They can't," he said. "It's really a wait-and-see kind of thing."

"I'm sorry," Amy said, because she was.

"Yeah, well."

"How's everything else? How's the menagerie?"

"Cats are fine. Roxy misses you."

"I miss her," Amy said.

"We all miss you."

"Should I come home?"

Judd paused. "Well, did you find the dog yet?"

God, the way he said it. It made her feel so small.

"Almost," she said.

He was quiet for a moment. "I think Uno's stable. You can see what Ferry thinks if you want."

"Does he know what's going on?"

"He knows," Judd said. "I don't know if he understands how bad it is."

"I thought it wasn't that bad."

"It wasn't," Judd said. "Now it is."

Amy sighed.

"I mean, I don't want to tell you what to do, but—"

On the one hand, she thought it was a good sign that Judd wanted her home, or at least hopeful—if he had been busy fucking Meret he probably wouldn't want her back on the same continent. But on the other hand, it felt a little manipulative (a little?), using Uno and Ferry to reel her back in as he'd done so many times before. But on the other other hand, she and Judd had known for a long time that this moment would come, when Uno's tortured body would finally crap out on her, when they'd be left to pick up the pieces for their child. Of course, ever since she'd gotten sober they'd talked about it less—they'd both assumed that the health benefits of sobriety would cancel out the decades of havoc Uno had wreaked on her own body. But of course bodies didn't work like that.

"I can't come home yet," Amy said, surprising herself. "But let me know if she gets worse."

"Why not?"

"I'm sorry?"

"Just—I mean, why can't you come home yet?"

"Lynne said she saw Meret crying outside Le Coin the other morning."

"What?" Judd sounded truly and very surprised.

"Did you break up with her?"

"Amy, there was nothing—I didn't do anything. There was nothing to break up." They were back to this. "I have no idea why she was crying."

"Did you fire her?"

"I told her I received those pictures and they were inexcusable and she was mortified. She said she thought she'd sent them to her boyfriend."

Amy was silent.

"Amy?"

"Okay," she said.

"I swear, I don't—"

"Whatever," she said. "It's fine. I don't care." And she thought she was probably telling the truth.

"Are you still mad?"

"This isn't about you, Judd."

"It's not about me?"

"This isn't about—" How to even begin to explain?

She heard footsteps and turned around. Andrei had come back downstairs, was standing in the doorway.

"I'm not mad," she said. "I promise. I'm just not ready to come home."

FOURTEEN

WHEN SHE WAS a little girl, Amy used to dream about her father, a man she knew little about and rarely thought about during the daytime. He'd been an orderly at the hospital where her mother was an aide; he and her mom were married for a total of three years. He split when she and her brother were two. "Just went out for cigarettes," her mom liked to say, not explaining what she meant. For a long time, Amy thought that was what had actually happened. He'd gone out for cigarettes and vanished into thin air.

In her dreams, her father was not particularly attentive, and in fact was usually unwilling to even acknowledge her. He would be a man on a sidewalk, two steps ahead. Or at the same Burger King she was, but sitting at another table. She'd seen a few pictures of him, had a general idea what he looked like (he'd given her and her brother their height, their lankiness, their whiteish-blond hair), but in her dreams he could and often did look like anything. A postal worker delivering packages to their house. A math teacher at her school, trying to teach her algebra in words she couldn't understand. Bill Clinton. The grocery clerk. But no matter what he looked like, she would know he was her father. She just couldn't get him to talk to her.

"Dad?"

In her dreams, following a tall bald man with a moustache across a busy downtown street, barely dodging cars, praying he would slow down to let her catch up but unwilling to ask him to.

"Dad?" Sitting a few seats back in a bus that was being driven by her father—she *knew* it was her father—but entirely unable to get him to turn around and look at her, even when he announced the next stops. She was scared; she didn't want to be on the bus without her mother, she wanted to ask her father to agree to take care of her until they reached her house, then he'd never have to talk to her again. But he refused to turn around.

She stopped having these dreams when she married Judd, which was one of the millions of reasons she was so glad she married Judd, but at the same time she worried that she had replaced her father with her husband, and if that were the case, how was she ever supposed to claim her own space in the world?

And sometimes she would dream of Judd sitting at the restaurant, and she would talk to him, but he wouldn't respond; no matter how much she wanted him to see her, to talk to her, he wouldn't. Was he refusing? Or was she invisible?

When she woke up from these dreams, she was disoriented, afraid. She would reach out for Judd in their big bed and he would hold her close, murmur to her until finally her heart would slow and her breathing would slow until she could fall back asleep. *Amy, Amy, I'm here, it's all right, go back to sleep.*

More than one therapist had suggested that her father's disappearance was her initial wound. Of course that sounded right, but she wasn't sure whether it mattered, particularly. We all walked around with initial wounds. Every human being on this earth. But didn't most of us find a way to heal, to walk around the world without so much discontent, at least by forty-six years of age?

"You have no idea what other people feel inside," said her second-to-last therapist, the nice one with the elaborate scarves. She was a good therapist, let Amy ramble or just sit in silence, didn't seem fed up with her or distracted. She was the one who told her she didn't have to write to her mother any more if her mother refused to respond. She was the one who told her yes, of course, she deserved to marry Judd.

"Losing your father as a young child is no small thing," her good therapist used to tell her.

"Half the people in the world don't have fathers," Amy said.

"That's actually untrue," said the good therapist. "And even if it were, that wouldn't make it okay." (Her name was Clarice, like the heroine of *The Silence of the Lambs*, and she worked out of a gorgeous apartment on the Upper West Side and occasionally hawks perched on her windowsill. And when she retired, she told Amy gently that no, retirement was what it sounded like; they couldn't keep in touch.)

Somewhere in Moscow, Amy thought, there was a girl without a father.

She looked at Andrei, his ski cap, his stubble, his new parka that was probably used, and felt a great outpouring of feeling for him and, for some reason, herself. She could not make sense of the feeling. It wasn't only lust, it wasn't pity—it wasn't sorrow or gratitude or hope. Just a feeling that the two of them were connected somehow on this ground in this place where neither of them really belonged. They could matter to each other.

"Irine texted me," he said.

"Where is she?"

"She went to the pharmacy to get some nitroglycerin. Her heart is—I do not know the word." He patted his chest rapidly.

"Palpitating."

"Palpitating," he said. "She wants me to find Maia."

In her mind, Amy started to frame a question: *Do you want me to, should I*, but then stopped herself. "I'll come."

He didn't smile, but he said, "Good."

Together, in silence, they left the house and walked down the hill, twisting and turning until the brightness of Rustaveli began to illuminate the trees around them. Since Andrei walked a half step in front of her, she could see there was a tattoo on the back of his neck, Cyrillic letters. She wondered if they spelled out the name of his daughter or his wife.

In the distance, they could hear a crowd, and a loud, thumping noise.

"Can we pause for a second?"

"Pause?"

"I need to catch my breath." The cigarettes must have been taking their toll, plus the cold air. She took a yoga breath, trying not to look ridiculous.

Andrei shoved his hands in his pockets. His expression was neutral. The wind was still, and the thumping sound from the bottom of the hill sounded expectant, even demanding. Amy was not afraid of what they would find at the bottom of the hill, but she wanted to be ready for it. The crowd earlier in the day—maybe that was why she was having a hard time catching her breath. She still felt the pressure of all those people around her.

"You are all right?"

"I was at the protest earlier today," she said. "By accident, I didn't mean to be. I just found myself in front of the square when the crowd started assembling. There were police, water cannons."

"You got hit by the water?" he said.

"No, I didn't get sprayed, I wasn't—I wasn't in danger. But I'd never been in a crowd like that before, so many people pushing toward something. I'm sure you've done this sort of thing before, but to me it was kind of, I don't know, a little frightening."

"I've never done this," he said.

"What?"

"I've never done a protest."

"You haven't?"

"What would I protest?"

"I guess—I just thought all Russians protested at some time or another."

"Do all Americans?" Andrei said.

"No, of course not. But didn't you protest Ukraine?"

He gave her a look. "I have never had any interest in going to jail, Amy."

"No, I didn't mean—"

"I am not a hero today either," Andrei said. "I am doing a favor for my landlady."

She nodded, didn't say anything else.

"We go?" Andrei said.

Amy pulled her scarf more tightly, continued following him down the steep road toward Rustaveli. The roar of the crowd pushed up toward them from the valley below. Lights beamed upward.

They turned one more corner and the entire boulevard came into view before them. A crowd ten times the size of the crowd this morning—twenty times, thirty times the size—filled Rustaveli Avenue and Parliament Square. People were holding up the flashlights on their phones and the entire street twinkled with tiny stars. There were red-and-white Georgian flags and blue-and-yellow Ukrainian flags and the blue flag of the European Union, twelve gold stars organized in a circle. Large police vans were parked in the middle of the street, but the crowd flowed around them as though they were islands in a river. The crowd shouted in indeterminable Georgian. Their signs were in Georgian, English, Cyrillic. They had flags wrapped around their shoulders, flags flowing behind them like capes. The bright lights of the police vans beamed down on them, and riot police with plexiglas shields and invisible faces lined the sidewalks.

"We'll never find her," Amy said, watching the river of people slowly flow by.

But it was peaceful—enormous and loud but peaceful—or at least there didn't seem to be any violence, the police watching, the crowd chanting, and Amy had half a mind to join them even though she knew this wasn't her fight. And even though Andrei did not protest.

But maybe? She looked to him to see what they should do, but he was just gazing, impassively.

So they watched the people marching past them, and Amy saw that there were children in the crowd and old people and people who looked like mothers and fathers. One person—no, two, in wheelchairs. But the bulk of the crowd seemed to be people Ferry's age, in their early twenties, unlined, beautiful.

And on the street where they were standing, ten yards away from the sea of people, two dogs lay on their sides, half asleep, unperturbed.

"Should we try to look for her?" Amy asked, but Andrei couldn't hear. She nudged him on the side, tried to mime looking for Maia. He shook his head, *Don't bother, I can't hear you,* and turned his face back to the crowd, mesmerized. What did he see there? Was this different for him? "Fuck Putin, Fuck Putin!" the crowd screamed.

Amy had protested twice in her lifetime: the Iraq invasion in 2002 and the Women's March of 2017, both times down Fifth Avenue, past the museums and mansions all the way to Washington Square Park. She felt righteous and alive both times, and obviously perfectly safe, lots of room to breathe, lots of fellowship among her fellow protesters, food carts lining the sidewalks. For the Women's March Lynne had knitted everyone those pink hats, and they took selfies and the police even took selfies with them, and the whole thing wasn't exactly a party but it wasn't a menace, either. What did they have on the line? They were protesting Trump and what he'd said about women, sure, and they were expressing their general displeasure with the way the election had gone, and they were sad about Hillary and the fact that

America would perhaps not get around to electing a woman president ever, or at least not in their lifetimes, and while all that was true and galling, they also agreed that the afternoon had been invigorating. It had been cheerful; it had made them feel good. Whether or not they effected any change—well, they hadn't *expected* to effect change! They had expected to come together, and they had, and then they had gone to happy hour at Le Coin and Judd had gotten them rosé and oysters on the house, of course. For the cause.

And Amy was thinking back to that moment—the oysters, the women sitting around the tables in their pink hats, rosy cheeked from the outdoors, they were all six years younger then and optimistic even in their despair—when a siren started bleating, blaring, the most piercing noise she had ever heard. Reflexively she took several quick steps back and almost tripped over the dogs who had been lying on their sides. They got up, offended, and took off in the opposite direction.

Andrei didn't move, however. He was still gazing into the crowd from his station as if he were watching a movie.

"Andrei?"

He couldn't hear her. She came back, touched his shoulder quickly, and he acknowledged her, nodded, pointed out to the sea of people. The police had stopped the march by lining up in front of the crowd like a sea of Darth Vaders, holding their plexiglas shields, and the horrible sirens were coming from the police vans behind them, but instead of dispersing (daarbiet! DAARBIET!) people were dancing, *dancing*, like they were at a nightclub or a rave. Just dancing in front of the police in these athletic, incredible poses, skinny twenty-year-old men and women, draped in their flags, turning the shriek of the siren into the pulse of a club track, and Amy looked at Andrei, who was smiling. The crowd had made space for them.

They would not find Maia, of course. She knew that. But they stood there anyway until they could no longer feel their fingers and their eardrums no longer recorded individual noises but rather just an oceanic roar and they watched the marchers march and the ravers rave, and when the police eventually lost patience and began spraying the crowd with their beastly water cannons, they felt stray droplets spray against their faces and still they did not move. She was still not brave enough to join them—she could not join them—but at least she felt the water hit her face.

IT WAS ONE in the morning by the time they got back to the house. They were hungry, frozen, exhausted, tingling. The dogs, asleep, snuffled and rolled over as they walked past. Some were snoring. Some moved their paws in the air as they slept.

"You found her?"

Irine, ghostlike, at the kitchen table.

"It was impossible," Andrei said. "There were probably five thousand people in the crowd."

Irine nodded. Her eyes were red and the ashtray on the kitchen table was overflowing. Next to it she had an open bottle of something, a small empty glass. Her phone. "I have not heard a word."

"Nothing?"

Irine looked at Amy, bleakly.

"Well, it was pretty peaceful down there, so I think she's okay," Amy said.

Irine waved away the smoke from her fresh cigarette. "Then why do you two look like you've been in a war?"

Nobody said anything.

Then, Andrei: "It was a long night. I'm going to bed. I hope she comes home." He turned and headed up the stairs.

Amy sat down at the table with Irine. Irine seemed neither pleased nor put out by the company. She slid her cigarette pack across the table.

Amy lit up and watched the smoke collect under the pendant lamp above the kitchen table. She should probably buy Irine a fresh carton.

"Marmar said she told you the story of my sister."

"Yes," Amy said. "I'm so sorry."

Irine took a long inhale on her Crown. Blew out the smoke in a stream. "For a long time I thought I would be okay one day, but now I know that you are never really okay after a thing like that," she said. "You do not really forget."

Her eyes had circles under them and her face looked grayish. She poured herself another drink but didn't take a sip. Amy hoped whatever heart trouble she had wasn't too terrible.

"Did you know," Irine said, "that when George W. Bush came here in 2005, I was in the crowd?"

"I didn't."

"Yes," she said. "It was very exciting. The American president! Nobody could believe it. My mother, Marmar, all of us—we walked down to Liberty Square together, and I remember the way people were streaming down the street. It was the first crowd I felt safe in since 1989. So many guards, you know? Nothing bad would happen."

Amy nodded.

"And it was worth it. Being in that crowd. His speech was so inspiring. Bush told us that we were free. That we were part of Europe now and for forever. He told us that what Georgia had done was an inspiration to the rest of the world."

Amy tapped the ash from her cigarette into the pile on the ashtray. Again, that strange sensation of being in a movie, of watching her life from a distance.

"I remember standing in that crowd, listening, thinking that the president was right, that the sacrifices we had made in our lifetime, that the marching, the starving, all of it—my sister's life—that it had all meant something. Because we were free. The American president was here in Liberty Square, something that would have been unimaginable when I was a child. I looked at that man and thought of my sister, I thought—I wish she were going to be here with us for this beautiful future we have fought for. I wish she could see this man in front of us. My mother and my aunts thought the same thing."

Irine wiped a finger under an eye, took a sip of whatever she was drinking. Amy got up and got herself a glass. "I was eight weeks pregnant then with Maia. I felt sick the entire pregnancy, but that day I was able to make it all the way to Liberty Square and back without feeling ill. I heard your president and I thought it was—what do you call that? I thought it was the intercession of God."

Chacha, which burned Amy's throat even more than the first time. "So this was 2005, right?"

Amy nodded, her tongue bristling.

"In 2008, Russia invades the northern part of our country. George W. Bush is still president."

"I remember."

"But do you remember what he does about this? Because we are a beacon of light and freedom? Because he is so proud of all that we have accomplished? Do you know what he does to protect us?"

Amy knew the answer but didn't want to say—

"He does nothing."

"Irine, the US was already in two wars at the time—"

"He does nothing."

"But in all practicality, there was no way the US could have—"

"Russia accused us of genocide against our own people. Genocide! That was their premise. Took Abkhazia. Took Tskhinvali where my father's people live. Their army surrounded Tbilisi for six days, while the city trembled. They could have demolished us in a second. And you Americans, with all your talk of liberty, you just watched all this happen and—tell me, did you even know all this was happening? Did you even bother to watch?"

Irine coughed wickedly. She really did not seem well. Amy had never looked up how to dial 911 in Tbilisi, and she had no idea where to find the grannies, but maybe Andrei knew—

"And then in 2014 Russia invaded the Donbas. And then it claimed Crimea for Russia. Just claimed it! Can you imagine! As if Canada just came and said, we'll take New York City, thank you, and nobody does a thing about it. You just let them have it!"

She began coughing again.

"Irine, maybe you should—"

"Last year Russia invaded the rest of Ukraine. And they are still there, just like they are still in Abkhazia and Tskhinvali and Crimea and if you think they will stop there you are as silly an American as I have ever imagined."

Amy poured some water for Irine at the tap, handed it to her.

"Marmar said you wanted to know if I am for the Russians," she said.

"What I meant was—"

"I am not for the Russians. But I am for reality."

"Of course." Amy tried to keep her voice gentle.

"This is not a free country. This will *never* be a free country. George W. Bush was full of bullshit."

George W. Bush, with his twang and his malapropisms, how impossible to imagine him here.

"We can cry and scream that we want to be part of NATO, part of Europe, but they will not have us as long as the Russian boot is on our neck. And we know by now that the Russian boot will never come off our neck, and nobody will help get it off no matter how many times we ask them to. Which means that the kids at the bottom of the hill can yell about it, can scream, can get tear-gassed, can get beaten, can go to prison, but we will always be Soviet here, even if we don't like to think that. And the more that we adjust to that reality, the more peace we will have."

"Irine, the future isn't written for any of us. It's not."

"And even more than liberty, what I want to have is peace." Irine wiped a finger under her eye again.

Amy pushed the water toward her. Irine ignored it.

"The only time in my life," she said, "that I almost died was when I tried to claim a liberty that was not actually mine. But for the rest of my life, even when it has been difficult—as long as I have accepted what is possible, I have always had peace."

Amy looked at her dim, purple-ish eyes.

"I want my daughter to have a good life. This is what all parents want, is it not?"

"Of course," Amy said.

"That boy of yours," Irine said, "this is what you want for him, isn't it?"

"Of course," she said again.

"Well your boy, your boy in America—he has a good life already written down for him. This is—this means, I am sure you worry, all parents worry, but your child goes to a university that, if I am to believe my eyes, costs more money for one year than I will make in my entire life. And when he is done he will have some kind of job, and he will make his own decisions about what he can do and what he can think and if he fails there will be someone to catch him, correct? You will catch him. Am I correct?"

To push back on Ferry's advantages or limitations—that wasn't the point of this, Amy knew. And anyway Irine was basically correct. Although he had been abandoned, again and again, by his drug-addicted mother. Although it was possible that he was going to lose her for good any day now. Although he would spend the rest of his life wondering why she had continued to use even though she loved him. Yet even with all that, he had been born into a luck that was incomprehensible for most people in any part of the world in any history of it. A luck she had once assumed would last forever. A house that wouldn't fall.

"My daughter is brilliant," Irine said. "She is the most brilliant— she speaks English as well as you can, and although she does not like to do it she can also speak Russian, and she speaks French. And on her most recent exams she got the highest grades in her entire district. Not just in her school. She is studying computer engineering, and the things she knows how to do—I can't even tell you. She can do math sums in her head that would take most people ten minutes with a calculator. She can look up at the stars and tell you the name of every one. In Georgian and in Greek! She knows more at seventeen than most people learn in their entire lives and she has only just gotten started."

"Yes," Amy said.

"But there are still things that she does not know. Things that she cannot know," Irine said. "Because she is seventeen."

"But maybe there's some beauty in that?"

Irine looked at Amy like she was a moron. "There is nothing beautiful in that," she said. "My daughter believes that it can be different. And what I am telling you is that it cannot be different, and the way to have a peaceful life in this country is to understand that it will not ever be different here. That if you want peace and safety you must compromise with the part of yourself that thought you deserved something more. You must tell yourself—"

And here, Irine seemed to run out of steam. She just stared off in the distance for a moment, over Amy's shoulder. Her eyes were watery, and her face was ashen.

When Irine began speaking again, her voice was close to a whisper. "I have tried to tell my daughter what my experience has taught me to be true. She can have a free life somewhere else or a peaceful life here, but she cannot have both. But she will not listen to me. She believes that everything I have lived through is worth nothing."

It was two in the morning. The cold had seeped into the apartment through the drafty windows and the chinks in the floorboards. But Maia's world could not be the world her mother lived in. This was not the way the future worked.

Amy thought about the distance between herself and Ferry, what she understood of the world and what he did. It was true, she knew, that she had seen and suffered through many things that he could not possibly understand. It was true that the world that she had tried to prepare him for in a million small ways was not the one in which he would live as an adult. She could not know the world as it would be. She could not know the world that was his. But still, she knew how the world could punch you in the gut when you were looking the other way. She did know that!

But she had never told him. She had only wanted to protect him from it.

Through the floorboards, a lone hound started to howl, and then another joined in, howling and then barking manically.

"She is home," Irine said.

Clomping up the stairs, opening the door. Maia in her beautiful gothness, her dyed black hair loose around her shoulders, makeup smeared down her face, her kneesocks ripped, her leather jacket looking way too thin for the weather.

"Shen gadats'q'vit'e sakhlshi misvla," Irine said.

Maia nodded. "I just wanted to let you know I'm alive."

"You wanted to let me know? Ras guliskmobt?"

"Before I go out."

"It's two in the morning!" Irine said. "Bad midikhar!"

"Out," Maia said.

"Maia," Irine said, and she sounded so tired. "Maia, please."

"Maia, maybe you should stay here?" said Amy, even though she had no business saying anything.

"Maia, gtkhov. Gtkhovt shets'q'vit'ot es."

"No, I'm not staying," Maia said. "I just wanted you to see I'm alive." She turned and went back down the stairs.

The downstairs dogs began to howl again.

In the dim light of the pendant lamp, Irine's face stayed unchanged. She lit another cigarette, and Amy watched her smoke it. There was nothing she could say to change anything and nothing she could say that would help, so she said nothing. And of course she didn't like this woman with the heart problem chain-smoking in the middle of the night, but who was she to stop her?

When her cigarette was smoked to the filter, she stubbed it out and poured the water glass over the smoldering ash tray. Then she stood and pulled the string on the pendant lamp, extinguishing it. Still, the moon beamed in through the kitchen window, so Amy wasn't in total darkness. She was able to watch Irine's thin form as she stood, rinsed her hands in the dripping sink, and disappeared up the stairs.

FIFTEEN

MIDNIGHT HAD COME and gone; it was now March 6. Amy thought it was important to keep track of the days, to keep her mind right.

She lay in her underwear in her single bed, trying to count the things she remembered and loved about the life she was six thousand miles away from.

She loved her block, solid four-story buildings, the elementary school, the bodega, the two vintage clothing stores, and, at the very end, her own sunny redbrick low-rise.

She loved Roxy and she loved the cats.

She loved the painting on the wall in the living room, the one she found in a general store in Hudson, New York, by the painter who had done a whole series while he was in prison (the painting was of dogs and cats).

She loved the old cast-iron pans that hung from the hooks in her kitchen. She loved making soup for dinner and eating it by herself in front of the old thirteen-inch TV they'd kept in the kitchen for way too long.

She loved sticking her feet into a hot tub of water at the end of shift, back when she used to have shifts.

She loved taking new students through tiny backstreets of Chinatown or Little India to the hidden little places, introducing them to hand-pulled noodles or cardamom pods or fava beans still in the shell. She loved watching them taste the not-too-sweet sweetness of a mooncake with its red beans buried inside. She loved surprising them with their own city.

She loved writing her small articles about what she knew.

And she loved the people she loved.

She loved Ferry, which was something she didn't even need to say, and she loved Judd.

Of course she loved Judd. The way he kissed her forehead, casually. The way he laughed with his whole body. The way he remembered everyone and everything about who she was. Even if he didn't always act like he remembered, he did. He brought home pints of Ben & Jerry's Mint Chocolate Cookie ice cream every month, as soon as a new box of tampons appeared in the medicine cabinet.

But of course all this was the sort of stuff a person was *supposed* to be attached to by the time she was forty-six years old. There wasn't anything brave or radical about loving who she loved or what she had.

Last night, Maia stood in the cold in front of the cops while Amy stood on the sidelines, and she worried that said everything about her entire life.

Of course, Maia's own mother had sat in the kitchen during the protest, smoking cigarettes. But Irine had once done her own marching, too, and had been terrified or crushed by where her marching had taken her, and therefore had really *lived*.

The night seemed quiet now; if there were still sirens on Rustaveli, Amy was too far up in the hills to hear them. This house, this small bedroom, felt like a cabin in a ship, floating through time and space, rocking back and forth between one destination and another. The dogs beneath her in the engine room. The grandmothers somewhere below deck. Irine, alone, in the heart of the ship, trying to steer it. And Amy upstairs, looking out at the inky water. The night in Tbilisi was black, Amy thought, like inky water, glittering from above with stars.

It was still so hard to sleep here.

In Tbilisi, two a.m. In Ithaca, six in the afternoon.

"Isn't it late there?" Ferry asked. He'd picked up the phone after just one ring. "Why are you awake?"

"I've never exactly adjusted to the time zones," Amy said. "I just wanted to hear your voice."

She imagined Ferry in his dorm room, window overlooking the golf course. He'd lucked out with a single this year, small but entirely his, and down the hall in every room seemed to be some buddy or another. The cafeteria on the ground floor almost never closed.

"Here's my voice," Ferry said. "Does it sound the same?"

"It does," Amy said. "Maybe a little older."

Ferry cleared his throat. "How about now?"

"Now you sound like you." Although he still sounded older.

During their last visit to Ithaca, Judd had taken them to a half dozen small wineries in the region, set against beautiful lakes; they tried the Riesling, less sweet than many others she'd had, and some gentle reds. They'd been dropping Ferry off for his sophomore year, late summer, and the roadways were clogged with farmer's markets, farm-to-table restaurants, tourists gawking at the sunsets and the bounty and then crowding into the charming lakeside restaurants to eat lake trout and corn from a field up the road. And then, after they'd eaten, Ferry took them to the Cornell creamery where they'd all had gigantic cones (the milk from Cornell's own cows!), two desserts a person every night. Judd wondering how neither Amy nor Ferry ever seemed to put on a pound.

That was only eight months ago, a marriage and a family that had seemed hard-won and assured.

"I heard about Uno," Amy said.

"Yeah, well," Ferry said. Then, matter-of-fact: "I guess it had to catch up with her eventually."

"Are you okay?"

"More or less," he said. Then: "Not really."

What were Amy's reasons, again, for not calling sooner? Only a feeling that he was twenty now, that she didn't have to try to soften every blow for him anymore, or that she couldn't. Or that everything seemed so far away from her, even him.

"It's kind of annoying, to tell you the truth."

"What is?"

"Just how she seems surprised by this whole thing. You can't abuse your body like that for half your life without any consequences." He sounded bitter; she had never heard this sound in his voice before. "Did I tell you she's been writing me letters?"

"From the hospital?"

"Yeah, these really long letters—she wants me to know more about her life, how she ended up where she is. And she wants to give me advice. As though she's someone I should be taking advice from."

"Well, she still wants to look out for you—"

"Name one time in my life she has ever, *ever* looked out for me."

"Ferry—"

"Name one."

"She's been sober now for seven years," Amy said. "That's a lot of work. And I honestly think you're the only reason she's been able—"

He cut her off with a snort. "Did you know she was actually *homeless* for a while? Born into a fortune and turns out *homeless*?"

The way he said that. "She always had a place to sleep."

"Mom, for two years she didn't have an address. Her parents kicked her out, none of her friends trusted her anymore. If Dad hadn't taken her in, she wouldn't have had anywhere to go. And he knew what would happen if he took her in! And she's actually telling me all this like she's proud of it! How he knew she would steal his shit and sell it, he made her promise not to, and then the second she arrived, she did it. Did you know that? Stole his kitchen knives which were worth like a thousand bucks and sold them for heroin."

"Ferry—"

"And she's writing this like it's something I should know! Like this is something I'd want to know about the person who fucking *gave birth* to me—"

"Ferry, she just wants you to understand—"

"I do understand. She wants to absolve herself, so she's dumping her shit on me."

"Honey, she's your mother."

"Like she was ever a mother."

"Ferry."

"Maybe I've never had a mother at all."

"Ferry!" she said. "Enough!"

But she could hear him crying softly on the other end of the phone.

"Listen, honey, don't read the letters if you don't want to. You don't have to engage at all. But I think she's just trying to explain herself, or make amends."

"She could have done that a long time ago."

But she had, Amy wanted to say. She had tried her best to be as good to you as she knew how to be. But she didn't think he'd be able to hear that right now, so instead she said, "I love you so much, honey."

"I know," he said. Then: "I love you too."

"You gonna be okay?"

"I think so," he said. "It's just—I'm so fucking pissed."

"I know, baby," she said. They were silent for a moment. She wondered if he was still crying. But then he heard a voice behind him, a few voices, and he said that his friends were there to go play basketball, that's what he wanted to go do, and she said great, and when they hung up she felt a heaviness in her gut, a sorrow.

The first time she'd met Uno: one afternoon after a brunch shift, she let herself into Judd's apartment; they'd been dating for three months and she already had a key. And there was Uno sitting on the couch, frail and blondish and red-eyed, either high or recently coming down from something. She wearing a black turtleneck; it was eighty-eight degrees outside.

"So you're the other Amy," she'd said.

"It's nice to meet you," Amy lied. The hand she grasped was as bony and freezing as a grandmother's, and Amy tried not to draw back quickly. "Have you been—have you been comfortable here?"

"I'm never comfortable," the woman said. "And when people are around me they're not comfortable either. It's too bad but it's a fact."

Amy admired the honesty.

"Do you love him?" Uno asked.

Who?

"Where is he?"

"Getting Ferry. At the babysitter's."

This was Ferry's mother.

"He's a good guy, you know. He has a good heart."

"I know," Amy said, nervous in this woman's presence; she disappeared into the kitchen to spend a long time making soup.

When Judd came in almost an hour later, Ferry in his arms, they found Uno passed out on the couch, silent and unmoving as the dead. She had just leaned back and closed her eyes and sat like that, upright, passed out, for hours. Ferry did not acknowledge her, but instead ran straight to Amy, jumped into her waiting hug, and she took him to his room and closed the door and they played with his toy trucks for three hours straight, while his mother sat corpselike a room away. It was all too weird, and not for the first time in this heady new relationship, Amy thought, what am I getting into? How can I do this? And then looked at Ferry and thought, it will be worth it, it's already worth it.

Those afternoons in Ferry's room were as close to her as yesterday was, as dropping him off in college, as searching for a dog in Georgia.

When she was younger, newly married, people had sometimes asked her if she wanted a child of her own, a "piece of real estate" someone had once described it, "that's just yours and Judd's." She knew why they wondered—clearly she had a maternal streak, and clearly Ferry wasn't entirely hers in the traditional sense. But she knew, in her bones, that she would never once want more than him, and in all these years she never had, because with this child and this child alone, she could be both his mother and more than his mother, someone bonded to him by the shared experience of complicated mothers, and because she understood him more clearly and loved him more dearly because she knew he needed her so deeply, and she knew that she could meet that need for him. She always did; she always would.

HE'D STARTED KINDERGARTEN on a beautiful fall Tuesday in 2009: new sneakers and a new backpack and had a new haircut and freckles across his nose. She and Judd walked him to school, hand in hand, and stayed with him for the first fifteen minutes taking pictures and feeling weepy until his teacher finally shooed them out. Judd had to go into Le Coin that afternoon, so Amy had stood alone at three p.m. with the other mothers and nannies by the school's elaborate wrought iron gate.

"Here they come!"

As though attending to a group of celebrities, the crowd of mothers hovered and fluttered as their children emerged through the gate, and Amy felt heartened by this exuberant display of parental affection, and then positively dazzled at the sight of her very own Ferry, walking out of the school with his overstuffed backpack and a shy grin on his face. He was still wearing a nametag on his shirt that identified him as FERRIS, which made him seem like a little businessman, both the nametag and the name itself (it was Uno's last name, a sop to her father, who disowned her anyway).

"How was it?" she asked, grabbing him and smooching him on both cheeks. Of course he had been to preschool and of course he'd had nannies and of course she'd rarely spent the entire day with him before but still she felt like she hadn't seen him in a million years, she'd missed him that much, and somehow he'd also gotten older.

"It was good!"

"What did you do?"

"Could you put me down? You're squishing me."

She planted him back on the sidewalk and together they walked, holding hands, around the corner and down Second Avenue, past the grocery store and the bakery and the drugstore. "You know you're going to learn to read this year."

"I already read!"

"But I mean *really* read. Long words, the newspaper, whatever you want."

"I don't think I want to read the newspaper, Mama."

"One day you might."

"I don't know," he said. "Can I get a boba?"

They were half a block away from the boba place they both liked; Amy pretended to think about it. "Have you been a good boy?"

"I've been medium-good?" Ferry said. "I forgot to put the seat up when I peed."

"Did you remember to wash your hands?"

He nodded.

"Good enough, then," she said. "Let's go."

But as they were leaving the boba shop, a shadowy figure, like something out of a horror movie, grabbed at her boy with a clawlike hand. While they had been in the boba shop the sky had turned cloudy and as the figure grabbed at Ferry, Amy suddenly had the feeling of being whisked into a nightmare. "No!" she shrieked, grabbing him backward, but it was New York and no one noticed.

"*He is mine*," the woman said. Uno, eyes bloodshot, her long hair in her face, her voice crackling, but Ferry stood still, holding tight to his boba. She was wearing a sweatshirt with the sleeves rolled up so you could see the track marks, smelling like death and God knows what she was on, and Amy realized she'd been waiting for this day to come for years without realizing she'd been waiting for it.

"Amy, stop it, you're frightening him."

But Uno wouldn't let go. She had tears running down her face now, and she held on to Ferry's arm but her grasp was weak, and Amy wasn't sure what to do here; she picked him up, Uno still clutching his arm. Could she run like this, Uno just hanging on? And then, like a hallucination, like a waking nightmare, Amy saw Uno grab a folding knife from her pocket—was she fucking kidding?—and open the knife with a shaking hand. "If you don't give him to me I will kill myself."

"Amy, Jesus—" She held Ferry to herself, mashed his face into her chest so he wouldn't see what his mother was doing. He dropped the boba and wailed.

"I swear to fucking God I will kill myself right here if you don't give me my child."

"Amy, come on, please—"

"*Give me my child*," she hissed, and the knife was steely in front of her; Amy's whole line of vision seemed to dwindle to the blade of the knife, and slowly, slowly, Amy felt her grip on Ferry loosen.

"Put down the knife," Amy said.

"Give me my child."

"Mom?" Ferry had turned his head, he saw his mother, he saw his boba on the sidewalk, but still, he stopped crying. Amy took her hands off the boy. "Mom?" It wasn't clear who he was talking to.

Uno had the knife back in her pocket and her hands on Ferry's shoulders and then she was hurrying him away like she was capturing a hostage and Amy had no idea what to do; with shaking hands she grabbed her phone and dialed Judd as she tailed them down Second Avenue and then Uno hailed a cab and pushed Ferry in it and Amy couldn't believe it as she hailed another cab and screamed "Follow that one! Follow that one!" like she was in some kind of crazy cop movie. The cabby turned to her and looked at her like she was insane—which one did he want her to follow?—and when Judd picked up the phone (she had to dial and redial to get him to pick up) she was sobbing, *Please, please, she took Ferry, please*—

And Judd knew what she was talking about, thank God, she didn't have to explain, and she realized her cab hadn't gone anywhere, was still stalled out on the corner of Second and Seventh.

"What's her address? Judd what's her address?"

Uno's townhouse was in Gramercy, just twenty or so blocks north. Amy gave the cabby the address. She tried to control her breathing but she could not.

What was happening to them? Was she hurting him? She wouldn't— she would hurt herself a million times over but she would never dare hurt him, would she? She wouldn't. She said she loved him more than life itself and they had always believed her. Uno had never been violent before. She had been distracted, asleep, sometimes almost vegetative, she had been careless, she had been anguished, she had been vacant or truant or almost dead. But she had never caused him physical pain. If she had, they would have cut her out of his life entirely (Amy would have insisted on it, biology be damned, she would have fucking insisted).

When they reached Uno's block, she threw two twenties at the cabby and slammed the door and she realized she was shaking as she raced up the townhouse stairs. She wasn't sure if she should call the police to meet her—would that make Uno act more rashly?—or if she should just wait for Judd on the steps or if she should try the doors herself.

She tried the doors; they opened.

"Ferry?"

The townhouse had a double-height entryway; her voice echoed. "Amy? Ferry?" She could hear the tremble in her voice: *please please please.*

She followed the hallway toward the low voices she heard, toward a kitchen. Marble, stainless steel, modernist lighting fixtures, light streaming in from the huge north-facing windows, and Uno and Ferry, their heads bent in the same exact way, their hair the same exact color, leaning together at the kitchen table looking at something.

Amy could feel her hands shaking.

Neither one of them looked up. She had no idea what to do; if she startled them, if she said something to them, would Uno—

"Dos?" Ferry said, looking up. "Why are you here?"

She felt the tears rush to her eyes. Her baby.

"I just—I wanted to make sure you were okay."

"I'm good," he said. "I'm showing Mom the pictures we drew of our pets at school. Some kids didn't have pets though so they had to draw pictures of their stuffed animals."

Uno did not look up.

"Okay," Amy said.

"But I drew Leo and Heidi and William and Junebug and Shawarma."

"That's great, sweetie."

"You want to see?"

"Of course I want to see," Amy said, and came over to where they were sitting and thought how easy it would be to take Uno by the thin neck and just crunch her bones. She was still shaking—*still!*— the adrenaline refusing to abate. Uno still smelled like whatever she smelled like, whatever she cooked with. It was a travesty to smell this way around a child.

"Those are great, honey."

"Can you tell who's who?"

"Well, this is Leo, of course," Amy said, pointing to the doggiest-looking drawing. "And then I guess this one is William, and this is Heidi?"

"Mom, no! Heidi is this one!"

"Of course," Amy said. "Silly me." She was so fragile, she could kill her with a strong slap. "Well, I guess I'll wait here for you two to finish up?"

"You don't have to," Uno said. "You don't have to wait."

"I think I do," Amy said, and Uno did not respond.

So she sat down at the table, breathing in and out and waiting for Judd to arrive, and when he finally did (ten minutes? A million years?) he stormed into the kitchen and Ferry shouted "Daddy!" And he carried him out in his arms.

And Amy went back into the kitchen to say something to Uno (*don't you ever, ever pull a stunt like that again or I'll throw you in jail*), but Uno was fast asleep on the kitchen table, drool pooling out of her mouth, and anyway none of it mattered, they had their boy, there was nothing else they needed.

SIXTEEN

IN THE MORNING, a brisk knock on the door. Maybe that's what had woken her up. A brisk knock, then another. Irine?

"Come in?" She was sitting in bed, still wearing the sweatpants she'd worn the day before. She could only guess what her hair looked like. The knocker knocked again.

"Jesus." She ran her hands through her hair, then cupped them around her mouth to test how bad her breath smelled (bad!). But she opened the door anyway. It was a granny, beckoning. Amy held up a finger, the universal sign for one minute, pulled her hair into something like a bun and followed her downstairs. Could she stop to brush her teeth? The granny looked at her expectantly, so Amy followed her down to the kitchen, where, on the kitchen table, sat a giant, an absolutely gargantuan, globe-shaped vase of flowers.

"What on earth?" Marmar? No—Bachana! It was Bachana.

"Your name," Bachana said and pointed to a card on the table.

Roses, hydrangeas, daises, tulips, so much greenery she could feed a cow breakfast. Bachana handed her the card.

Just thinking of you. J.

God. She never called him J.

"They're from my husband," Amy said. "In New York."

"He misses you?"

"I suppose," Amy said, although the flowers didn't feel like a missing-you kind of gesture as much as they felt like a demand.

"What you do with them?"

A fair question—they took up half the table.

"Do you want them?"

"Me?"

"Like, do you want to put them in your room? I don't think I have room in mine for all these flowers."

"I don't have room," Bachana said. "Who has room?"

And Amy felt herself flood with embarrassment. How had Judd found out how to send her a bouquet in Tbilisi? Was he trying to show off their American extravagance? Did he have any idea what things looked like on the ground over here? And with Maia gone, and who knew what Irine was doing, and this insane display of disposable wealth, it was so tone deaf.

She caught herself. No, of course he could not know what things looked like on the ground over here. She had never told him; he had never asked.

"They are very beautiful," Bachana said. "So many roses. I never see so many."

"Yes," Amy said, looking again at the card. *Just thinking of you.* All these flowers and this was the best he could think to say.

He'd been with Meret while she was here. He had to have been. Why on earth would he have sent these flowers otherwise? Amy waited for her gut to roil in jealousy or disgust, felt faint surprise when it didn't. In fact, all she felt was a cementing of the distance between whatever New York could offer her and whatever she could do here in Georgia.

"We will fix it," Bachana said. She turned, pulled some wine bottles out of the garbage bin in the corner of the room.

"What will we fix?"

"The big size." Bachana rinsed out two bottles and filled each with tap water. She then brought the bottles to the kitchen table and expertly pulled a few roses from the bouquet, a bit of greenery, some dahlias. Artfully, she arranged two small bouquets in each wine bottle.

"You like?" Bachana asked.

"Beautiful."

Soon she and Bachana were rinsing and filling bottles—they spread eight out on the table and yanked enough flowers for all of them. Outside the window, she heard barking and yipping; one of the other grannies had let the dogs outside for their afternoon fresh air. Amy thought she should probably walk some of them. As much fun as they had humping each other outside, it wasn't really exercise.

"What do you think?" she asked Bachana, showing off one of her vases, this one filled with hydrangeas.

"Yes, good," Bachana said. She finished planting a few sprigs of delphinium among the roses in her bottle. "This is nice, yes?"

"Lovely," Amy said. "You should keep that one."

Fifteen years ago, Amy and Judd had walked from the East Village to their courthouse wedding. Somewhere on the Bowery they came across a bodega with a half dozen buckets of flowers by its side door: roses and tulips, of course, but also dahlias and peonies, anemones, orchids, and callas. Judd stopped her. "You need flowers," he said.

"Oh, come on," Amy said. She had promised herself she would be businesslike throughout this; she would be controlled. She would not let this new thing she was getting, this new family, this new life, make her collapse with emotion. She was holding tight to Ferry's stroller.

"'Come on' what?" Judd said. He was wearing a suit, he looked so handsome. She was wearing a white silk blouse and white jeans.

Out of the bucket: fragrant lilacs, white daisies, a lily of the valley. There was a sleeve of butcher paper; Judd wrapped them. "For you," he said. In return, she plucked an orchid for his buttonhole and another one for Ferry to hold.

"Now we're a proper wedding party," Judd said.

She kissed him, still holding tight to Ferry's stroller. As safe as she had ever been in the world.

Bachana held up her vase to the light streaming through the kitchen window. The light beamed through the silky petals of a pale pink rose. "Your husband often sends you flowers?"

She thought of the orchid in Judd's buttonhole. "He used to."

"But no more?"

The ceremony had been brief. Ferry had fallen asleep in his stroller. Jorge, the dishwasher, had popped some nonalcoholic bubbly in the courthouse lobby ("I wasn't sure we could bring booze in here."). They went out for lunch, went home for a nap, were back at the restaurant for dinner service.

"We've been married for a long time," Amy said.

"Ah," said Bachana. "And you are not happy anymore?"

"Happy?" Amy considered it. "I guess sometimes. But I just couldn't go on the way we were going, you know? I felt like I couldn't stand one more day with him. So I guess that's not very happy." She slid a rose into the vase she was working on; the stem jammed. "I was always just—I was the support beam of our marriage. I wanted to see what would happen if I went away." Amy picked up another bouquet, turned it this way and that. Some baby's breath here? Or here?

"There was another woman?"

"Another woman?" God, she was so obvious. "Probably. Maybe. I'm not sure."

"There are always other women," Bachana said.

What kind of marriage had *she* had? "I guess that's true."

They were quiet for several minutes, completing their vases, taking tulips out of one, moving hydrangeas into another.

"Men all over the world are the same," Bachana said. "They always chase after other women. They cannot help it. They have a drive to— how do you say this? To populate the world."

Amy laughed. Men *were* the same. No, she did not miss him.

"New York, Tiflis, no matter," Bachana said, shaking her head. "My husband, when he was alive, he had so many women!"

"But you stayed together?"

"Yes, of course," Bachana said. "I just tell him, you can do what you want but if you bring me another woman's baby I'm throwing it in the river."

Amy laughed again; Bachana wasn't smiling but she had a mischievous look in her eyes. "And if you bring me disease I throw *you* in the river."

Amy nodded. "Fair enough."

"So we agreed," Bachana said. "No baby, no disease. Flirt, do what you do, I don't ask. You come home at night, you earn your wages. I don't ask!"

"And it didn't bother you?"

"Not so much—sometimes I flirt too! There used to be more men in my life, too. Aren't there men for you? You are so pretty!"

"No," Amy said. "I've been faithful to my husband."

"Ah," Bachana said. "For us," she continued, "we were not as faithful, but we come home to each other every night. It was okay. We were married for twenty-eight years. I think it was a good marriage for most of those years, you know? We understood one another."

"What happened?"

"He died. Almost seven years ago, cancer of the stomach."

"I'm sorry."

"Well, everyone dies," she said. "At his funeral, I look at the women there, I think—was it you? Or you? But I was curious, not angry. I felt so sad for him, at the end. There was so much pain. Stomach cancer is very terrible."

"I'm sorry," Amy said again. "I really am."

Bachana fidgeted with one of the vases. "We had known each other since we were children. At the end I held his hand. I said to him, thank you for this life that you have given me. I am not angry about anything at all. I don't know if he heard me at that point."

Bachana was smiling now, at the memory or at Amy.

"Did you two have children?"

"One, a son. He lives in Kazakhstan, works on oil pipeline. I visit him two years ago, but I did not like it," she said. "Very hot and dry. And the food!" She wrinkled her nose. "But he makes a living and sends money sometimes."

"You must miss him."

"Of course," Bachana said. "And I miss my husband too. It surprises you what can happen."

"Everything surprises me," Amy said. "All the time."

"Come, we deliver flowers. You can carry?"

"I can carry."

They gathered up the wine bottles in their arms, and Amy followed Bachana down a different passageway out of the kitchen, this one wallpapered in a maroon paisley pattern, the strips of paper peeling haphazardly. A short staircase up and then Bachana pushed open a narrow wooden door. "Marmar," she said. The room was small and spare, with a twin-sized bed and a small chest of drawers. A wooden cross with drooping arms dangled from a chain in the window.

"Huh," Amy said.

They placed a vase of flowers on the chest and went to the next room, Natela's, which looked much the same as Marmar's, same cross and everything, and then they placed a vase in a tiny spare room where Zazi lay sleeping on a rug.

"Bad dog!" Bachana said. "You should be downstairs!"

Zazi looked up with a guilty dog expression and fell back asleep.

"We give Irine next."

"Is she home?"

Bachana shook her head. "She went to work. We let dogs out together this morning, maybe five? I don't think she slept at all."

"God, that's the worst."

"Maia is making her very crazy. I say to her I'm glad I had son. I don't think I could manage daughter."

"I know what you mean."

"We do this quick, okay?" Bachana said, opening the door to Irine's room, and Amy suddenly felt like she was trespassing, like Irine would not want her in this room, which was messy, unmade bed, clothes on the floor, smelling faintly like smoke and some kind of strong perfume. A formal portrait of a family hung on the wall over a bureau: Irine, a small Maia, a handsome, dark-eyed man. Nobody in the portrait was smiling.

"Is that Maia's father?"

"Yes," Bachana said. "But he left a long time ago. I don't know why she keeps picture."

"He left?"

"Another woman," Bachana said. "Remember how I told you? All men the same."

She put a vase on the bureau, which made a strange tableau, the wine bottle of flowers underneath the family portrait.

"How long ago did that happen?"

"Oh, many years. Maia was two."

"That's when my father left," Amy said. "I mean, that's how old I was."

"Your father left?"

Amy nodded. "We never saw him again."

"He is alive?" Bachana said.

"I really don't know," Amy said, surprised by a passing breeze of sadness. But why? It was fine, it had been fine, it was how it always had been.

"Maia's father died in car accident after he left. With other woman in car. Terrible accident. Car fell down the hills, a big explosion."

"How awful!"

"No, we were happy. He was a bastard." Bachana adjusted the vase on Irine's bureau. "We go?"

"Um, sure."

They had three vases left; Amy followed Bachana up another short set of stairs. She walked more quickly than Amy would have expected—"We go in here?" "No, that's closet"—and then down another hallway.

"My grandfather build this house, did you know?" Bachana said. "Three houses next to each other, he combine them. But he did not know anything about architecture, as you can see."

"When was this?"

"Maybe 1900, maybe a few years before? It was before Soviets, I know that. You could still purchase property. My grandfather had money, then lost money, then had money again. You know? Always doing different jobs."

"I know people like that."

"He bought these houses when he had money," Bachana said. "Then he lost it all again doing—what do you call it? With horse races?"

"Gambling?"

"Gambling, yes. But then, when Soviets came, he got job with city gas company, was able to keep the house. He had to bribe someone lot of money for the job. So we had big house but no money. Sometimes Soviets put other people in house with us but sometimes they didn't. People coming and going."

"Was it like this your whole childhood?"

"Oh yes," Bachana said. "It was how I meet my husband! That room was his and his mother's when he was a boy. His father died in the war." She pointed at a doorway.

Amy tried to imagine if she would have married Judd if she'd known him since he was a child. Would she have loved him more then, or less?

Bachana shrugged. "It was how things used to be. Not like where you are from, where everyone has own house," she said.

"Not everyone," Amy said, then considered. "But, I suppose, most people."

"You know," Bachana said, holding her flowers against her bosom, "I always feel sorry for Americans. Having to always to think about money. Having to buy so many things all the time." She knocked on the door they were standing by and pushed it open.

"Maia."

"I'm not sure—"

"Go on," Bachana said, ushering her in. "It is disaster but we don't stay very long."

Maia's room, once Bachana's husband's boyhood room, was larger than most of the others and a total mess, but Amy understood it immediately as a walk-through history of the person Maia had been and who she had become. She had seen rooms like this before, had even had one, sort of, when she was a teenager. The walls were still the baby pink of a little girl, but they were covered in adolescent posters: Che Guevara and the Ukrainian flag and Keith Haring and "Fuck Putin" and the European Union flag and Barack Obama and Rihanna, which was frankly a bit surprising. And posters of bands she'd never heard of.

Amy had the same sense of trespass that she'd had in Irine's room, but for some reason that sense of trespass was not matched by an equal urge to get out. She was too curious. Lacy black underwear strewn across the floor. A silver bra. Black combat boots with yellow laces. Ripped jeans, a ripped jean skirt, a backpack, phone chargers, paperback novels, socks.

Taped to the wall by Maia's bed, a small photograph of the same image that was on Irine's wall: mother, father, child.

"Do you think Maia remembers her father?"

"I don't think so," Bachana said. "She was too young."

Amy wondered if that was something she could talk about with Maia, that she too was fatherless and always had been. Or would Maia care? Something about this room made Amy feel in touch with her own impoverished younger self, the person she had been before she knew she'd escape Minnesota. A person who thought her ambitions would only ever be realized in her head. She had been a mess, too. She had liked to draw and liked to read. Of course Maia was much more driven than she had been, was much more willing to fight.

"It is such garbage pit in here," Bachana said. She stooped to pick up some T-shirts, dropped them in a bin in the corner. "She does not take care of anything."

Amy put the vase of flowers down on Maia's desk, next to journals, books, papers covered in flowery Georgian script. A large pile of Polaroids and a kitschy miniature Polaroid camera. Lipsticks, eyeliners. Pencil drawings of cats with wings, cats holding swords, dragons. They weren't bad, actually. Drawings of beautiful women, some of them naked. A chemistry textbook. A math textbook.

Amy couldn't stop herself—she rifled through the Polaroids.

Maia and her friends at a nightclub. At a restaurant. Maia in this very bedroom, smiling coyly. Her shirt and silver bra straps hanging off her shoulders.

And then photos of another girl, naked from the waist up, on Maia's bed.

And then several close ups. The girl smiling. A come-hither smile. A selfie of the two of them kissing, topless.

Well, of course.

Did Irine know? She must. If Maia was trying to keep a secret, why would she keep these Polaroids out?

Or was it a dare? To see if her mother would see what was hiding in her own house?

The other girl was beautiful, long brown hair, clear brown eyes. No tattoos. Amy thought back to the last time she saw pictures she wasn't supposed to see and felt a tingle crawl up her neck. This was no business of hers.

Bachana was still tossing clothing into the bin. Amy slid the racier Polaroids back in the middle of the stack and tried to make the stack look disheveled in exactly the same way it had been before she'd gone snooping.

"Come on," Amy said. "We shouldn't go through her things."

"Such a messy girl," Bachana said. "I do her laundry but last time I try she yell at me to leave her things alone."

"Kids like to be private."

"You be glad someone do your laundry!" Bachana said. "We have two more flowers. One for you, one for me?"

"That sounds right."

She and Bachana parted ways in the kitchen, and Amy brought her vase up her own winding passageway. At Andrei's door, she paused for just a moment, then knocked. "I have a present."

He was sitting at his computer like usual, spartan room, neatly made bed, no photographs on the walls or in frames, no disorder of any kind. A duffel bag in the corner. His winter coat on a hook.

She wondered what he would say if he knew what she'd just seen. She couldn't tell him. In his part of the world this sort of behavior could cost you your family or your job (sometimes in her part of the world, too).

So instead, she said: "I brought you these."

"Flowers?" He looked at her, a crinkly half-smile.

"It's a long story," she said. She put them down next to his computer and then took a step away.

He picked up the vase and held the flowers to his nose. "They don't smell."

"Hydrangeas don't really have a strong scent."

"This is what they are called?"

"Hydrangeas," she said. "Those puffy blue ones." She approached his desk again, fluffed the flowers in the vase, aware that she was performing for him and intruding on him at the same time.

"Ah," he said. Then: "You are looking for the dog today?"

She sighed. What else did she have to do here? What else was there to do? She wanted to find Maia, to see if she was all right, to say I know who you are, I know about your father, I know about your girlfriend, I know why you are fighting. I can be a friend to you. But she didn't have the courage.

"Yes," she said. "I'm going to leave in a few minutes."

He nodded at her. It was a beautiful day out, or rather afternoon, the sun streaming in, the birds twittering outside.

"Do you want to come with me?"

"I will."

"You will?"

"Where are you going to look?" he asked. "Have you been to Mtatsminda Church? Are you still having a hard time with your breath?"

She was offended. "I'm not having a hard time with my breath. I just didn't want to walk so fast last night."

He gave her another half-smile, those perfectly shaped lips. "Meet me in the kitchen in ten minutes. I show you where you should look for this dog."

SEVENTEEN

SHE BRUSHED HER teeth, slapped on some deodorant, untangled her hair, and then, after taking a closer look, shoved a baseball cap on her head. On her way to the kitchen she almost tripped over Zazi.

"Who let you up here, anyway?" she asked. Zazi looked aggrieved.

Andrei was already in the kitchen; the table was still scattered with greenery and the fat glass globe her bouquet had come in. "These were your flowers?"

"They were just too big," Amy said.

Andrei smirked, and she could almost hear him think *American,* but she didn't say anything and neither did he. Zazi followed them as they walked downstairs. "Is he coming?"

"I think he is." She had a leash in her backpack, attached it to a patient Zazi's collar, and they let the small mutt lead them down the street and up, this time, toward the hills that overlooked Tbilisi.

If she told him about Maia, if she said, *I think I know why they fight all the time, I think I understand*—she would probably just be doing it for the gossip of it, or to have something to talk about with him. Which was one of her bad habits, the way she would spill secrets when she was nervous or wanted something to say. But there was nothing Maia would gain from having Andrei know about her, and therefore it was irresponsible to tell him. And if Irine didn't know, how terrible it would be for the American stranger and the Russian lodger to know something Irine didn't about her own daughter.

But also, *also,* it was possible she was misinterpreting—or maybe over-interpreting—the photos. Ferry's friends' approaches to sex and sexuality and gender were so different from her own, so fluid as to be basically a puddle. His friends looked like anything, man, woman, in-between, and dressed like one another and went to the prom in a big group and, Ferry said, slept with everyone, no matter the gender— well, *he* didn't, that wasn't his thing (he said and she believed him)— but basically teenagers were so much less anguished about sex than she had been and so much more open to doing it with just about anyone or nobody at all. And proud of it. Perhaps that was the way of teenagers all over the world these days?

And how well she remembered her brother's anguished time in the closet, his celibacy throughout high school, how he preferred to be friendless rather than have any friends who might know his secret, how, even now, he couldn't believe his own fortune to be married to someone he loved.

She was self-conscious about her breathing as she followed Andrei up the windy streets, but she was now used to the way he walked in silence, a step or so in front of her. Zazi was a commanding walker, too, but every so often he would stop to sniff a bush or pee on a par- ticularly enticing patch of grass and she would have a chance to catch her breath. Andrei would vanish into the distance while she waited for the dog to do his business. Which was okay. She had a sort of radarlike way of sensing where Andrei was.

The breeze blew the fur on Zazi's back straight up, and he lunged or barked at each passing dog or bird, or sniffed eagerly at the ground to smell the messages that other animals had left in their urine. Up, up they climbed, higher than anywhere that Amy had climbed so far in this strange city. The buildings were starting to recede and now they were traversing a path through some scrubby brushland, pine trees ahead, and Amy thought that it was possible Andrei had no idea where he was going and was just interested in pushing her off a cliff. Which would be a surprise! But anything was possible here!

"You okay?" he called from fifty paces ahead.

"I'm great!" she called back as chirpily as possible. From here the path jutted up steeply. Zazi was cruising jauntily ahead of her, yanking her upward, and she had half a mind to let him off the leash so he could bounce ahead but of course that was the most common way for dogs to get killed.

"Zazi," she said, "just give me a second? Please?"

The dog returned to her side, stood next to her, looked up with an obedient expression.

The air was cooler up here, and thinner, or maybe that was just her imagination, and it smelled like juniper. Above them, all she could see were rows of evergreens, and she was sure that behind her lay an impossibly beautiful view, but she wasn't particularly interested in turning around. She had forgotten that, under extreme circumstances, she could be a little bit afraid of heights.

"Doing all right?" Andrei asked, lumbering back down the path and lighting a cigarette.

Smoking during a hike like this!

"Want one?" he asked.

"Sure," she said, withdrawing one from his pack and letting him light it for her. She wondered if the trees were dry up here, if there were forest fires. She wondered what they would do if a spark suddenly caught. She wondered about her lung function and what all this smoking was going to do to her airways and to her face. She hadn't even put sunscreen on today. She hadn't even brushed her hair.

"You're not looking at the view," Andrei said.

"Not yet," she said.

"It is a nice one," he said.

"I'm sure," she said.

"Do you not like to look at views?"

"I'm just focusing on the path ahead," she said, trying to avoid his half-smile. "Where are we going again?"

"To a church on the side of this mountain," he said. "It is very nice. They have a lot of dogs up there."

"They have a lot of dogs everywhere."

"Yes, but they also have beautiful views." Andrei took a final drag, then flicked his smoldering cigarette butt into the distance.

"You realize you could start a forest fire that way, right?"

"What do I realize?"

"You could start a fire."

He just looked at her.

"Don't you have forest fires in Russia?"

Andrei snickered and began walking back up the trail. She hadn't yet finished her cigarette, which was almost certainly for the best. She shouldn't be smoking entire cigarettes here or anywhere. She stamped it out and then picked up the butt carefully by the end. Because there were no trash bins, she stuck the butt in her pocket.

When she and Zazi caught up with Andrei again, he was standing outside a brownish-gray stone church that seemed to have been planted among the trees by a mysterious giant. To the side of the church was a graveyard, each headstone different from one another, some somber and sturdy-looking and others fabulously ornate, and almost all of them huge. Amy followed Zazi to a tombstone that looked like a giant man leaning over from his pedestal as if to embrace them. Quietly, with some dignity, Zazi peed on the pedestal.

Because the ground she was standing on was flat, and because the tombstone was freaking her out, Amy finally turned to assess the view of the valley below. It was indeed beautiful. And because the day was clear, she could see all the way across to the hills on the other side of the valley, to what she imagined was Asia.

"I think I see your dog," Andrei said.

"You do? You see Angel?"

"I think I do," he said, and even though she didn't believe him she followed him around a bend to where several more graves were assembled and, asleep among them, lay a runty brown dog with short legs and pointy ears.

"Andrei, do you even know what Angel looks like?"

"She looks like a dog, yes?"

"She's white, first of all."

"So this is not her?"

Zazi was barking excitedly at the presence of the brown dog, who opened one eye in irritation. "It is not her."

"I'm sorry," Andrei said, but the twinkle in his eye suggested that he was, perhaps, flirting.

She grinned. "I don't think you actually are."

The gravestones circled the church; Amy and Andrei followed the path around, rousing a few more sleeping dogs (black, black and gray, sort of yellowish) and passing graves that looked like grapevines, like stern old men, like gates, like angels. Andrei did not seem particularly interested in any of them, but Amy paused to look at each and try to make out the inscriptions (impossible; half were in Georgian and the other half Cyrillic).

"Who do you think these people were?"

"Writers, politicians," he said.

"Were they famous?"

"Who can say?" He paused in front of a Cyrillic gravestone. "It says this man was the first translator of Pushkin into the Georgian language. I'm not sure that makes you famous though, even here."

"I read Pushkin in college," she said.

"They assign Pushkin in the United States?"

"Tolstoy, Dostoevsky, Chekhov," she said. "Advanced World Literature my senior year."

"I'm impressed."

She smiled at him, and he smiled back.

"So who was this guy?" She pointed to a figure of an enormous angel carrying a child draped in greenish metal robes. "Another translator?"

"The mayor of Tbilisi in the 1930s," Andrei said.

"Pretty fancy gravestone for a mayor."

"Soviet mayors had big jobs," Andrei said. "They had to figure out which bribes to accept, who to report to senior authorities," he said. "Who the Jews were, who the capitalists were."

"The Jews?"

"Of course the Jews. And sometimes the Catholics too."

Andrei sat down on a bench near the church wall, shook out his cigarettes. Amy sat next to him, calibrating exactly how many inches she could put between them.

"And also you had to make sure nobody was coming for you and what to do about it if they were," he said. "All while pleasing the party officials. Best case you were fired. Worst case, the police came to your door."

"Oy," Amy said.

"Yes, but I should say that this is not how I grew up. By the time I was a kid, all that was gone. We didn't really have a system anymore."

"It was the same sort of chaos they had here," Amy said.

"I suppose," he said. "People who thought they would have jobs when they finished high school—there were no more jobs. And the inflation meant that whatever you had was suddenly worthless. There were no more police, there was nothing."

He offered her a cigarette but she did not accept; really, the smoking had become too much. But after they sat in silence for a minute she changed her mind and took one.

"That's why they love him, you know," he said. "He made them feel safe again."

"I know," Amy said.

They sat next to each other on the bench for a several quiet minutes, but it was a nice kind of quiet, the wind in the trees and the animals flitting about the graveyard and Zazi sighing at their feet.

"What did you think about Americans?" she asked. "When you were a kid?"

"About you?" He laughed. "Americans love to know what other people think about Americans. Every American I've ever worked with, they always want to know what do you think of our food? What do you think of our cars? They want us to be impressed."

"Are you?"

She held her breath.

"Sometimes."

Zazi was dozing at their feet, and a few yards away was another dog, stretched out in the sunshine, but not Angel. Of course not Angel. She was suddenly certain she would never find Angel. But right then, on this bench, she did not feel like a fool.

"To tell you the truth, we have everything that you have in America, and some of it is better. My guess is that maybe even a lot of it is better. Our subway is better. Our bread."

"Hmmm," she said. "Do you have skiing?"

"We have skiing."

Amy hated skiing. "Do you have pizza?"

"Excellent pizza."

"Do you have baseball?"

He chuckled. "Nobody in Russia has the least bit of interest in baseball. But if we did, I guarantee you our stadiums would be top-notch. Did you see the Sochi Olympics?"

Amy never watched the Olympics. "I heard you guys did a pretty good job."

"I don't know," he said. "I never watch the Olympics."

She laughed.

"Of course, not everything is better. Air, water, traffic, our politics. It is all quite bad. And if you are poor, it is even worse than that."

"But you are not poor," she said.

"I am not," he said. "In many ways, in fact, I have wealth."

If she had dared reach out to Andrei, if she had taken his hand, if she had touched his face—the wind whipped against them every so often and she could use it as a pretext, somehow, dead leaves flying at her, to lean into him. She knew how to do it, she used to do it. She could maybe even make him think it was his idea. But she wouldn't do it. She was enjoying being with him too much to want to break the spell of being with him, to want to even risk breaking it.

Still, he saw her sneaking a look at him. "Yes?"

"Yes?" she said.

"You were thinking something?"

She did not want to know about his wife; she wanted to know everything about the wife. "Tell me about your wife."

He took a drag of his cigarette, blew smoke toward the sky.

"She worked for Colgate-Palmolive."

"The toothpaste people," Amy said.

"Toothpaste, detergent, yes."

That was not what Amy had expected. "She didn't mind working for an American company?"

"Why should she mind? She made a decent salary. But Colgate closed its Moscow branch after the war started, so she found a new position at a Chinese firm. They pay more."

She sold toothpaste for a Chinese firm. Amy had expected an artist, a painter. Or, for some reason, a shabby housewife. "What's she like?"

"What is she like?"

"What's her name? What sorts of—I don't know, what does she look like?"

His eyes wrinkled a little bit. "Her name is Lena," he said. "She has some Korean family somewhere, so she has black hair. So does our daughter. And brown eyes. But our daughter has blue eyes, like me."

"Lucky girl."

He smiled. Those eyes.

Lena.

"Where did you meet?"

"Online," he said.

"I didn't know Russians had online dating."

"We have all the things you have, Amy."

"I know, I just—" Actually, she still didn't know.

"We texted for a while and then we met at a bar for the first time. I was surprised at how she looked, even better than the pictures she sent me. That was the first thing I said to her. She said I looked worse than the pictures I sent, but that's what she'd been expecting, so she was not disappointed."

How on earth could he have looked worse? "When did you get married?"

"When we discovered she was pregnant," he said. "I didn't see myself getting married, but she was traditional, and then her father told me that if I didn't marry her he was going to crash my car with me in it." He smiled. "So we married."

"Was it a nice wedding?"

"It was a very nice wedding," Andrei said. "And then she had the baby two months after that." He flicked away his cigarette. "She was a very nice baby."

He shook out another. He was going to get cancer; did all men in Russia get cancer?

"Did you ever want more?"

"More what?"

"Kids?"

"No," he said. "She was all we wanted. We didn't think it could ever be any better."

"I know what you mean," she said.

On the telephone wires strung in the distance, Amy could see a few crows settle and squawk. Or maybe not crows—these birds seemed bigger, even from a distance.

They lifted off the telephone wire as a single unit, squawking again as they passed overhead.

"Does your daughter get your emails?"

"She does," Andrei said.

"What do you write to her about?"

He didn't say anything for a moment, and Amy thought that she had finally asked too much.

But then he said: "Mostly I write about life on the front. The battlefront. Battlefield? I'm not sure how you say it. I believe she currently thinks I'm in Donetsk. She thinks I'm a soldier."

It took Amy a moment. "Ah."

"I tell her about members of my battalion. I tell her how we won the latest fights, how the Ukrainians are welcoming us like heroes, that sort of thing."

Amy nodded at him, kept her eyes on the valley.

"It is what her mother wants," he said. "When I video with her, I turn off all the lights and tell her that my fellow soldiers are sleeping in the barracks." He was leaning forward with his elbows on his knees. "Or that they've all gone to a hospital or to a school or something. To help save the Ukrainians."

Amy stayed quiet.

"Or she shows me the drawings she has made at school. I'm holding a gun, or I'm rescuing an old woman from a Nazi. She's a good artist."

Amy wondered if a day would come where he had to tell her the truth. If not, he'd be spared, but if so—if so, at least he'd get to see her again.

"She makes me promise her that I won't get hurt."

"How do you respond?" Amy asked.

"I am happy to promise that," he said. "Since I will not be getting hurt."

She didn't say anything else, and neither did he. She thought: *The valley below us is open like a thousand questions.* The thought ran into her mind but she wasn't sure what it meant. But it stayed there, circled around.

Across the world, parents and children writing letters to each other, creating a reality they thought the other person wanted, or simply lying. To what end? To protect what? And what did they destroy along the way?

Zazi was paying attention to a small black bird, and Amy was afraid he'd get up and chase after it and she'd have to follow. But she didn't want to stand up, didn't want to make Andrei think that she judged what he was saying or thought worse of him, because she didn't. He loved his daughter enough to lie instead of disappear.

"I'm sorry you have to do this."

"It is okay," he said. "It is not what I would have chosen, but I am glad that she is proud of me."

"You're a good dad," she said.

He looked at her then, and although he wasn't smiling, his glowing eyes seemed to lift at the edges.

Amy felt the air between them start to hum again, and the urge to take this man into her arms was almost overwhelming, but she had no idea what he would do, and that had never been her thing, she had never really been forward like that, and then he looked away from her, and the moment ended as quickly as it had started.

She wanted the moment to return. "Do you ever—"

Which was when a particularly ambitious bird dashed in front of them to grab something from the ground. Amy tightened her hold on Zazi's leash, but even a thirty-pound dog had the strength to move a woman a hundred pounds heavier when it was after something. Zazi pulled her off the bench toward the church, in the direction the bird had flown. Chasing him, she tripped on several stones buried in the grass and almost wiped out, a romantic comedy moment the afternoon didn't seem to call for.

Zazi stood at the tree trunk and barked furiously at the impudent bird, who stood on a branch, chittering.

"Let us go into the church," Andrei said, coming up behind her. "It is peaceful inside."

She and Zazi followed Andrei around the bend a little further until they came to the wooden double doors carved with intricate symbols. Zazi planted himself in the doorway, unwilling to come any further. Amy tied his leash to a sapling.

The air inside was filled with the smell of incense and swirls of smoke from what seemed like one thousand burning candles.

Andrei said, "There is never anyone here during the week."

"Then who lights the candles?"

He shrugged. "It is a mystery."

The church was not one of the grand stained-glass affairs Amy had seen in Paris and Rome, or even the more modest, wood-and-stucco ones she'd attended for weddings and funerals in the United States. This building felt like the home of a deeply religious grandmother, cluttered with candles, gilt portraits, heavy wooden furniture, velvet chairs, alcoves, statues, and candelabras. Toward the altar was a semicircle of life-sized icons, painted with gold and silver paint, creepy in their dead-eyed stares. The floors were cracked tile and the walls were painted with scowling angels and above the altar an image of God floated in a mist of brownish clouds. Below Him hung one of the drooping crosses.

"You've never been in an Orthodox church before," Andrei said.

"I haven't." She approached a life-sized painting, in the corner, of a woman holding a small child on her knee. Her skin was olive; her eyes were defiantly black.

Andrei stood next to her, but he was looking down at his phone, not at the painting.

In the dim light of the church, the woman's halo glowed.

"They consider them family, all of these saints," Andrei said, gesturing to the life-sized portraits that surrounded them, each with its own glowing halo. "They're like the parents and great-grandparents. They help you get your messages to God. If you find the right one to pray to, you'll get the results you want."

Amy moved from saint to saint and tried to figure out who did what as the smoke swirled around them, and the motes of dust floated in the thin light filtering through the stained glass. There was the old man with the lamb: the saint of shepherds? The young man wearing a crown made of pearls: the saint of wealth. The woman holding a cross with a grapevine wrapped around it. She locked eyes with the icon and waited for a sense of peace or understanding to wash over her, or even a guess as to what she should pray for. Maybe the grapes meant agriculture. She kept looking at her, though—her beautiful face, the delicate lips, the folds of her white gown. The halo around her was bigger than all the others, and she seemed to have a message barely hidden behind her lips.

She turned to say something to Andrei, but was surprised to see his eyes closed in front of her, his lips moving rapidly.

The sense of trespass was sudden and deep.

She moved away to let him pray for what he needed to pray for.

Outside the church, in the clean, cool air, Amy untied Zazi and stood for what felt like many minutes, leaving Andrei inside the church to ask for intercession.

The birds were at it again, flying and squawking, and Zazi stayed by her feet while she scratched the top of his head (good boy, such a good boy), and she thought about how some saints were holy fools, she had read that once somewhere, that a holy fool was someone who rejected the customs of the world to pursue godliness in all things, and that the truest holy fools were animals, because they had no need to participate in human life, they were incapable of society's failings and all of our failures, and they were therefore divine.

When Andrei emerged from the church, his eyes had tears in them, and Amy couldn't help herself—she reached out for him and folded him into her arms.

EIGHTEEN

THAT NIGHT, THE darkness seemed to come earlier, falling without any preamble. She dropped Zazi at the house, kept walking down the hill, and by the time she got to the bottom the sun had vanished behind a distant horizon.

The protesters were again milling about Rustaveli. There was no march yet—they saved that for later, when the moon was higher overhead—but Amy could see them preparing signs, flags, boots, waterproof coats. Whatever objectives they had screamed for yesterday were still unrealized. They would, therefore, keep screaming, and scream again and scream again until someone of importance blinked.

Amy was tired, she was hungry, she knew this wasn't her place. She walked down Rustaveli, past Liberty Square, past Stalin's seminary, down a few streets and then a few more until she came to a neighborhood she'd never seen before. Streetlights glowed. The area felt welcoming, or at least less tense than the street in front of Parliament Square. There was an almost Parisian feeling here, couples strolling

hand in hand, that sort of thing. Cobblestone sidewalks. A few restaurants beckoned, but when she peeked inside she saw clamorous groups
feasting together and she couldn't bear to be alone among them.

She kept walking.

It was the dogs of Tbilisi's witching hour, as the dogs she had pre-
viously only seen sleeping were now up and wandering about, visiting
the couples who were sitting outside under the heat lamps, begging
them for food. People seemed obliging, dropping bits of bread or meat
to the waiting dogs, who knew to take it gently. They had clearly
reached an agreement with the people who visited the restaurants on
these streets; you take care of us, we will be pleasing to you. And the
dogs did seem pleasing and easily pleased, sitting at attention, looking
up at the diners with their large, liquid eyes.

She was disgusted with herself and her circumstances; still, she
reached into her bag for a bully stick. A dog came up to her, a smallish
one, gray and spotted like an Australian shepherd, but small, with a
flat face. The dog sniffed at the stick once or twice, and Amy let him
take it from her hands, and he lay down with the stick between his
paws and nibbled it gently, looking up at Amy every so often with
arched eyebrows, a canine expression of gratitude. Amy crouched
down with her elbows on her knees, knowing that this dog would not
hurt her, that she could get close. That the dog's presence would be
calming.

The dog chewed gently on the stick but kept it tight between its
paws. She could not take it back. Nobody could.

Had she really come here to save Angel? Had she really thought
herself capable of finding one dog among the thousands in this sprawl-
ing city?

Was it possible she was as naïve as all that only a single week ago?

On the hilltop, mere hours ago: she had put her arms around
Andrei, had felt him relax into her for a moment, for a heartbeat. They
were the same height and she put her forehead against his and felt the

heat of his neck on her palms, and his arms were behind her back, and she knew what would happen here and she wanted it to happen, it was fine, she was betraying no one—in fact to *not* do this was to betray only herself.

They breathed like this, Zazi patient next to them, outside the church's doors. She felt the wind blow against her legs. She waited for him to kiss her, she turned her head slightly. All he had to do was move his.

Together, they breathed for several seconds. Her whole body tingling. She could have moved her lips just a millimeter, but she wanted him to be the one to do it, to kiss her first. They would make it back to the house somehow. They would make it to her tiny bedroom, or to his.

She kept her eyes tightly closed. He still smelled like the incense of the church, and his brand of Russian cigarettes, and whatever soap he used, and the sweetness of the air outside.

She told herself to remember this moment. She felt that her life would change forever.

And then: he pulled away. In fact, he took several steps back. He said, "Thank you"—and what was he thanking her for, exactly?

"Thank you?"

He looked at the ground. She said nothing.

"You must understand," he said. He was still several steps away. "I love my wife."

She must have looked perplexed.

"I would not be here," he said. "I would not do this if I did not love my wife."

"I don't—what wouldn't you do?"

"And you love your husband too," he said, and she wanted to know why he thought that, had she ever even *mentioned* Judd? And she was so embarrassed that she thought she might keel over but she didn't, she just picked up Zazi's leash, and said that maybe it was time to take him

home. Andrei said that he thought he'd stay on the hilltop awhile, that
he hadn't yet found whatever he had come up here for.

"We are both searching, Amy," he said.

But what on earth was he searching for? Had he ever shown any
indication of looking for anything?

And she thought about the tattoos and the beautiful eyes and the
long freezing walks without a coat and how she'd thought he was one
sort of person but actually he was just another *husband*, that's all he
was. Some lovesick husband. He belonged to someone else, and he
came from a monstrous place.

She led Zazi away from the church, trying not to run; she couldn't
trip and further humiliate herself. It turned out there was an easy-to-
follow path down the hill, they hadn't needed to bushwack their way
up the side of the mountain. The sky was a luminous, accusatory blue.
The same blue (of course) as Andrei's eyes.

God. Humiliating.

She had never been rejected like that, certainly not by a man that
she wanted, a man she'd embraced from the core of herself. Whom
she'd felt so deeply connected to. Her cheeks burned from shame and
from the wind slapping them as she hurried down the path.

And Judd, her husband, the father of her child, the man she was
tethered to, a man who had betrayed her and was possibly betraying
her at this very moment (evening here, almost dawn in New York—
maybe that's what those flowers were for? Maybe just another piece
of guilt-ridden performance art?): how insane that her *husband* could
have whatever woman he wanted without breaking a sweat. How was
that? Why was that? A man in his early fifties, a good fifty pounds
overweight, and sure he was a restaurateur, and sure there might be a
certain glamour attached to him, but come on, Meret, *you're twenty-
three*. You're broiling hot. You're really going to give it up to this fucking guy? *This guy?*

She was so embarrassed she thought she might just die.

Now the shepherd was finishing up its bully stick, looking at her gratefully. Well. At least something appreciated her.

She looked up to where a man on the nearby sidewalk was holding a menu. He waved at her, beckoned her in, and despite her rage and embarrassment she was also so incredibly hungry (she had actually eaten nothing yet today, was that possible?), and he said something to her in Georgian and she shook her head.

"Me ar vlap'arak'ob kartulad."

At least after all this she could speak a little Georgian; she could say, "I do not speak Georgian."

"Would you like to eat inside or outside?" he replied, smoothly. "I can turn on the heat lamp for you. It is very comfortable."

She did not want the outside world to see that she was alone. "I'll go inside, thanks."

He set her up in a corner table with a gloriously misspelled English menu and a basket of bread. She washed up in the small restroom, took a close look at her own face. Her cheeks were wind-chapped. Her lips were dry. The wrinkles around her lips were deepening, and the crease between her brows. But she could look closely and still see what Scott had seen in the Limited dressing room decades ago. The person she had been was still in there. The woman she had become. She was still a person worth seeing. She knew she was. She had to be.

The restaurant was half full, and from where she sat she could watch the two waitresses march in and out of the kitchen with plates full of khachapuri, shishlik. She ordered the cheese khinkali and the red bean lobio and a glass of red wine that she knew might turn into a bottle.

It was the humiliation, yes, but it was also the sense that it should be otherwise. That men who had been sent away by their wives should not remain faithful to their wives. That she had been right there, connected to him, that they had connected, that she had seen him weep in the church and wanted to hold him in her arms. That he should have let her.

She wanted to love him. She wanted to change his life.

Or maybe she was ludicrous.

The khinkali came, fragrant with garlic and mushroom, six of them fat and pleated on a long white plate. She remembered how the woman at the restaurant on her very first night had taught her to eat them—hold it by the topknot, take a nibble, be careful not to let the juice spurt all over you. Amy took a nibble, and the juice dribbled down her chin. It was okay, it would be okay. She'd leave here, go back to her real life, who cared anymore.

On the table, her phone started to buzz.

"Hey," she said. "Good morning."

"I was thinking of you," Judd said. She heard the sleep still in his voice. She knew he was alone.

"What's happening there? How's the menagerie?"

"They're fine," Judd said. "They miss you. Want to say hi? Here, I'll put you on speaker."

He did, and she said hello to the dog and the cats, closing her eyes and imagining Roxy on the bed, confused about why she could hear her voice but not smell her, and the cats were probably sprawled across the room, too, could hear her, too; cats supposedly had better hearing than dogs, and equally sharp senses of smell.

"Did they look at the phone?"

"They did," he said. "They're bereft."

"Come on," she said.

"Fine," he said. "Maybe that's just me."

"Thank you for the flowers."

"Hey," he said. "I'm glad they got there."

She sighed, looked around the restaurant to see if she was annoying anyone with her one-way phone call. She and Judd both hated it when they'd see customers barking on their phones during the dinner hour, but nobody here seemed to care one way or the other what she was doing. She popped the rest of the khinkali in her mouth and chewed in Judd's ear.

"So yesterday afternoon my dad came in," he said. "I decided to take him out for Georgian food, turns out there's a new place on Fourteenth Street. I wanted to get a sense of what it was like where you are."

"Ah," she said. That was sweet. "And what did you think?"

"Totally authentic, as far as I could tell. Half the people there didn't speak English. Arthur and I sit down and are like, what's good? And they brought us some of everything, even more than we had ordered, salads, kebabs, that amazing bread filled with cheese."

"Are you sure they were Georgian? Because all Georgians speak English."

"They were Georgian! They were so friendly they made us nervous. Did you know they're doing orange wine over there? It's like them and California, that's it. I had no idea."

"I think they invented it here," Amy said. "Orange wine."

"That's what they said! They've been making wine over there for six thousand years!" He sounded amazed.

"It's a pretty old country."

"And did you have the dumplings?"

"I'm eating them right now."

"You are? You're kidding," he said. He got so animated about food, it was funny. "They make them vegetarian? You're not eating meat, are you?" Hope in his voice, maybe she'd retreated.

"They do make them vegetarian," she said. "These are mushroom."

"And they're good?"

"Yes," she said. "They're really good."

The doctor had said, when she'd gotten him to go—god, what was that, six years ago now?— he'd said Judd should really lose weight, his cholesterol was borderline, his blood pressure was not quite ideal, and now, six years later, he was certainly heavier, and had eaten six more years' worth of heavy food, and had not seen a doctor since. And Amy thought that she shouldn't encourage him to eat like this, but on the other hand the joy he clearly got from food and from eating had to do him some equal and opposite good?

And for a moment she forgot about humiliation and about Andrei and did what she was supposed to do, cared for her husband.

"Did they have pickled walnuts?" she asked. "They do a lot of walnuts here."

"Yes, yes, and all the bean dishes," he said. "And the chicken with garlic. I don't think there's any way to really bring Georgian food into the restaurant, it would look like appropriation, but I'm wondering if there's some kind of spice mixture or something, some way to capture—"

"You could do orange wine," Amy said.

"We already do orange wine."

"You could do Georgian orange wine."

"I should talk to the guys," he said.

"You should," she said. She lofted and then nibbled another khinkali, quite a feat while she was on the phone. "I wish you were here," she said, surprising herself.

"I do too," he said.

Her mind flashed to the pressure of Andrei's forehead against hers, where it had left an invisible, burning mark. She blinked to try to make the burning go away. It did not.

"I should probably go," she said. "I'm being rude." To whom? To whom was she being rude?

"Did you talk to Ferry?"

"I did," she said. "He said that Uno's writing him letters."

"I read one," he said. "She's telling him all about her childhood, about what it was like when she was trying to get clean. I don't know why she's doing this to him. It's making him upset."

"She loves him," Amy said. "She wants him to know the real her. And I don't think she understands—"

"Maybe you could email her?" Judd said. "Explain it?"

"You want *me* to explain to Uno why she shouldn't write her child letters?"

"No, no, you're right, forget it. I think she's just losing her mind in the hospital. But her boyfriend's coming to visit from Singapore, so that's good. It'll give her something else to focus on."

"That's good," she said.

"Come home soon," he said.

"I will," she said. She hung up before he could ask her what soon meant. She wiped her hands on her napkin and turned her attention back to her remaining dumplings, knowing, if she'd had her way, she wouldn't be eating anything at all right now, that she would be somewhere with Andrei, in his bedroom, her bedroom. That she never would have picked up the phone. Her forehead still burned where he had pressed against her.

SHE'D SAT AT the table far longer than she'd planned on, buoyed by the excellent food and the wine and the waiting for a check that never materialized. Finally, as her knees started to grow stiff from sitting, she threw too many lari on the table and headed out the door, waving at the staff who waved back, cheerfully. On the street outside the restaurant, exactly where she'd left him, was the Aussie she'd met before.

"Were you waiting for me?" she asked, bending down to rub the bony spot on the dog's delicate dark gray head. She wished she'd thought to bring out her leftovers for him to eat. The dog looked up at her lovingly, but without expectation. His fur was soft and slightly springy, like someone had brushed it.

The wine and food had warmed her, or perhaps it was just the distance from this afternoon's humiliation. She headed back in the direction she thought she'd find home—she could have taken out her phone, but she wanted to test her own sense of direction. It had been almost a week in Tbilisi, after all. Shouldn't she have some idea where she was? The Aussie followed at her heels.

"Hey, dog, do you know Angel?" she asked. "Have you heard of her? She's famous."

The dog looked up at Amy, pleased to be acknowledged.

"Do you have an interesting backstory, dog? Do you need to be rescued?"

The dog trotted along next to her, reserved, pleasant. He stayed by her feet as she walked down one cobblestoned block into the next, turning around once to find herself back on the block she had just left, when she heard, in the distance, a sort of rumbling noise. She knew what the noise was, and she knew it pointed the way home.

"Do you want to come with me?"

But the noise was too much. The dog disappeared into the darkness of an alleyway as soon as Liberty Square came into view. The square was flooded with people; a gateway had opened and there were even more people than had been there last night, and even more police, and even more tanks. There was no way around them, or through them, and she was certain the mass of people backed all the way up to Rustaveli. The thudding, thumping noise matched her suddenly pulsing heart. How would she get home? She stood one hundred meters away, down a sidestreet where the crowd would probably not bother to go, but if they did, she would be washed away by the tide of them.

Perhaps the best way to go home was to simply go through?

The square—the oval—was surrounded by roadways filled with marchers moving at a slow clip, somewhere between a slog and a trudge. Many of them were holding posters and flags, and a group ten people across held up a banner that said, in English, WE WILL NOT GO BACK.

On either side of the roadway were police (or were they soldiers?) lined up like stanchions, faceless behind their visors, dressed entirely in black, holding shields emblazoned with the world POLICE, in English. They hemmed the protesters in, and Amy wondered if their hearts were hammering behind their uniforms, too. They had clubs in their belts, and Tasers.

How old could they be? Why were they here supporting the government? Why weren't they on the side of the young?

Amy looked at the map on her phone to see if there was a way around the protest—there was, maybe, but it took her up into the hills, and she wasn't sure if she'd be able to follow the unlit path. She took a few steps back and was instantly unsure of herself. The night had gotten so dark.

She could, perhaps, go back to the restaurant—they were nice there, she could sit—but would they let her stay all night? The thought of ordering more food made her ill.

She wondered if it was time, after all, to return to New York. She had been in Tbilisi for a week, managed to make a fool of herself, somehow alienated her host, and hadn't solved any mystery whatsoever. Angel was lost to the mists. Ferry was going through something painful, and Uno might need her help again.

Nobody would have to know she'd come home early. She could play it off like it had all been some wonderful adventure, and not a strange, lunatic foray into a world dealing with infinitely more complicated problems than her own.

There was a narrow space behind the cops on the sidewalk that she thought she could make it through if she squeezed. She wouldn't draw attention to herself.

All the dogs that were usually on this path—where were they?

In the middle of the square, people were taking turns speaking into a megaphone, and every so often a roar would go up from the crowd. Amy took careful steps around the square, trying to stay in the narrow space between the cops and the buildings that lined the sidewalks, trying not to draw attention to herself, still wondering if she should turn around and head up into the hills. Every so often the crowd would roar with an intensity that made her freeze, scared of what was happening or what the cops might do. But they stayed where they were, statuelike, unaware that she was moving quietly behind them. She was almost certain she was moving in the right direction—it had to be this way, wasn't it? Along Rustaveli? The crowd kept marching, kept screaming, and she felt like it was at her back, propelling her forward, and she was afraid of what would happen if she turned around.

And then a shriek from the crowd, and the sound of glass breaking, and Amy in her nervousness tripped over something on the sidewalk, and finally one cop in the wall of cops turned around and noticed her and said something sharp that she didn't understand.

"Please," she said. "Me ar vlap'arak'ob kartulad, I speak English."

Was she able to be heard? The cop was inscrutable behind his visor. She said it louder, "Gtkhovt, please, please—Me ar vlap'arak'ob kartulad, just English, not Georgian—" and for whatever reason this pissed off the cop and he grabbed her by the shoulders and threw her into the crowd like she was a trash bag he'd found on the street. Tears sprang to her eyes. Her shoulders pinched where he'd grabbed her.

And now, suddenly, she was in the middle of it, swept into the ongoing tide of the protesters, in the heat of the screaming crowd. People were chanting things she didn't understand but underneath the rumble she heard words she did: *Freedom* and *Fuck Putin* and *No USSR*. And underneath their winter caps and their scarves the protesters looked like people she knew, looked like Maia and her friends at the restaurant, looked like the teachers at Irine's school. They were linking arms and they were shouting. And someone grabbed Amy's arm, and even though her shoulder definitely felt sore she let her arm be grabbed and she decided that she would not be scared, she would yell and march along with them. She would try to understand.

The march took her in the opposite direction she wanted to go, back toward Liberty Square. It was easy enough to move with them once you figured out where they were going, once you decided to keep your eyes on the people in front of you and not on the wall of faceless cops with their shields and their Tasers, once you pretended the tanks weren't there, once you stopped thinking about Irine's sister and the eighteen people killed in this very spot by Gorbachev's goons in 1989 and instead you thought about the present, only about the present. If you lent your voice to the voice of the collective.

You could be part of it if you screamed "Fuck Putin!" and "Fuck Stalinism!" and "We Won't Go Back!" and if you looked at the young people around you who looked so much like your stepson that it was almost like he was there marching with you—if you made sure your footsteps moved in line with everyone else's, if you raised your voice and let yourself feel part of something instead of apart from everything, it was easy to keep going. It was easy to keep moving.

She marched and shouted. She moved in time with her fellow marchers. A man in front of her wore a Ukrainian flag draped around his neck and the flag occasionally flew up and brushed against her forehead, against the very spot that Andrei had burned with his touch.

Andrei's wife was a Putinist, a Putinista, did anyone ever call them that? Lady Putinists? She felt some of the crowd's delirium infect her. Arms linked with strangers' arms, she marched around Liberty Square and back down Rustaveli, toward the parliament building with the drooping cross and the massed troops of cops and the tanks. But she wasn't afraid. Why be afraid? She screamed obscenities into the sky and the crowd screamed them along with her. In the hills above her, a TV tower glowed red and white. She wondered if news agencies were picking this up. She wondered if anyone in the world knew this was happening besides the people right here with her, now.

They proceeded down Rustaveli, past the Nike store, the Adidas store. The stores were not boarded up the way they were in New York during the George Floyd protests. Nobody had thought to put plywood in front of the plate glass. Which seemed to say to Amy that this was fine, this was going to be fine, this was healthy pro-democracy shouting and it was good to be part of it. If she couldn't find Angel, she could at least do this.

Which was when she heard an explosion.

Something in front of her—how far in front, she could not tell—had exploded, and now smoke was pluming up into the sky, and a mass of cops (or were they soldiers? They seemed so profoundly *in formation*) marched toward the crowd with their shields in the air, and screaming that had been joyful was now suddenly terrified. Protesters were running in different directions. Amy's eyes started to burn. And the cops were grabbing people and throwing them against the walls, or throwing them against tanks, and Amy was terrified of being grabbed again but it was so smoky and her eyes were burning so horribly that she didn't know where she was going, and she thought *I am a tourist I am a tourist* but didn't scream it because she knew it didn't matter in the least.

Anyway nobody would hear her.

She tried to stumble off the street but there was nowhere to go; Parliament Square was blocked off in one direction and the crowd blocked any escape route in the other direction. She wasn't sure if she was supposed to rub her eyes or not—would that increase the burning? She wasn't sure if this was tear gas or a smoke bomb or if someone was going to start tasing or worse.

God, it fucking burned. The skin on her face felt like it was crawling with tiny electric ants.

Through streaming, narrowed eyes, she could see that the crowd was dispersing, dispersing, daarbiet. She followed them, through a narrow channel away from the cops and the crowd, and found herself climbing, half-blinded, up on a platform near a McDonald's of all things, and someone handed her something and gestured that she should pour it into her eyes.

"What?" she shrieked.

The woman looked at her.

"English? Please!"

"It helps!" the woman said, gesturing. "The burning!"

Amy poured the liquid into her eyes and it was white and cold and it did relieve some of the sting and a drip dribbled into her mouth and she realized it was milk.

She pressed her palms into her eyes. Her face was cold and sticky with milk. When she opened them again they stung a little bit less. She saw police actively beating the protesters with their clubs while others stood around them screaming words she could not decipher. Some of the cops were dragging protesters away from the avenue and toward their vans, were throwing them into the backs of vans. Where were they going to take them? Where would they be detained?

"You need more?" asked the woman next to her, gesturing toward the milk.

"Madloba!" Amy said. "Madloba." And she poured more milk in her eyes.

"I have to go," the woman said. "You keep this." And handed her the container.

The woman climbed down from the platform then, leaving Amy to try to figure out where to go next or what to do; it seemed impossible to go anywhere, though, so maybe she would do nothing? Watch this insane Bruegel scene in front of her go on until it ended, and then hurry her way back home? Wait till the burn wore off? Pretend none of it was happening at all?

She picked up her phone. She could document this. Yes, that was something she could do.

She took a photo, then another, then turned on the video and let it unspool in front of her, for posterity, but also separated by her camera so that she didn't feel like she was a part of this as much as she felt returned to her rightful place as a mere observer. And the phone blocked the smoke from her eyes.

The protesters kept coming and the police kept catching them, almost willy-nilly, and the smoke bombs blew up every so often and the police kept coming forward in formation as though executing a plan for war. The red button of the video blinked on and off, capturing all of it. She swung her camera up toward Liberty Square, where the marchers kept coming, and then back toward Rustaveli, where the police kept coming.

But then the camera caught someone she knew.

Jesus.

Dragged back by her elbows, screaming who knows what up to the sky, kicking and trying to make herself immobile, it was Maia. Clearly and undeniably. Maia, in her Doc Martens knock offs, in a T-shirt that had Putin's face on it crossed out in red, Maia, who suddenly looked ten years younger and ten times smaller than she did in her kitchen, who had a line of blood on her face and whose eyes were closed against the smoke bombs and who was screaming with her mouth open up to the stars.

Fuck, Maia.

Amy was not a brave person. She knew that about herself. She was not brave and she was not reckless but still she jumped off the safety of the platform and raced back into the crowd, toward Maia, who was being dragged toward one of the black police vans.

"NO!" she yelled as she pushed through the crowd—was it possible she had pushed one of the cops? She had certainly pushed one of the cops out of the way with both her arms in front of her, she was running and forcing herself through the crowd, eyes still blurry, until she found Maia, who was kicking her feet in the air, refusing to be thrown in the back of the van.

"NO!" she screamed as a cop tried to grab her from behind; she somehow slithered away. "NO! *I am American! I am American! I am American!*"

And somehow, for some reason, that did the trick. The cop paused. *"You will not take her! I am American!"* and she grabbed Maia around the waist but then the cop pulled her back toward the van, the rear doors to the van were wide open and the cop backed up into it and tried to pull Maia in, too, from behind and Amy jumped up into the van before the cop could hoist Maia in. The cop looked at her from behind her shield.

The cop was a woman.

"You will let her go," Amy said, her heart racing, unsure of what she was going to say until it was out of her mouth. "I am American and I am telling you, you will let her go."

The cop said something to her in Georgian; she reached toward her belt for her club or her Taser, keeping one hand on Maia's neck. But at the same time Amy reached into her belt bag and grabbed her wallet.

The cop watched her, unmoving.

Amy withdrew one thousand American dollars from her wallet. She was shaking. What had the British man said? *The consequences can be extraordinarily severe.*

What could that mean?

It did not matter what the consequences were. Maia was bleeding pools of dark red blood from the mouth and the nose.

"You will let her go," Amy said.

The cop looked at the money.

"You will let her go," Amy said, shaking but trying to keep the shaking from her voice. "Now."

The cop reached out and plucked the ten American bills from Amy's American hand, and she let go of Maia's neck, and then she pushed Amy out of the van, and she ran, and Maia ran, and they didn't stop until they were halfway up the hill, and when Maia finally turned to her, Amy saw that her nose looked like it was sitting at a strange angle and one of her front teeth had been knocked out of her mouth. And there was so much blood.

"Maia," Amy said. "Let's get you home."

But Maia didn't say anything, just spit out of the corner of her mouth and ran back down the hill toward Rustaveli.

NINETEEN

"DID YOU SEE her?"

Irine at the kitchen table again, wreathed in cigarette smoke.

Amy shook her head. "It's peaceful down there," she said. "I'm sure she's fine."

UPSTAIRS: TIRED, COLD, heart still hammering. She peeled off her jeans, looked at her phone to see what kind of flights were possible. There was a twenty-three-hour doozy through Istanbul, another seventeen-hour one through Paris. She would call the airline, see how much it would cost to change her flight. She didn't have that much money left in her account, but she probably had enough.

It was almost midnight again—it was always almost midnight here—but she knew herself well enough to know there'd be no sleeping. Still, she closed her eyes and leaned back on her pillow.

She tried not to think about what might have happened had the cop wanted to punish her instead of taking her money.

Her phone buzzed.

"Ferry! I was just thinking about you," she lied.

"So Dad is going to tell you that you need to come back, but I just want you to know you don't have to."

"What are you talking about?"

"Uno is going downhill," Ferry said. "The, um—I guess the drugs stopped working. She might not make it. She took a sudden turn last night and now the doctors are telling us to prepare for the worst."

"Ferry—"

"It's okay," he said. "For some reason, I feel okay about this right now. I don't know if I'm just in shock but I feel like it's going to be all right. Whatever happens."

"Honey." Her breath caught. Here she'd been playing like some kind of war hero while her real life was happening without her. "Oh honey. I don't know what to say."

"Yeah, well," he said, "that's because there's nothing."

Was he crying? It didn't sound like he was crying. But he sounded older than he ever had, even older than the day before.

"Ferry, I can be there tomorrow."

"No, please. Believe me. What I'm saying is that I want you to stay where you are. I want you to finish doing what you set out to do. I feel like—this is something I need to do for myself. I need to see her out, however this goes."

"But I can be there for you."

"I know you can," he said. "And you will be when you get home. But right now, I just—I want you to finish doing this thing. You've always given up your life to take care of Uno. And of me."

She hadn't wanted him to know that; of course he knew that.

"You don't have to do that this time," he said. "No matter what Dad says." He laughed. "Anyway he just wants you home because he misses you. Not because he thinks you can save her life again."

"Ferry, honey," she said. "I'm not going to let you face this alone."

"I'm not alone," he said. "And even if you were here I'd still have to face this. But it's okay. I'm going to be okay. I'm trying not to be angry with her anymore. Just accept her for who she is. Who she was."

"Ferry—"

"And it matters to me that you set out to do what you went there to do."

"Sweetie, I came here to do something ridiculous."

"Please, Mom."

How easily he called both her and Uno Mom; he always had.

"I love you."

"I love you too," he said. "Thank you."

She looked down at her body. Her filthy clothes. Well, she supposed, this was probably how it was always supposed to end. She clicked over to the airline and spent $1200 to change her flight home, leaving the next day.

SHE WENT TO the red-tiled bathroom to wash her face, brush her teeth. In the mirror, she saw raw cheeks, red-rimmed eyes, white-ish stains on her chin from where the milk had dripped down. She still smelled like smoke, too, alongside something chemical and strange. If she hadn't been so tired she would have showered; she could shower in the morning.

"Amy."

She turned. She had managed to forget about him for almost three hours.

She was wearing her sweatshirt, no pants, no makeup, she was damp-faced and her palms were still sweating. But she turned to him anyway, stood there to face him, his beautiful face.

He looked at her too, almost frozen.

"Yes?" she said.

"I—"

He didn't finish the sentence.

She took two steps toward him.

And in the next second: his stubbled cheeks, his perfect lips. He put his hands against the sides of her face and his mouth on hers and she opened her mouth, she raced to unbutton his shirt. She stopped thinking, this wasn't something she wanted to think about. She only wanted to feel.

They found their way to her tiny bedroom, her jeans already on the floor.

She was surprised at how easy it was, how natural, even in this strange place, even still smelling like some sort of chemical bomb. His body was strong and lean. He took over her body and she thought that she hadn't submitted to a man like this in a very long time and she was happy to do it. She didn't worry about anything hurting, anything feeling stiff or strange like it did sometimes at home. She didn't worry at all; she was so happy to let him do whatever he wanted. He kept his mouth on hers, then moved his mouth to her breast. She unbuttoned his jeans, threw them to the floor on top of hers.

She thought, ridiculously: I have never had sex before on a twin bed.

Soon, then, he was inside her, he moved inside her, they moved together, he kept his mouth on hers, and was it her imagination or did he say her name again and again, *Amy, Amy*? She had her hands on his ass, pulling him in toward her.

Sometimes she came when she had sex with Judd and sometimes she didn't, she'd tell him not to bother trying to make her come, *it's a freebie*, she'd say. But now her body was responding with something she hadn't felt in decades, a kind of helpless pleasure, an inability to resist or to stop herself. There was no work involved, there was nothing involved but letting her body do what it wanted to do. She had forgotten it could be like this. He was so sweaty and his sweat poured onto her face and her body.

She rolled over on top of him and pressed against him and it was not like making any decisions; she felt incapable of making decisions. She was just following the script her body was writing.

She came and when she did she bit his shoulder to keep from crying out, and then she came again and bit him again, harder.

He clasped her, he brought her closer, she felt him shudder.

She lay down next to him and he kissed the side of her face.

"Amy," he said again, but that was all, and she was grateful. She would not say anything to him, and she did not want him to say anything to her. Anything he could say—about his life, her life, this strange place, his family, what they were doing, whatever was happening around them—she didn't want to think about it. She didn't want to hear about it. Whether or not he had intended this to happen, whether or not he felt guilty about it, she didn't care. She wanted this and she wanted to hold on to it for as long as humanly possible.

He lay beside her, squished in next to her on the tiny bed. She knew that if she fell asleep, that when she woke up, he'd be gone. She tried to stay awake next to him for as long as she could; her eyes were closed but she would not let herself sleep.

What time was it? Two in the morning? Three?

She could stay awake all night next to him, surely. If she stayed awake next to him he would not dare to leave her alone.

She breathed in and out, matching the pattern of his breath. He was asleep. He was breathing deeply, clearly deeply asleep, pressed next to her. He did not snore, he did not twitch, but the way his chest moved in and out against her, he must have been sleeping. He still held her close.

Well then. Okay. If he was allowed to sleep, she too could sleep.

She felt her brain begin to send out strange thoughts and images, surreal spools of action, she was on a plane somewhere above the Atlantic, and she had Andrei with her, and she was going to bring him home to New York and explain it to Judd. She loved him, she loved both of them, it was a different kind of love, surely he understood? Hadn't he felt this himself, over and over?

But when she turned to look at Andrei in the seat beside her he wasn't on the plane anymore at all; instead it was the small Aussie shepherd from outside the restaurant, and she said to the dog, *but you're not Angel*, and the shepherd just looked at her closely, forgivingly, as the plane started to shake.

The plane was shaking, trembling in the sky, like an in-cabin earthquake. All around her, passengers were screaming. She grabbed the shepherd and put it in her lap, stroked its fur, tried to stay calm. And when she looked at the dog again it was Angel. She'd found her after all. *You!* She said.

And then she looked again and it was Roxy, and the plane had stopped shaking, and she was home.

She opened her eyes. Sunlight flooded the room, and Andrei was gone.

TWENTY

THE HOUSE WAS empty, or seemed to be empty. If Andrei was in the house somewhere, she'd know it; she felt unnaturally attuned to him, like there was an invisible wire buzzing and snapping between them no matter how far apart they were. She did not know what she would say when she saw him again, and in fact was not certain she would see him again. She wondered if she would still feel that buzz once she got on a plane. She wondered if she would feel it for the rest of her life. Her skin was still humming, and when she'd showered she'd found pale bruises on her thighs and the round of a bite mark on her breast.

Would Judd notice this, when she got home? Would he think to look at her that closely, or think to ask?

Andrei had not been in his room when she knocked or when she pushed the door open. But for the first time, his window shades were open, and light filled his room, and the breeze blew in through the open window.

It was strange that she did not feel guilty about what happened, nor did she feel any longing for it to happen again—it could not happen again. She was leaving so soon. But if she saw him again in the flesh, if they were alone, she wasn't certain if she would be able to keep her body calm. And what would he do? Or would he act like none of this had ever happened?

Where was everybody?

She sat down at the kitchen table and opened up a video of Angel. Even now, she thought, she could still cover some ground; there were so many places she had yet to search, so many options she could still comb through. Was it really possible that Russians had kidnapped Angel? She could put up signs in Cyrillic, she supposed, she could— she had nine hours left.

No, it was enough. Enough already. The dog had vanished to the winds. And she wondered, thinking back to the woman in the park (could that have really only been ten days ago?) if she'd thought she was talking about Roxy, if even the woman herself had thought she was talking about Roxy, but it was really poor good Angel who was lost. Poor Angel who the woman had a psychic connection to.

She thought maybe she believed in psychic connections now.

She would have to pack soon; her clothing was dingy and smelly, and she thought it might be best to just toss out the jeans she'd been wearing yesterday instead of trying to rehabilitate them in the wash. She'd meant to find a laundromat, she'd meant to find a dog, she'd meant to find something to justify her trip to this part of the world, a hero's welcome or a sense of purpose or a reason to not be so mad at her husband anymore.

Her skin tingled. Andrei was somewhere nearby.

She remembered, from her tour with Bachana, how to find certain rooms (or at least she thought she did?), and although it seemed presumptuous of her, her flight left in nine hours; she wanted to tell them she was going, and she wanted to make sure that Maia had come home.

The hallway that led out of the other side of the kitchen went up stairs and down stairs, like she remembered; the paisley wallpaper peeled where she remembered. She walked slowly, listening for signs of life; when she got to a door she thought might be Maia's, she knocked and then opened it, slowly. The room was empty. Zazi, somehow, had escaped the basement again and was lying on the unmade bedclothes, but the rest of the room looked thoroughly unvisited from the last time she'd been in there. The roses were already starting to droop in their makeshift vase.

She had never ever planned on being unfaithful to her husband. She had never thought such a thing was possible for her to do. When he had cheated on her, when she had caught him, and even when she had only suspected he'd been unfaithful, she had never thought of revenge (or at least not bodily revenge, or even an emotional entanglement). She had thought only of escape, of getting out of this unholy mess of her life, of making something new for herself because whatever else this first life was (was it her first life? Her second or third?) it was clearly, irredeemably broken.

Moreover, she had always assumed that Judd had discovered what was broken in her, and had sought to escape that himself by burying himself in much younger women. He lusted after women who weren't old enough yet to have fallen apart. Women who were barely women at all. And who therefore stood in opposition to her; she thought they'd been a *response* to her.

But she knew now with great certainty that whatever Judd had done in the past (and god knows maybe even this morning?) really had nothing to do with her, because what had happened with Andrei had nothing to do with him. She was rebuilding herself here by herself, not in response to anybody else. She was attempting, for the first time in forty-six years, to act according to what she wanted, not just what she needed.

The feeling of Andrei's rough cheek against her skin would never leave her. The pressure of his lips. His thighs, his ass under her hands, his eyes. And although she knew she would never have him again, she knew, too, that he would be with her always. That connection could look like anything and be everything.

She glanced down at her phone, at an old image of her and Judd, and felt nothing more than gentle nostalgia, the nostalgia for a life that had held together as long as she didn't pull at its threads. A life that would be hers again as soon as she stitched the threads back together. All of it, as much as she could have of it (not Judd's faithfulness, necessarily, but his home and his money and their child) would belong to her again and Andrei would be lost to time, to a past that might never have even really happened.

Downstairs, she heard a door open and shut, and the howl and whine of the dogs—someone they knew had walked in. She walked down the rickety stairs to the front door. It was Maia, looking bruised and tired and satisfied.

"Maia, are you—everyone was so worried. Call your mom, please. You have to call her."

"I did," she said. She plopped down on the floor and let the dogs embrace her.

"When did you call her?"

"She knows I'm okay."

"Are you? You look—"

"I know," Maia said. She was missing a front tooth, not one of the middle teeth but the one right beside them on the right, and her nose was definitely askew. But she was smiling.

"I was really worried, Maia. When I left you, I didn't know—"

"But as you can see, I am fine." She stuck her tongue in the space in her mouth. "I mean, I will have to go to the dentist."

She was surrounded by the dogs, on the floor, all eleven of them were rumbling about, sniffing her, licking her, so happy that she was home. They must have known, too, when she was gone, when she was unsafe. Dogs knew that. They too had invisible humming wires that connected them to everyone they loved.

"They retracted the law," Maia said.

"What do you mean?"

"They announced an hour ago, they were retracting the foreign agent law."

"What?" Amy said. "You won?"

"For the moment," Maia said. "There will be more."

She had her arms around one of the dogs, who was licking her ardently on the cheek; her cheek seemed a little bit swollen, but she didn't push the dog off, and in fact seemed to welcome her, drew her in closer. The dog was white, Lab-shaped, medium-sized, very fluffy. The dog stopped licking Maia's face for a second and looked directly at Amy with her beautiful, expressive brown eyes. Had this dog been one of the pack the whole time Amy had been in this house?

"Maia—"

The dog sat, looked straight at her. She felt a strange wave inside her gut, a wave of confusion. And something like anger, and also an odd sense of relief. She reached out her hand. The dog moved toward her and licked it.

She had seen this dog before. Its familiar shape, its fluffy white fur. She had seen this dog many, many times.

"Maia?"

It was her, she was sure of it.

"Maia," she said. "Is this Angel?"

Maia busied herself rubbing the dog's white fur.

"Has she always been here?"

Maia sighed. She pulled the dog into her, onto her lap, where she sat, contentedly.

Could it really—"Is it?"

"Amy, it's not like—"

Had she been in the basement the whole time? Been one of the heap of the dogs? Running outside with the group?

"Like what?"

"My mother did not think you'd notice," Maia finally said. "She said Americans don't see the obvious. Or they don't look for it even when it's right in front of them."

Amy felt her insides crumple in humiliation; she actually gasped. Then she said, "Your mother tricked me."

"She did not think—it's a long story."

The dog came over and began licking her hand; *Angel* was licking Amy's hand. This dog, this hero of Georgian democracy, or at least of Georgian children, this beautiful animal, this holy fool.

"Maia—Maia, Jesus Christ," Amy said. "I feel mortified."

"Please don't," Maia said. "If she'd told you, you never would have come."

"Yeah, but—"

"And she needed you to come. She wanted to meet you," Maia said. "She wanted to know you."

"She wanted to use me?"

"Please don't think of it that way."

Amy couldn't move because the dog was now content under her hand; despite herself, she was rubbing Angel's chin. But her gut was twitching.

"You see, it was just one small thing and then another small thing," Maia said. With her missing tooth, her esses sounded a little muddled. "As you know, after my mom fired Eteri from the school, there was a huge outburst."

"Eteri is the teacher?"

"In fact, Eteri was my girlfriend," Maia said.

The photos. Well, that had been obvious.

"We met at my mother's school one day when I was volunteering, just doing some art projects with the little ones, and then she got me involved in this pro-democracy group. So that's how I became part of this movement. And we started dating, too."

Angel nuzzled into Amy's palm.

"Of course my mother did not like any of that," Maia said. "Not that I was dating a woman, not that I was involved in the democracy movement. And then my mother had to fire her, and then Eteri broke up with me, and my mother and I couldn't stop fighting. It was terrible. I blamed her for everything."

"So how does this lead to Angel?" Amy said. "I don't understand."

"That week she fired Eteri, she found some blood in her doghouse— that's what she said at least—and she was worried kids were bothering her, throwing stones or something. So she brought her home."

"What?"

"My mom had always loved Angel. She thought that Angel was actually sent from heaven—she's the one who named her, you know? *Angelozi*. So she took her home, just for a night, just to keep her safe. And she wanted her close. You know that feeling, right? When you need a dog to be close to you?"

"Didn't she already have like ten dogs at home?"

Maia shrugged. "I don't think she really thought about what would happen next. But Angel just joined the pack, and it made my mother so happy to have her, and even though everyone was searching for her she never—I don't know. My mother thought that maybe she could just bring her back, but she could never bear to do it. She gets very attached to her animals, you know?"

"So she kidnapped her?"

"Not kidnapped, no. I mean again I think she always meant to bring Angel back. But then you started sending money, so—"

Oh god, the money.

"I think she thought—" Maia shrugged. "I think she thought

you could help us," she said. "I think she thought Americans have a lot of money and good intentions. Even when they don't understand anything."

"I can't believe this."

"Please don't hate her."

"She used me, Maia."

"But don't you understand where she's coming from?" Maia said. "Don't you see? She needed you."

"She needed my money."

Maia was quiet. Then she said, "Amy, she always told me, if you don't think about the future, what else is there to think about?"

Amy looked into Angel's dark brown eyes. She had loved this dog for a very long time. She had flown across the ocean for her, to rescue her. She had seen in her all that was maternal and loving, which had helped her see that in herself. She pulled the dog in the way she often did with Roxy, and felt the dog's soft fur under both her hands, and rubbed the sweet spot on top of her head.

"Are you okay?"

"I'm okay," Amy said, and for a long time she let the dog's breathing comfort her. Maia didn't say anything, but she didn't leave.

After a while, Amy looked up. "Do you want to come study in the US?"

"I'm sorry?"

"Just—" Amy wiped her cheeks with the back of her wrist. Angel curled up in a circle of white at her feet. "I could maybe make that happen? Or help you work there or something?"

"No," Maia laughed. "I'm Georgian. My future is here."

"Your future could be anywhere," Amy said. "You're so young."

"Yeah, but if I went to the US I'd always be dependent, right? I wouldn't have any money, I wouldn't have any connections—besides you, I guess, but you have your own family. But even if you— What

I mean is that I want to build the future I want in the place I want to live. In my home."

Amy understood. She brought Angel's face close, scratched under her chin. The dog smelled a little gritty; she could use a bath, but she was going to leave that job to Maia and the other women of this house. "I'm leaving in a few hours," she said. "Heading back to New York."

Maia nodded. "I understand," she said. "I'm glad you came here. You helped us a lot."

"Honestly, I didn't do anything," Amy said.

"Actually," Maia said, "you might have saved my life."

They sat there then, in the quiet, until finally Amy rubbed Angel's head one last time. Then she stood and walked out of the house, down the hill to Rustaveli, which was quiet, clean, and ordinary under a bright blue sky. The stray dogs had assumed their places. They would all be fine without her.

She walked down the street a few blocks, past the McDonald's and Parliament Square and the drooping cross, past the subway stop and the paths up the hill, to where she thought she'd seen a bank the other day—yes, there it was, with an ATM inside. She punched in 3000 lari, and the machine flashed red: she didn't have 3000 left in her account. God. In one week she'd spent everything she'd salted away over the years. She'd once thought of this money as her escape fund.

Oh, what did it matter anymore? She punched in 2500 lari, and—success!—received the money in crisp yellow notes. She put the lari in her belt bag, tucked into a secret compartment, then grabbed a spinach pastry from one of the windows that opened onto the street. She ate most of it on her walk back to the house, saving the last bite for Angel.

HER CLOTHING WAS packed away. Her dog treats were stashed in her backpack. She went to her room with the small bed and the wood-framed window, stripped the sheets, folded the blankets. She ripped a piece of paper out of her notebook and wrote the word *Madloba* on it, and also, in English, *good-bye*. Then she folded the paper around the 2500 lari, brought it down to the kitchen and placed it in the middle of the table where she thought Irine would find it. The faucet dripped to its own beat.

"You are sneaking out?"

Irine was in the doorway opposite, smoking, gray-faced. Amy felt a surge of anger that quickly subsided into shame.

"Angel was here the whole time," she said.

Irine said nothing.

"What a strange thing to do," Amy said. Irine looked at her blankly. "What a mean, strange thing."

Still, Irine was silent.

"Was it fun for you to watch me run around trying to rescue an animal who had never gone missing?"

Irine tapped her cigarette ash onto the floor. "I don't think you understand."

"What don't I understand?"

Irine inhaled on her cigarette, then blew out the smoke. "I am sorry about Angel. I didn't mean to trick you."

"You didn't *mean*—but you—"

"I wanted to meet you, I hoped you would come. I could tell you were a useful, hopeful person. And I didn't think you'd be so—so serious about finding a dog."

"You didn't think I'd be *serious*? Irine, I flew across the ocean!"

"I know. But I thought once you were here you'd meet Maia and you'd want to help bring her to the United States."

"Maia doesn't want to come to the United States! She's fighting for democracy here! For this country's freedom! That's all she wants to do! She's told you that so many times!"

Irine walked forward to the kitchen table, where the ashtray sat. She ground out her cigarette. For a minute, she was silent, and Amy could hear her shallow breathing. Up close, Irine looked so very tired. "I can't believe you've spent all this time here," she finally said, "and seen what you've seen and still understand nothing."

"Enough with that already," Amy said. "I don't have to—"

"I have explained and explained to you and you still refuse to see."

"Give me a break," Amy said. "You live with Maia and *you* still refuse to see! Don't you understand what she's trying to do? Or are you really some kind of—some kind of Soviet stooge?"

Irine laughed, a bitter, choking sound. "No more than you are, Amy."

"Excuse me?"

They were silent for several seconds.

Then: "Your husband makes the money, am I right? Or his family makes the money, you're not even sure? And all you have to do is wake up every day and decide if you feel like eating this or that, or if you feel like walking your dog here or there. Or teaching, or not teaching. It doesn't matter. You are taken care of. You do not have to make any hard choices. You have a roof over your head no matter what. You have a warm coat in the winter no matter what. All you have to do is overlook the fact that your husband treats you badly."

"Irine, that is absolutely not the same—"

"So forgive me if I want a few of those same things in my life."

"That is a totally false binary—"

"Forgive me if I have learned the hard way that having a goverment tell me what to do or even what to think is worth it, in the end, if I know that my daughter is safe and I have a roof over my head. You would make the same bargain in a minute. You've already made the same bargain for less."

Irine picked up another cigarette but did not light it. "I think," she finally said, "I think it was not possible for an American to ever really understand our life here. I should not have expected you to."

"You made a fool of me," Amy said.

"And you of me," Irine said. "Without even knowing you were doing so."

The lari was on the table but Irine did not seem to have noticed it. Amy could pick it up, put it in her backpack, and be on her way. But Irine was right; she didn't really need it. She'd be home soon. Irine could spend it on the dogs or whatever the grannies needed. She could get that faucet fixed. And Amy could leave with the dignity of having paid for her room and board.

"I have to head for the airport."

Irine lit her cigarette. "Thank you for coming to stay with us," she said. "I wish you a safe flight."

Amy walked downstairs past the dogs, past Zazi and Phil and dear Angel, who was curled up in a furry halo of white. How could she not have seen her before? What had always been so clearly in front of her? "Angel," she said, "be a good girl," and the dog looked up. For a moment they locked eyes, and then Angel lay back down on her front paws, and Amy left for home.

THREE

PARIS

TWENTY-ONE

THE THING ABOUT a cockamamie last-minute flight to New York from the Caucasus is that you end up with an eight-hour layover, and even if that layover is in Paris it's a bit of a nightmare if all you really want to do is go home. Which Amy decided she did. She could imagine the apartment, what it would look like even if the housekeeper had come, Judd always messed it up as soon as Nadia left, a trail of dirty socks, nobody would change the cat litter (she could never ask Nadia to change the cat litter). And Judd had probably been eating all his meals at the restaurant or at the halal cart on St. Mark's, which meant that there was nothing in the fridge. And probably a pile of laundry, plus her own laundry, and whatever Uno needed in the hospital. If she still needed anything.

She wondered who was coordinating Uno's care. Was it the boyfriend in from Singapore? Or was it Judd? She imagined she'd take it over as soon as she got home; she was probably still listed on some of Uno's paperwork. She had always taken care of the details, figuring out how to get the billing charged to Uno's accounts, or to get reimbursed from Uno's trust, how to hire someone to take her to meetings after her release, that one time she found a permanent caregiver.

Amy wandered through the long, glass-enclosed hallways of Charles de Gaulle and thought about how nervous she'd felt in this very place one week ago. How ambitious. And also how, that time, she'd been trapped in the airport, but this time she had a long enough layover to go into the city, so at least that was something?

She boarded the train from the Charles de Gaulle platform and watched as the stops clicked by toward the city until Sacré-Cœur appeared in the distance on top of its glorious hill.

All those years ago, the first time Judd had cheated—she'd thought that maybe she'd live here once. A studio, a one-bedroom, near a florist and a bookseller.

Well, maybe in life number three.

She got off the train at Luxembourg Gardens and stood for a moment, agog at the orderliness of the street, the bourgeois peace of the place. Restaurants on the corners, a shop selling macarons, a shop selling adorable brightly-colored children's clothing. Bustling shoppers, aimless tourists. She took a seat at a café with a striped awning and black-aproned waiters and couldn't believe this city existed exactly like it did in every movie. It had been—how long?—ten years at least since she'd been here, but she remembered it all as though it had been yesterday. Nothing here really changed. Nothing here needed to change.

She stretched out her legs under the table; she was wearing gray jeans, black sneakers, felt grungy next to all these glamorous women. It really was the best-dressed city in the world. None of the teenagers here were goths; they'd done that twenty years ago. Now they all wore wide-legged jeans and striped tops.

She had taken out twenty euros at the airport; it was all she had left.

"Madame," said a waiter.

"Q'ava, madloba," she said, and the waiter looked at her; she wasn't making sense. "Un café," and the waiter smiled faintly and turned away. She knew he didn't speak Georgian. She just didn't want to lose the sound of it.

The waiter brought her coffee, a tiny cup, a tiny square of chocolate on its saucer. The weather was beautiful, springtime. She was two thousand miles from Tbilisi and twice as far from home. She closed her eyes to see if she could still feel the thread that connected her to Andrei. To her surprise, it was right there, humming inside her. She sipped her coffee, nibbled her chocolate. She wondered how long she would be able to feel the hum inside herself. She wondered if there was a way to make it stay forever.

But lunchtime was coming and it was clear the waiter wanted her to surrender her seat for more profitable customers, so after an hour or so with her coffee she got up and crossed the street toward Luxembourg Gardens. The garden, surrounded by tall black gates, was filled with green pavilions and stately tennis courts, statues and neatly mowed lawns. The only dogs here were on leashes. The only stray animals were the beautiful strange banded pigeons of Paris and the frisky, oversized squirrels.

She found a path toward the small pond in the middle of the park where the children still played with small toy sailboats, took a seat in a green chair and watched the children push their boats around from the sides of the pond with their long sticks. It was already one in the afternoon. Soon she'd have to return to the airport to finally make it home. She was out of money, she was out of time.

The children by the pond were giggling, chasing each other, the only sounds in an otherwise strangely quiet park. She remembered when Ferry was like this, big-bellied, running around in his little shorts. His soft blond hair.

She called Judd. "I made it to Paris. I'm sitting in the Luxembourg Gardens."

"Thank God," he said. "You're out of there."

And immediately she was angry. "What do you mean? Out of where?"

"Ame, every day you were in Georgia I was worried," he said. "I was following what was happening there on the news. Did you know they were having massive protests while you were there? Right downtown or something?"

A squirrel dashed between the green chairs to grab the remains of a tourist's croissant. "Huh," she said.

"That wasn't anywhere near where you were, right?"

"What, the protests?"

"I mean, it was far away from wherever you were staying?"

She thought of the video she had on her phone, how satisfying it would be to send it to him. But instead, she just took a breath. "Yes," she said. "Far away."

"I don't know, these lunatics can't get their act together anywhere in Eastern Europe. It's like, Jesus Christ, people. It's 2023, figure your fucking government out."

"That's what they're trying to do."

"Yeah, but—"

"They're trying to figure their government out. They want to be free. That's what they're fighting for."

"Okay, fine, I'm just saying you don't need to—"

"Their word for it is *tavisupleba*. It means 'self-rule.' Like you get to be the lord of yourself. It's what they've been struggling for for centuries."

Judd made a hmph noise. "Okay."

"*Tavisupleba*," Amy said. "It's a beautiful word."

"They can fight for their freedom after my wife gets home, all right?"

"Judd, if you don't think about the future, what else is there to think about?"

Out of the corner of her eye she saw a dog without a leash. The dog was sleek, black, probably cared for. Certainly it had an owner somewhere.

"What does that mean?"

"How's Uno?"

"It's a fucking mess," he said. "I've been trying to organize everything—you know her crazy family insurance thing, when you get home I'm going to need you to unravel the way her plan works. The hospital has already started billing her. And I'm afraid we're going to be on the hook since her brother won't talk to her anymore, and I think we're her guarantor?"

"You have the money," she said, mildly.

"It's like hundreds of thousands of dollars."

"You have the money."

Judd barked a laugh. "So I told her fucking brother, I told him what's going on, and he won't give me a straight answer about whether or not he'll help. And nobody else seems to know what to do about the insurance. But her brother always liked you, right?"

"I never met her brother," Amy said.

"Didn't you?"

The dog was loping its way around the pond. Nobody was following it.

"No," she said. "I never did."

"Then how did you figure out what to do with her insurance?"

"I made a lot of phone calls," Amy said.

"Hmm," said Judd. And the more she watched it, the more it seemed that the dog didn't belong to any human, and in fact maybe it wasn't so well cared for? Because now that she was watching it, she was almost certain she could detect a slight limp. "You know, I found your credit cards in Ferry's desk."

"Why were you looking through his desk?"

"Why would you go to a foreign country and not bring any credit cards?"

"I didn't—" She couldn't remember what she was thinking, only that she needed to be free. "I can't remember."

Judd let this inanity pass. "Well, you'll be home soon. When do you have to get back to the airport?"

She looked at her watch. Her flight was in a little more than two hours, and the lines in Charles de Gaulle were dismaying, interminable. "Is she comfortable?"

"Uno?"

"Yes, is she—is she in distress?"

"She seems stable right now," Judd said. "I mean, I think we're on a downhill slide but you'll probably be back in time to see her alive."

"She's not in pain?"

"No."

"Is she conscious?"

"Most of the time, no," Judd said.

"And Ferry's okay?"

"I think so."

"Is he still angry?"

"Sure," Judd said. "But he's working through it. He's gonna be okay."

"I love that boy," Amy said.

"I know you do. We all do."

The dog was circling back toward Amy. "Pssst, psst," she said. The dog approached; it definitely had a limp. She pulled a pig's ear out of her backpack. "Hey," she said. "Hey, for you."

The dog took it gratefully, and instead of running away with his prize, he lay down on his belly and began gently nibbling.

Amy resisted the urge to pat his head, not wanting to disturb him while he was eating. Now that she was on her way home, now that whatever had happened with Meret was almost certainly in the rear-view mirror, things would be the way they'd always been.

"Who are you talking to?"

"There's a dog," she said.

"God, Amy, it's enough already. Another dog?"

"Yes," she said.

"It's time to come home."

She didn't say anything.

"Amy?"

"I haven't figured it out yet, Judd. I still don't think I've figured it out."

"Figured out what?" Judd said.

But she wasn't sure she could explain herself without getting tangled up in the words. So she stayed quiet. *Tavisupleba, tavisupleba.*

"I love you, Amy," he finally said.

"I love you too," she said.

And then she hung up the phone.

And when the dog finished his pig's ear and began to trot away in a new direction, Amy followed him through the garden. They passed statues, they passed pigeons, they passed the gates, and soon enough they were in the streets of Paris. The dog paused at the streetlight. It knew how to cross the street. It knew! The traffic stopped for the dog, and Amy followed.

She had a leash in her backpack, but no collar, but she could make the leash into a slipknot if she could just catch him. He walked quickly toward the end of the broad street, in the shadow of tall limestone buildings. "Hey!" she shouted. "Hey! S'il vous plaît." The dog kept moving. "Gtkhovt!"

And he stopped and looked at her, quizzically, one canine eyebrow raised higher than the other. As if to say, are you coming?

She was coming. She was almost there.

"Wait for me!" she said. Angelozi, angel, wait for me! But before she could arrive, the dog disappeared around a corner. Amy hurried to catch him, graceful down the sidewalk, tying an invisible thread to wherever the dog might have gone.